WE
GOT THE
BEAT

ALSO BY JENNA MILLER
Out of Character

WE GOT THE BEAT

JENNA MILLER

Quill Tree Books
An Imprint of HarperCollinsPublishers

For Nelson, who showed me I had a voice
and encouraged me to use it.

CHAPTER ONE

"YOU CAN DO this, Jordan Elliot."

I stared at my reflection in the school bathroom mirror, letting out my fifth deep breath. Or was it sixth? Whatever. I was hope and terror wrapped in the body of a fat sixteen-year-old lesbian. Typically wavy shoulder-length brown hair was straightened. Lipstick was applied for the first time in months. Glasses had been cleaned more than once. My usual nerdy-casual look took a back seat to a professional black blazer, blush-pink top, and dark jeans that said I was confident, but serious.

And none of it mattered.

My appearance wasn't going to make or break my future. Mx. Shannon had already chosen the newspaper staff roles, and whether or not I was at the top was no longer up for discussion. Still, I wanted to look good for the moment they announced I'd be editor in chief as a junior. Or managing editor. Hell, I'd even take news editor. No matter what happened next period, my life was about to change. I could *feel* it.

"You can do this," I told myself again.

"But what if you can't?"

I whirled around as Mackenzie West exited the last stall and stopped at the sink next to mine to wash her hands. I took in her summer-tanned skin and blonde hair that fell down her back in perfect waves. Two years since our falling-out, and she was *still* the worst. Not that we'd talked outside classroom obligations since then, but this interaction and the grin on her lips was enough to confirm it. I glared to make up for the fact that words weren't coming to me—a first.

"You should probably stop the pep talk so you're not late for class," she added before I could think of something clever, grabbing a paper towel to dry her hands.

"What do you care?" I asked, my eyes narrowing. Just because she was my nemesis didn't mean I had to acknowledge it, or her.

"I—"

"Forget it," I said before she could get in another snide comment. "Just forget it." I collected my bag from the floor and headed out of the bathroom.

"See you around," she called after me.

Escaping into the hall, I groaned, impossibly furious at her words. She'd barely spoken to me, and I was already on edge. So much for positive breathing exercises.

The *Davenport High Observer* classroom was full of chatter as I slid into a chair next to Audrey Lim. She was Korean American, bisexual, and had the most infectious laugh. We met in middle school during the first day of gym class—which we both hated—and decided to eat lunch together after—which we both loved. She got me addicted to K-pop and I got her addicted to *Doctor Who*. Somehow the combination translated to *best friends forever*.

On Audrey's left was my other bestie, Isaac Berman, who was straight and came from a half-Jewish (dad), half-Christian (mom) household. He was mostly raised Jewish but still celebrated Christmas—or Chrismukkah, as his dad called it. Our moms had bonded as neighbors over being pregnant at the same time, so we were friends from day one. When Isaac's family upgraded to a nicer apartment building, mine followed. We learned how to walk, talk, and ride bikes together. Our parents exchanged recipes from old family cookbooks. The Elliots taught the Bermans all about hot dish, and the Bermans showed the Elliots how to make matzo ball soup and challah.

Looking them over, I could tell they were as nervous as me about the newspaper positions, so I held back my urge to throw an anxiety spiral at them. Audrey was also gunning for a top-editor position, and Isaac wanted to be the next photography editor—because taking pictures was the only reason he was in newspaper. He didn't obsess over writing stories like Audrey and I did; for him, his photos *were* the stories.

Agree to disagree, Isaac. Words were *everything*.

Top spots typically went to the seniors, but there were more juniors this year and too many positions to go to seniors alone. And after two years of working our asses off with late-night planning sessions, taking on extra stories, and each winning an award at the newspaper conference last year, the three of us were feeling pretty confident.

The *Observer's* front wall was entirely whiteboard, while the back was full of storage cabinets that we shared with the Yearbook Club. Long tables and chairs filled the rest of the space. I eagerly sat front and center with my friends. Off to our left was a small office, and our right housed the lab with prehistoric computers that would freeze without warning in the middle of saving a document. It was dated. It was glorious. Magic happened in the lab. In short, it was our sanctuary.

Mx. Margo Shannon stood in front of the class as everyone calmed down. They were in their late twenties and the only teacher with an undercut. They'd started teaching the same year I started high school and newspaper, so we'd grown up here together. And although I was still two years from graduation, the idea of leaving them and newspaper class behind one day already felt bittersweet.

"Okay, class, I know you're all eager to find out your roles and beats, so I won't keep you waiting," Mx. Shannon said as they started passing out papers. "I seriously considered each position, and not everyone who wanted an editor spot was able to get one. I'll be available after class if anyone wants to talk."

Audrey was practically bouncing in her seat by the time the papers made their way to us, and a rare smug smile tugged on Isaac's lips. They were shoo-ins for top spots, and I wasn't even a little surprised when I saw *Opinion Editor* next to Audrey's name and *Photography Editor* next to Isaac's. But as I got to the bottom of the editor list, I realized Mx. Shannon's mistake.

I wasn't on it.

How was that possible?

My eyes trailed down the page until they locked on my assigned beat for first semester: *Volleyball*.

Audrey's and Isaac's faces were a mix of excitement, confusion, and empathy. They knew how big a deal this would be for me. I wasn't mad about their positions because they truly deserved them, but I felt an uncomfortable twist of jealousy that was new to me. We got jealous of other people sometimes, but not each other. Feeling it now made me want to scream at myself.

Mx. Shannon explained the importance of everyone having a part to play to make a newspaper successful, but I tuned them out and stared daggers at the list. Volleyball beat. I'd never played the sport outside gym class, and I hated it. Okay, I miraculously had a killer serve, but I'd never dive or jump for a ball. And the team was full of girls who had some kind of cult-like friendship.

Volleyball. Beat.

Jordan. Elliot.

This was my nightmare.

I took Mx. Shannon up on their offer to talk after class since it was the last period of the day and I had nowhere to be—and because I wouldn't be able to sleep tonight without answers. I was still hoping there'd been a mistake, but I knew I was wrong the moment Mx. Shannon said, "I'm sorry, Jordan, but it wasn't a mistake."

I huffed a sigh, fighting with myself to stay calm despite still wanting to burst into tears or yell. "I don't understand. I thought I'd crushed it these past two years."

"Oh, you totally crushed it." Mx. Shannon smiled warmly with a look that said *I have bigger plans for you*. They nodded to an open chair in their office, and I collapsed into it immediately. "But I want you to go outside of your comfort zone this year."

"Isn't that what I did freshman year with track and cross-country?" I asked, raising my brows. "No offense to sports, but this feels like a step back, not forward. How am I going to get into Columbia with this kind of résumé?"

They chuckled, shaking their head. "This is different. The volleyball team stands a good chance of placing first this year, and I want my best writer on it since we're cringe at every other sport. And don't worry about Columbia. I wouldn't put you in this position if I thought it would jeopardize your future."

How could this *not* jeopardize everything I'd worked toward? We weren't the school to attend if you wanted a sports scholarship—except volleyball, apparently. And wasn't sports writing more of a formality in high school? Did anyone even care about it outside the team, and maybe their families? Would Columbia?

The rest of Shannon's words sunk in. "You really think I'm your best writer?"

"I do," they said. "If you're serious about being an editor, we'll revisit that discussion at the end of the school year. And you can still pitch me other stories. But if you want to be a journalist, you should be producing more pieces for your portfolio this year, not editing them. Covering a winning team will help, even if it's not what you want to write about professionally."

Their plan didn't make up for the fact that most of my writing this semester would center around volleyball, but arguing was pointless. Shannon didn't make half-ass decisions, and their constant support of me helped. If getting an editor position senior year and looking good for college meant crushing the volleyball beat, I'd have to make it look like I gave a shit about it in the first place.

"Okay," I said slowly, forcing a smile. "I'll be the best volleyball writer this school has ever seen."

"I was hoping you'd say that," they said. "Now get out of here and work on believing it."

How well they knew me.

"Thanks, will do." I grabbed my backpack and stepped into the hall, getting immediately bombarded by Audrey and Isaac.

"What did they say?" Audrey asked, her voice full of hope. "It was a mistake, right?"

"Afraid not," I said, summarizing the conversation before shrugging. "So, I guess I have to write about smacking balls around for four months. My favorite."

Isaac snorted, resting an arm across my shoulders. "I'm sorry, Jo. That sucks. Especially the balls part."

"It's trash," Audrey added. "We should report them for neglecting student potential."

"We're not reporting them for doing what's best for the paper," I said, rolling my eyes. The idea was tempting purely out of spite, but considering the heaps of admiration I had for Mx. Shannon, I had to trust them with this one. "But I don't want to think about it anymore. Are either of you free to hang?"

"Can't," Audrey said. "Dad gets back from his work trip tonight, so Mom and I are baking his favorite treat once I get home."

"I'll allow that, but only if you bring us some honey cookies tomorrow," I said, knowing all about her dad's sweet tooth.

"Obviously."

I laughed, looking at Isaac. "You in, or are you going to mooch a ride home and disappear the moment I park in front of our building?"

Isaac groaned. "Okay, I've done that, like, twice, and for good reason."

"There's no shame in not being able to poop at school," Audrey said, smirking as she leaned up to ruffle Isaac's thick black hair.

"That's not why!" Isaac swatted her hand away. "I hate you both."

"No, you don't!" Audrey said in a singsong voice as she did a cheek heart and turned to walk off toward her locker. "See you tomorrow, besties!" We waved goodbye.

"I *do* want to hang out," Isaac said, smiling sheepishly. "But

I got partnered up with Olivia Davidson for an English project, and she wants to get started immediately. We're meeting at the QB, like, any minute."

I groaned at the mention of my nemesis's best friend. Olivia had always been nice to me, but I didn't trust her friend choices. At least the Quilted Bean, the craft-store-slash-coffee-shop, was only a couple of blocks away, and I wouldn't need to drop him off and risk running into people I'd rather not see outside school. "Okay, well, good luck with that. See you tomorrow?"

"You know it."

I stood in the hallway after he'd left, debating my next move. I could kill time at the bookstore before my parents got home from work, but I didn't have a lot of fun money to spend at the moment, and I'd gotten enough dirty looks over the years for reading in-store without buying anything. There was also the fact that my goldendoodle, Pond, hadn't gone out since Dad walked her during his lunch break. Knowing I'd hate to rely on someone taking me to the bathroom, I decided to go home. Pond did *not* like to be kept waiting.

CHAPTER TWO

THE BEST THING about dog parks was seeing all the different breeds that frequented it. No matter who was there, Pond was equally excited because every dog had the potential to be her best friend. That was the good part. The bad part was dealing with the owners. Unless we were blessed with an empty park, I was left to endure small talk while Pond played.

Today, I was stuck on a bench next to Cindy. Instead of opting for one of the other five open benches, the middle-aged woman sat beside me because, presumably, I'm a human with ears. Her dog, a corgi named Queen Elizabeth II, was fun to watch, and Pond loved her, but I did *not* love Cindy. No matter how little I added to our conversations or how hard I tried to focus on Pond, she'd keep talking. Mostly I'd hear about her love life, or lack thereof, and all her dreams. People talked about dreams a lot at dog parks.

Mom told me once that I have the kind of face people find approachable. I'd never had the heart to tell her that I'm approachable because I'm fat. As the only fat person in my immediate family, I didn't expect them to understand. They'd try to make me feel better by telling me people don't look at me differently, but them not doing it didn't make it true for everyone. I knew the difference between judgment and acceptance. It was the little things people did in response to my fatness that made it obvious who thought they could take advantage of me. When there's a park filled with strangers and I'm, more often than not, the chosen victim, it's obvious. I don't radiate joy or have an overly friendly demeanor. But people oftentimes think of fat people as the lonely castaways who would welcome any attention—even negative attention—so there I was talking to Cindy about her latest online dating disaster. You know, because a teenager could totally relate.

"You're young, but inviting a man up on the first date is never a good idea," she said, as if my lesbian ass needed to know that.

"Do you think I'm approachable because I'm fat?" I asked before she could launch into the details of his ghosting.

"What?" Cindy laughed, shaking her head furiously. "Of course not! And you're not fat."

There it was—the denial. And her voice had raised. I was totally right. "Well, I *am* fat. A doctor confirmed it medically and everything." I shrugged, knowing Cindy would be more bothered by this reality than I was.

Cindy scoffed. "You know what I mean."

I didn't, but the goal wasn't to have a long conversation, so I focused on sealing the deal. "I'm also a lesbian, so it's never a good idea for me to invite a man anywhere, you know? Would be pretty awkward all around."

She was perfectly flustered now, her cheeks turning scarlet as she let out a breathy laugh. I didn't think Cindy was homophobic by any means, but too many differences mentioned face-to-face tended to rattle her generation. "Of course, dear, of course," she said quickly as she gathered her things. "I should go. The Queen has an appointment soon. See you next time!"

It was like clockwork. I'd humor a person long enough in hopes they'd go away after a minute. When that didn't work, I'd say something to make them uncomfortable and leave. After that, I'd see them across the park on another bench, and they'd pretend to look busy on their phone or with their dog when I'd wave at them. I expected this to happen with Cindy the next time we crossed paths.

I'd successfully driven away every person I'd met at the dog park. It wasn't that I hated people—though, sometimes I did— but I wanted fifteen minutes of silence while Pond pooped, got her energy out, and made a new friend, or seven. Unlike her, I didn't want more friends, and I didn't need to hear a woman ramble about hetero sex. Hard pass.

"Have a nice day!" I called, waving dramatically as Cindy hustled off to collect her dog and be on her way.

Pond continued making the rounds, and I took out my phone to research the volleyball tags on Instagram. Before I knew it, I was on Mackenzie West's account. We weren't following each other, but we hadn't blocked each other either. I doubted she looked at my account randomly, but that didn't stop me from checking in on her life sometimes.

The most recent picture was from yesterday, the first day of junior year. She stood in front of her house with Olivia and a few other girls, wearing matching volleyball uniforms and smiling as if it was the greatest day of her life. But that was how she always looked in pictures—like every day was the best day, a new opportunity to live life to the fullest. Hashtag blessed.

It was bullshit. A lie. A facade. At least that's what I'd come to learn the summer we hung out nearly every day, before I made a habit of pushing new people away.

We met at the exact park bench I was sitting on now. After exchanging names and talking about our dogs for a minute—hers a black dachshund named Sabrina after the Netflix show—she told me her story. She'd just moved to the area from Arizona with her parents, and they were temporarily living in a building near mine while their new house was being built. She'd start freshman year that fall, same as me, and she loved volleyball and poetry. Something about the combination had surprised me, but we'd hit it off in those first twenty minutes while our dogs chased each other around the park.

I snapped out of the memory as Pond nearly barreled into my legs, barking excitedly in a way that meant she'd pooped and I needed to take care of it. With a relieved sigh, I stopped looking at my nemesis's face and followed Pond to her business. At least one of us was having a good time.

* * *

Not even a minute after I got home, Dad walked in with groceries. One of the biggest victories in my life was having married parents who didn't hate each other. They had their moments, but I'd seen more fights go down at Audrey's house than mine, and her parents were generally quieter and around each other less.

"Hey, JoJo," Dad greeted, setting two reusable totes on the counter as I refilled Pond's water bowl. "What are we feeling for dinner? Spaghetti or potpie?"

"Potpie if it's homemade and not the frozen boxed kind, otherwise spaghetti," I said, giving him a look. We were all guilty of cutting corners in the minimal-effort meal department, but real potpie was a thousand times better.

"Oh, it's the real deal," Dad said, sounding scandalized. "I'll get it started while you tell me about your day. Did you hear about the paper positions yet? Actually, hold that thought."

"Dad—" I started, but he held a finger up as he pulled out his phone.

Before I could crush his moment, "We Got the Beat" by the Go-Go's started to play. It was a tradition that went back to his high school journalism days—you know, when they had to print hundreds of copies of every edition and have layout nights with actual paper. His teacher played the song before handing out the list of beats for the semester, and Dad leaned into it so hard that he played it every semester I came home to announce my fate. He also played it anytime he made a recipe with beets, but that was another story.

As a former editor in chief, he was beyond excited for my time to shine. And considering I'd obsessed over my future staff title the entire summer, he was almost as invested in the result as I was. He sang along with the music and danced in a very dad way, and I wanted to curl into a ball and cry more and more with each line.

When he reached the end of the chorus, I hit my limit. "We don't got it!" I yelled over him and the music, replacing the final words with a negative.

"What?" His face fell as he stopped the song. "What do you mean?"

"I got assigned the volleyball beat," I said, shrugging. "No editor position."

Dad gasped, and not to humor me. He was truly as shocked as I'd been. I could see it all over his face as his hazel eyes widened. "I'm sorry to hear that. Did Mx. Shannon say why?"

I groaned, launching into the explanation Shannon had given me earlier. "It's obviously a huge disappointment, but there's nothing I can do about it. I'll just write some damn good stories about . . . volleyball. It'll be great."

Dad rested his hands on my shoulders, smiling proudly like a parent would do after his daughter tried making the most out of her dreams being crushed. "Good attitude. You'll go far with it. And I bet if you called Casey, he'd have all kinds of wisdom to share."

I snorted at the suggestion, doubting my almost-perfect older brother had anything to say that would help. I loved him, of course, but we'd never succeeded in the *understanding each other* department. He'd also never been in newspaper and never failed at anything in his life, so this was clearly an attempt to bring us closer together. "Right. I'll think about it. Thanks, Dad."

"You got it. Now, let's make a delicious potpie so your mom can relax when she gets home. She called me during lunch and sounded like she was about to murder her boss."

I laughed at the image. I didn't fully understand Mom's job, but she worked in sales for some massive health-care company. She traveled and worked late a lot, so I grew up more with Dad around, which made her time at home feel special. Dad owned a local comic shop that also sold nerdy memorabilia and games. He always made a point to be home around the time I got in from school—unless he was hosting Dungeons & Dragons night on Thursdays, in which case I didn't see him until after nine.

Dad switched to a playlist that consisted mostly of early 2000s punk rock before we got to work on the potpie. I cut a couple of carrots to boil and made the rest of the filling as Dad prepped the crust. We were in our element when we didn't have to talk about work or school or my current anxieties—though sometimes we did talk about those things. Dad was my go-to for the big conversations. We leaned on each other. In a way, he was like my third best friend. Or my first. He just *got* me.

But not even Dad and his old music could keep me from thinking about what had happened at school. I liked dancing and swimming at the lake, but competitive sports were the last thing I wanted to write about. The worst part was that Mack was on the team, but at least it was big enough where I wouldn't have to focus on her. She'd be just another player. I could write about her generally when I had to and force our thorny history aside.

We were halfway through eating when Mom finally got home. Pond barked and whined at the sound of a key entering the lock, and she was a puddle of emotions by the time Mom was inside. "It's like you never see me!" she joked before walking into the dining area of our apartment. "Dinner smells delicious."

"We hadn't made potpie in a while," Dad said. "JoJo put together a salad, too. How did the rest of your day turn out?"

"Ugh, don't ask," Mom said as she took off her navy blazer. Her dark brown hair was up in a tight bun, and her nearly flawless skin was covered in makeup. I personally thought she looked beautiful without it, but try telling that to a woman who'd been on various fad diets her entire adult life and obsessed over every article of clothing she bought. I knew better than anyone that it wasn't fair to judge people by appearances, even if how she talked about herself rubbed me the wrong way sometimes. Like, if she thought negatively about her own body, what did she think about mine? But since she'd never said anything bad to me about my weight, I made a point to push down those thoughts whenever they came to the surface.

"How was school today, sweetie?" Mom asked me after kissing Dad and joining us at the table.

"It was okay." I wanted to leave it there, but Dad gave me an encouraging look. "I got the volleyball beat for newspaper."

"And an editor position, right?" she asked, raising a brow. "Which one?"

"No editor position." I added what I'd told Dad before shrugging. "But it's fine. I'll get through it."

Mom pursed her lips, and I could tell my attempt to act chill had failed. She had a habit of reacting to things that affected me in a bigger way than I did. "You know what? It's not fine. I'm going to call the school in the morning. You worked too hard to be passed over. Columbia won't be impressed by having the *volleyball beat* junior year. I mean, what's next, *orchestra*?"

Dad laughed. "Says the woman who fell in love with an orchestra nerd."

"And you're such an incredible violinist, love, but my comment stands," Mom said, reaching over to squeeze his hand. "Sports beats aren't impressive unless your dream is to work somewhere like *Sports Illustrated*."

Now it was my turn to groan. On top of Mom's too-intense reactions, she was obsessed with being the best. She strived to pass that down to her children, as if it was an admirable trait like kindness or snark. If anything, competitiveness made me feel sick. Of course I wanted a top spot. Of course I wanted Columbia. But I wasn't going to resort to sketchy tactics to get there. Or whining.

"Mx. Shannon said I can still pitch them other story ideas," I said. "It doesn't have to only be about volleyball. But even if I don't have time for other stories, they know what they're doing, and I trust them."

Mom scoffed. "Well, I don't. They're clearly holding you back when you deserve to shine."

I let out a slow breath before responding to that one. "I know you want all of us to be top-notch winners, Mom, but have you considered the possibility that maybe the students who got editor roles worked just as hard as I did, or even harder? I mean, Audrey and Isaac got editor roles, and they worked their asses off."

"But you worked harder," Mom said dismissively, ignoring the swear word that she and Dad only corrected every so often. "I'm still calling the school. What kind of mother would I be if I didn't stick up for you?"

"Let's hold off on calling the school," Dad said, chiming in at last. I respected him for letting me handle my life, but he also knew how Mom was with me and that I needed backup sometimes. "Anything could happen. Maybe JoJo will uncover a juicy story within the volleyball world, and it'll be written so well that Shannon will beg her to cover bigger stories. Maybe one of the editors will drop out second semester and she'll take their place. Or maybe they'll die."

"Dad, oh my god!" I laughed despite the last possibility being far from funny. "No one is dying, and I seriously doubt any of them will drop out. All of the editors are serious about journalism. They're not going anywhere."

"Still, I think this will be a good thing for you," Dad said, shrugging off his dark humor before looking at Mom. "I know you don't like to hear this, but sometimes there's a hidden gem buried underneath disappointment. And even if there isn't, JoJo writes amazing stories. She'll find an edge and crush it."

I beamed at his words. For as much as my parents loved each other, they had a lot of differences. Mom was aggressively competitive while Dad enjoyed the fun of the game. Mom went hard on her health kicks while Dad lived more moderately. Mom made comments about her weight around me while Dad . . . well, didn't. Not once. I loved that about him. But with Mom, it could be a lot.

"I'm sure she will," Mom said, a tight-lipped smile forming as she looked at me. "I just want you to be happy, sweetheart."

"I know, thanks," I said before going back to eating. Relief settled over me as Mom tore her eyes away and finally told Dad about her work day and complained for the rest of the meal about cutthroat coworkers and awkward clients. I'd listen to her bitch all night if it meant shifting focus from me.

I texted Audrey and Isaac in our group chat after getting through some reading for English class. Teachers didn't understand that we needed to be eased back into the swing of demanding schedules and piles of textbooks. Rude.

Jordan: To no one's surprise, the parents had differing opinions on my newspaper announcement.
Audrey: Let me guess . . . Laura was super happy for you and squealed in excitement and Clark was all frowny face
Jordan: You know them SO WELL!

Isaac: Complete opposite then?

Jordan: Complete opposite! Mom threatened to call Shannon
and give them a lecture. Imagine it.

Audrey: Oh, I can. Shannon would tell Laura what's up and
look like a damn hero.

Jordan: True. Maybe I should tell my mom to call them.

Audrey: Hahaha do it!

Isaac: I have some other news that you might want to hear
from me instead of someone else. But also it's not a
big deal!

I laughed at his fake assurance. Every time he said something
wasn't a big deal, it definitely was.

Jordan: Hit me with it

Isaac: Your BFF Mackenzie West made captain of the
volleyball team. Olivia was gushing about it at the QB.

Of. Course. She. Got. Captain.

Why wouldn't she? Mack got everything she wanted, so why
not get a captain position instead of letting one of the seniors
have it? My rational side would say she probably deserved it, the
way I would've deserved an editor role, but screw that. This was
just another mark against her.

Jordan: Gross but not surprising

Audrey: She'll be even more insufferable now . . . yay?

Jordan: Yay.

Isaac: At least you lucked out this semester and have no classes with her?

Audrey: Uh not me! I'm in THREE of her classes. And trust, she's even more insufferable when she's speaking French.

Jordan: merde

Jordan: But she's not your nemesis, so does that matter?

Audrey: Your nemesis is my nemesis!

Jordan: A TRUE FRIEND

Isaac: I still think she's hot. Not as hot as Olivia, IMO, but still.

Jordan: I'm throwing you in the pit.

Audrey: The spiky side! WTF Isaac

Isaac: You know I'm right Audrey!!

Audrey: Yes but I'm not going to say that to our wounded friend! Where's your loyalty?

Isaac: I deserved that. No rest for the wicked.

I laughed, knowing I couldn't blame Isaac for his opinion. Mack *was* hot. Aesthetically, she was damn-near perfect. Of course that meant she had another mark against her. Damn-near perfect was almost as infuriating as perfect.

I opened Instagram to see what she had to say about it. A new picture showed her standing in front of the volleyball net in the school gym. She was wearing a Davenport Wildcats tank top and black shorts, her hair in a high ponytail. A turquoise volleyball rested at her hip, and her other hand was raised in the shape of a C. Her caption read: I'm honored to be the varsity volleyball captain this year! Hard work really does pay off, but I wouldn't be here without the support of my team and coach. Here's to an amazing year of fun, friendship, and victory!

She'd posted the picture a little over an hour ago, and she already had more likes than anything I'd ever shared. But that wasn't what set me on edge—it was the fakeness of her post. Her friends and fans no doubt fawned over it and left adoring comments to prove it, but the Mack I'd known was far from who she showed everyone else. Or maybe the person she'd shown me had been the lie.

I forced myself to stop reading the comments after the first dozen and refocused on my homework. As Dad always said, tomorrow was a new day full of opportunities.

CHAPTER THREE

SOMETIMES DAD'S POSITIVE outlook on life was really annoying.

As hard as I tried to see the next day at school as an opportunity, I struggled to find it. Every period dragged on like me in gym class. By the time I entered the newspaper room, I was ready to escape to my bed with Pond. Mx. Shannon planned to walk us through our goals for the semester as well as any requirements they had. Audrey was already chatting it up with her fellow editors when I arrived, but Isaac waited for me in our usual spot. "Thanks for not ditching me for the cool kids," I joked. But also, not really.

"We're the cool ones," Isaac said, nudging me. "But how are you? I know Mackenzie making captain is pretty shitty for you, but it's not like you'll have to be around her *every* day."

I shrugged, trying to ignore how upset my new reality made me feel. "She'll be as insufferable as the rest of the team. But it's only for a few months, and then it's on to a brighter future—you know, like baseball. Instead of moving up in the world like I'd imagined, I'll be moving down. Shannon must really believe in my potential."

Isaac's brows perked. "I think you're forgetting a key piece of covering sports."

"I already made it clear that it's terrible and the last thing I should write about," I said. "What else is there?"

"One of your assigned stories will be to write a story on the team's captain," he said, his voice laced with concern. "So you and Mackenzie . . ."

He trailed off as I stood and stormed into Shannon's connected office, my heart racing. "Can I talk to you?" I asked, shutting the door behind me.

"Of course," they said, looking up from their work. "This a closed-door conversation?"

I nodded, taking a deep breath and releasing it slowly as I fought back tears that threatened to spill. "I'm not saying this to whine about being on a sports beat, but I can't cover volleyball. I forgot about the captain feature story, and it just so happens that the new captain is my nemesis."

Surprise flooded Shannon's face, and their pause made me think they were seriously considering changing my beat. "Why is the captain your nemesis?" they asked instead.

I sighed, working extra hard to keep myself in check. The last thing I wanted was to be difficult around someone who'd been nothing but honest and real with me since day one. But the thought of being near Mack that much threatened hives across my skin. "I don't want to talk about it. But trust me, it won't be good if I have to, like, follow her around and ask her questions and stuff. I did that all of freshman year with track and cross-country, so you know I'm good for it, but I can't do that with Mackenzie. There's too much bad blood."

Shannon leaned forward, their tone gentle. "Does she make you feel unsafe?"

"No," I said slowly. "It's not like that. We just don't like each other. Like, at all."

"I hear you," they nodded. "And I'm sorry you have a nemesis, but if it's not a matter of safety, I'm going to insist you stick with volleyball."

My stomach dropped. "Even if the story ends up being a complete failure because she won't cooperate with me, and it makes me *and* the paper look bad?"

"Let's not give her that much power," Shannon said, clearly trying their best not to look amused or annoyed. "I can only assume she'll want to look good for the feature story, right?"

I didn't like where they were going with this. "Right."

"Exactly, so it'll be just as important to her that you get along this semester. Maybe it'll give you a break in whatever war has been waged, which, by the way, surprises me. I can't imagine you having a nemesis."

"She started it," I mumbled before shaking my head. "I shouldn't have to be fake nice to a person who's made me feel like crap for two years."

"You shouldn't," Shannon agreed. "But don't think of it as

being fake nice. Think of it as being professional. Serious journalism comes with many challenges, including interviewing people you don't want to. But that's part of the job." A proud smile formed. "You know, this could turn out to be my best decision all year."

"I'm really happy for you," I said dryly. "But I'm on the verge of having a panic attack here, so can we not celebrate?" Okay, maybe it wasn't quite panic attack level, but my heart was racing. And I hated that Shannon knew me well enough not to take the bait. If they thought I was truly on the verge of a mental breakdown, they wouldn't hesitate to pull me from the beat.

"This experience is going to do wonders for your career—I can feel it," they said. "You'll win all kinds of awards later in life, and I hope you think back on this moment when I pushed you to do the hard thing instead of coddling you like I've done in the past."

I opened my mouth to argue, but fair. I'd gotten my way on a lot of things last year, including writing an exposé on lawn gnomes that made the paper look ridiculous. "Is this punishment for the gnome story?" I asked.

"Hell no, that was perfect." Shannon chuckled, shaking their head. "This is nothing more than an opportunity to set you on the right path toward a career in journalism. And honestly, you might be surprised by what you learn this semester."

I doubted it, but there was nothing else I could say to convince them to give me a different beat. "To be determined," I said, forcing a smile. "Thanks for the chat."

"My door is always open."

I nodded and left their office, returning to my chair next to Isaac. "Sorry for walking off," I said, pulling out my notebook in case some brilliant idea came to mind.

"All good," Isaac said. "How'd it go?"

"You're right. I'm doing a story on my nemesis." I sighed, slowly succumbing to reality. "My future in journalism rests on the shoulders of Mackenzie West."

Isaac snorted. "Nah. You'll write a kick-ass story like you always do, and the whole world will know your name because of it . . . or at least the whole school."

I smiled a little at his enthusiasm, determined to make it work. It would be the best story I'd ever written. It had to be.

If I wanted to make editor next year and get into Columbia, I couldn't afford to fail.

After school, I wandered to the gym to familiarize myself with the world of volleyball. Coach Pavek taught U.S. and World History and had her moments of intimidation, but we'd always gotten along well enough. And by well enough, I mean I didn't suck at her classes and she never had to yell at me like she did with other students.

"Elliot, what are you doing here?" she asked as I approached, an amused expression on her face. "Got a question about your reading assignment?"

"No, Coach," I said, calling her by her preferred identifier. I didn't blame her. Coach sounded so much better than Ms.

Pavek or Sheila. "I got assigned the volleyball beat for newspaper, so I thought I'd come check out how practice works."

Pavek stared at me for a too-long pause, her eyes narrowing. "You going to make us look bad like last year? I don't appreciate volleyball being considered a lesser sport, you know. It's cutthroat."

Coach and Mx. Shannon had it out over a story that Coach claimed was unprofessionally written and full of negative bias. After some yelling, Shannon reminded Coach that we wrote the truth, and losing three games in a row couldn't be reported as a win. I was sure she'd never forgotten the perceived slight. Apparently, she hadn't forgiven it either.

"I'll report the truth, Coach," I said, trying to sound confident that it would result in us both getting what we wanted. "Also, I'll need to do a feature story on Mackenzie since she's the new captain and all that."

"Right, of course," Coach said with a dismissive wave of her hand. "She'll like that. Good for the ego."

Something about her words made me think she also saw through Mack's act, and it caused a light grin to appear on my lips. "Great for the ego," I confirmed. "Anyway, can I get a copy of the schedule? I plan on attending a couple more practices on top of the games."

Coach snorted, grabbing a small pamphlet from her clipboard and handing it to me. "I doubt this is a dream topic for you. I'm impressed by the dedication. No one else bothers with the practices."

The compliment would carry me through the semester. "Thanks, Coach. And you're right— it's not a dream topic, but I'm committed to making the most of it."

"Good, because I won't have another ruthless story written about my team."

There it was. I pushed a laugh down, nodding. "Crush the competition and you'll get the very best stories."

"Deal," she said as if she could fully control the fate of the team, let alone the competition. "Well, take a seat wherever. I need to get things rolling."

I nodded and sat on the sidelines. Coach Pavek blew her whistle and called the team together as they trickled in from the locker room. After taking out my newspaper notebook and turning to an empty page, I glanced up and saw Mack's eyes on me, her unreadable expression pulling me back to two years ago.

The annoying thing about memories was that they showed up when you'd rather forget they existed.

First, let it be known that I wasn't always a dog park curmudgeon. I used to feel excited about the possibilities of a new day at the park. I used to sit and talk to the other dog owners. I used to play with the other dogs.

And then I'd met Mackenzie West the summer before ninth grade, and everything changed.

We'd started planning our park outings so we'd run into each other on purpose. Before long, we were hanging out at each other's homes and going to nearby movies and restaurants.

Casey even drove us to hiking trails a few times, though I'd make him go ahead of us on the path so it could just be me and Mack. And we texted constantly. You know, real friend stuff.

By the time school started, it was like the entire summer had been a fever dream. We'd gone from giving pep talks about high school and her volleyball tryouts the week before freshman year to radio silence. Mackenzie West didn't want to be my friend anymore. She didn't need someone like me because she'd found her people. People like Olivia and the volleyball girls and football boys. People who went to parties and knew all the best spots to make out around town. People who played sports and got noticed by upperclassmen like my brother's "cool" friends. People who noticed her in a way that "mattered."

I thought our summer had mattered, but I'd learned the truth our first week of high school when she'd called me her "summer stalker" to her new friends. People I'd known since kindergarten laughed in my face over the word of the new girl, and she let them.

Isaac and Audrey hadn't hung out with us that summer due to conflicting schedules and, honestly, me just wanting to connect with Mack solo before bringing her into the group. But when I'd told them about the fallout, about those two words sketched into my memory forever, all their previous good thoughts and encouragements about her dropped. They couldn't believe someone would treat me like that, and their loyalty kept Mack barred from their minds ever since.

I snapped out of my internal pity-party as Mack laughed at something Coach Pavek said. I let out a slow breath and focused on my notebook, writing *Volleyball Beat Notes* at the top.

For the next two hours, I switched back and forth between watching the practice and taking notes. I wrote down all the terms I heard, the names of the players, and who was good at what. Olivia had a wicked spike that I didn't expect from someone so small, and Mack had the best serve by far. And the way she made it look effortless, made everything look effortless . . . that was why she was the captain.

Or maybe it was because she got everything she wanted.

Or maybe she had the kind of personality that people easily fawned over and listened to.

Whatever the reason, I started to feel less and less certain of my ability to write a story about her that would make us both happy and help me get an editor position next year. But that was what she did to me—made me doubt myself—so I tried pushing those feelings aside out of spite.

When practice ended, I gathered my things and stood to leave, but Mack was there before I could quietly disappear.

"What are you doing here?" she asked.

"Oh, girl, I totally forgot to tell you!" Olivia said as she stopped at Mack's side. "Jordan is covering volleyball for the paper, and she'll be writing a feature story on you. Isn't that great?"

"How did you know all of that?" I asked, my brows shooting up. Olivia was nice, but she never took an interest in me, and vice versa.

"Isaac told me when we were working on an assignment yesterday," Olivia said. "He talked you up a lot."

"He did?" This was news to me.

"Of course! We also agreed that maybe this situation is a good thing. You and Mackenzie can get past any little grudges and move on."

Little grudges? I was going to kill Isaac, his heart eyes for Olivia be damned.

Mack laughed before I could respond. "I think we're old enough to be over past grudges, Liv. Right, Jordan?"

No.

"Sure," I said, forcing a smile. I'd need her to cooperate with me, so I might as well cooperate with her. Even if that laugh had been a thousand percent fake and I still hated her.

"Perfect," she said, her eyes shifting from me to Olivia. "I'm going to talk to Coach. Meet by my car after showers?"

"You got it," Olivia said, flashing Mack a cheery smile that shifted slightly once she was gone, and her focus returned to me. "So, Isaac is really cute. Did he have some kind of life-changing experience over the summer that made him come out of his shell?"

"No," I said, an easy laugh breaking out at her words. Sure, Isaac *was* cute, if you were into the male species, but he looked the same as he had three months ago. "I think you just noticed him for the first time. He's better one-on-one sometimes." *Especially when he has a crush*, I wanted to add, but didn't for his sake.

"Right, of course," she said quickly, her eyes widening. "Please don't tell him I said that. It was just a question."

"Sure, just a question," I said, smiling back at her. "See you around, Olivia."

"Yeah, see you!" Olivia's hair did a little swish as she turned to jog toward the locker room.

I glanced down at my notebook where I'd filled in a few pages of notes and added something unrelated but very important.

Olivia has a crush on Isaac!!!

CHAPTER FOUR

BEING NEARISH TO Mackenzie West for more than ten seconds called for greasy food.

I parked in front of our favorite eatery simply called The Diner to meet Audrey and Isaac. Their editors' meeting ended long before the practice, so they were already eating fries when I slid into the booth next to Audrey.

"How'd it go?" Audrey asked carefully after the waitress came by to take my order of a chocolate shake and another round of fries.

"I doubt it was as exciting as the editors' meeting, but it wasn't too bad," I said. And by *wasn't too bad*, I meant *I'm beyond jealous that I'm not in the editors' meeting and would rather gouge my eyes out with that fork than spend a semester with Mackenzie West.* "And Isaac, please don't talk to Olivia about me and Mackenzie. It's dated bullshit that I'll have to look past if I want to survive."

"Sorry," Isaac said, tapping my foot under the table. "But Olivia is just so . . . you know."

"No, I *don't* know, Isaac," I said, tapping back.

"Yeah, we *don't* know, Isaac," Audrey said, grinning and batting her eyelashes. "Please, tell us more about Olivia."

Isaac groaned, no doubt regretting his word choices around his terrible, terrible friends. "She's basically perfect, okay? We were talking about the assignment, superfocused on that, but then she saw Mackenzie's Instagram post about the captain news and started rambling about it since it was no longer a secret, because apparently she *had to* keep it a secret . . ."

"Isaac!" I laughed at his own rambling. "The point?"

"Right, the point. I'd mentioned you having to write about the team all semester, which made me realize the feature story part. And then Olivia got into your old history and gossip and all kinds of shit, but her eyes were doing that thing and I . . . *The point* is you have nothing to worry about. What went down freshman year, even though extremely shitty, is in the past. Mackenzie will want a great article, too, so she won't be a problem."

"Yeah, she'd made that pretty clear after practice when Olivia told her the news," I said, rolling my eyes. "What do I do?"

"You play nice right back," Audrey said. "And really, you already have an upper hand. You probably know her better than most people at school from that one summer alone."

"What's your point?" I asked, not wanting to think about that summer ever again.

"She obviously trusted you. Even if she turned into a monster the second she entered the school, she still gave a shit about you before then."

I snorted. "I'm pretty sure she was using me to have a friend before meeting her *real* friends," I said, popping one of Audrey's fries into my mouth since mine hadn't arrived yet.

"I don't believe that," Isaac said, smiling gently. "You told us everything about that summer, and it didn't sound like you were a desperation friend, Jo. You mattered to her."

"Then why didn't it last?" I asked, my tone firm as I fought back other emotions. "Obviously I'm not the coolest girl in school, never have been, but I don't have any marks against me either. The three of us are in the middle—not popular, but socially acceptable to be around."

"Then something else happened." Audrey shrugged. "I'm obviously not defending her, Jo, but I don't think it's as simple as you being the temporary convenience friend. This isn't some unrealistic teenage revenge movie. You're not Janis Ian."

"I still can't believe my mom made us watch *Mean Girls* last month. Talk about old-school," Isaac said. "Also, no one is getting pushed in front of a bus. I want to make that clear right now. I won't help with any life-threatening schemes, even if no one actually pushed Regina George."

"Okay, Buzzkill Berman," Audrey said, leaning over to poke his cheek. "Anyway, I was saying that if she's going to pretend all is well in the world with you two, you should use it to your advantage."

"How?" I asked, still not following.

"Take the things she told you back then, and dig deeper," Audrey said. "Find an angle to write about that goes beyond her being good at sports or whatever other safe bullshit she wants to talk about. Something that will show your dedication." She grinned, nearly bouncing in her seat as her eyes gleamed. "Maybe even find dirt to get back at her for everything she did to you. Take her down. It's a win-win."

"Absolutely not," I said quickly. "I'm not stooping to that level. And even if I wanted to, Shannon would never let something like that go live."

Audrey deflated. "Okay, fine. But I still think there could be another angle without going too far—one that would make your article stand out."

My shake and fries arrived, and I thanked the waitress before letting Audrey's idea sink in. I *did* get to know Mack that summer. It was possible she might let her guard down enough to let me back in. It could end up being worth the effort if I got a major story out of it that would help me with my goals. But I wouldn't slip over to the dark side and use Mack for some kind of scandalous revenge story.

"I'll think about it," I said, not wanting to commit either way. "But let's go back to talking about how much Isaac is in love with Olivia."

Isaac threw one of his fries at me. "We're done talking about that."

"Aw, come on! I think you should ask her out."

"Ask her out, ask her out!" Audrey cheered loudly, resulting in dirty looks from the other diner patrons. She giggled, leaning toward Isaac and lowering her voice. "Ask her out."

"I hate you both," Isaac grumbled before drinking more of his shake.

Audrey and I laughed, and I reached across the table to ruffle his hair. "Fine, pine in silence and see how that goes."

"Maybe I will," Isaac said firmly, confirming he was done indulging us for today.

Audrey took the hint and started talking about the editors' meeting instead. She and Isaac carried on a conversation while I zoned out to consider her idea again. I wasn't a manipulative person, and I didn't like the idea of being deceptive—not even to the girl who'd gutted me mentally and emotionally. But if Mack was going to put her best interests first and ignore the pain she inflicted on me so she could get a perfect feature article, I could do the same to write it. We weren't friends—I didn't owe her a damn thing.

Whatever it took, I would prove myself as a serious journalist who wasn't afraid of backstabbing girls like Mackenzie West.

The next day, Mack showed up at my usual lunch table seconds after I sat down—like she was waiting for me. "Hey, Jordan."

I didn't know if it was her presence or her cheery tone that alarmed me, but it wasn't something I wanted to deal with before food. "People can see."

I met her eyes in time to see her roll them. "I don't care about that," she said. "I came over to invite you to a party Friday night at my house."

"A party?" I choked out a laugh. "Why?"

"The team will be there," she said, shrugging like the invite was a perfectly normal part of being on the volleyball beat. "I thought you'd want to get to know everyone better outside of school and upcoming matches, you know?"

Yes, Mackenzie West, I know exactly what you're doing. She was already playing the game, and she was damn good at it. That made me not want to go, but going could help me find a story worth telling.

I sighed, my eyes scanning the room in the hope that Audrey and Isaac were on their way over, but they were nowhere to be found. "I don't know about that," I said, looking back at her. "Getting to know the whole team doesn't really have much to do with writing about the sport. There's only room for one feature player story, and you already have that."

"Yeah, I know."

She looked . . . frustrated? I couldn't figure out her angle, but I didn't want to get into that. I wanted her to go away so I could eat and talk to my friends and not have to think about her again until necessary. "If I say I'll think about it, will you leave me alone?"

"Yes, of course," Mack said, smiling more as she ran a hand through her perfect blonde hair. "Your friends can come too, if that'll help sway your opinion."

"It helps," I said. "See you later."

"Yeah. See you."

She looked practically giddy as she walked off, leaving me at a loss for words. What the hell was that?

"What did *she* want?"

I returned to reality after an unknown number of seconds, seeing Audrey and Isaac staring back at me. "Um, she invited me to her party on Friday?" I said, still not fully believing it. "Something about getting to know the team. You're both invited, too."

"Yeah?" Isaac glanced toward the volleyball table, a light smile forming on his face. "Think Olivia will be there?"

"I doubt Mackenzie would host a party without her bestie."

"Damn boy, you've got it *bad*," Audrey teased, nudging Isaac before raising a brow at me. "Is she trying to out-nice you or something? What's her angle?"

"I don't know," I said, glad someone understood. "But I'm sure she's trying to get on my good side again by acting all buddy-buddy. Or maybe it's her way of getting Isaac to the party for Olivia."

"That's obviously not it," Isaac said, his cheeks turning a deep shade of red. "But we're going, right? I've heard her parties can get pretty intense, like the time someone ended up in the hospital after jumping off the balcony."

"Or the time my dad and I had to pick my brother up there on the Fourth of July because he was vomiting in the tub," I said, my nose scrunching at the visual from this past summer.

"Or the time Tanner Munroe got arrested for selling drugs," Audrey added, looking as giddy as Mack had a minute ago. "Or all the hookups and breakups and makeups . . . oh my god, we have to go!"

I laughed at Audrey's enthusiasm. None of us were party

kids, but we'd also never been *invited* to the kind of event that would make us party kids. "You really want to go?" I asked.

"Totally," Audrey said. "Plus, this is a good first step. You didn't have to insert yourself into her life for our plan to work. She came to *you*. So just be your charming self and she won't suspect a thing. It's perfect."

It was impossible not to laugh at her scheming. "Do you hate her for something I don't know about?"

"I hate her for leading your friendship on and hurting you," Audrey said. "No one gets away with that, even if it took years for us to come up with a good revenge plot. And I decided we're calling it Operation Mack Attack."

Isaac snorted. All our little schemes over the years had some kind of operation tied to them, courtesy of Audrey. Operation Ungrounding. Operation Homecoming. Operation Save the Dogs. The older we got, the more invested Audrey became, and Isaac and I were too amused to stop her. "You should've been in drama instead of journalism," I teased, nudging her foot. "And okay, we'll go to the party. Can I eat now?"

"Yes!" Audrey said, almost knocking her shake over while raising her hands in cheer. "This is going to be so good for you. Operation Mack Attack is on!"

I steadied her glass, knowing she was already making plans in her head. No matter how invested she got, Isaac and I could rein her in if needed. And this wouldn't be a true scheme anyway, just me writing a solid article, so I was confident things wouldn't get out of control.

I waited in Mx. Shannon's office after class the next day as they said goodbye to a few students. They hadn't sounded mad when asking me to stay behind, so at least I had that going for me. But after the past couple of days, anything was possible.

After closing the door behind them, Shannon sat across from me at their desk. "Your mom called me this morning."

I groaned. Mom hadn't said anything else about calling the school, so I'd taken her plan as a false threat, but I should've known better. "I didn't ask her to," I said. "In fact, I specifically told her not to call you. I'm sorry."

Mx. Shannon chuckled, shaking their head. "Don't be sorry. It's refreshing to see parents taking an interest in their kids. And she's one of the only parents who gets my title and pronouns right every time, so I guess I can let her *try* telling me how to do my job."

Despite Mom's imperfections, she was good for that. Granted, knowing such things didn't warrant a trophy, but at least she supported people for who they were. Letting her daughter fight her own battles was another matter entirely, apparently. "Well, I hope you didn't cave. I have a plan."

"A plan?" Mx. Shannon raised their brows. "Care to share?"

"There's really nothing to share. I've just figured out a way to handle my nemesis. The paper will get solid volleyball stories and a feature that will put all other features to shame. But I might need some extra time on it. Can we could hold off on having it due until later in the semester?"

"Do what you need to do. There's no real timeline as long as it gets done and you're covering the sport as outlined otherwise. And I trust you."

I wished they hadn't smiled when saying that. The party would mark my official entrance to the dark side, and they wouldn't be smiling if they knew what that might entail. But I meant what I'd said—my plan wouldn't cause problems for the paper. And if it did, at least it would get people talking. Really, it depended on what I learned about Mack. But I would find *something*. I wasn't turning back now. I wouldn't throw away my chance to shine.

CHAPTER FIVE

POND MADE ME pay for not taking her to the dog park yesterday. It didn't matter that I was at another volleyball practice or
that Dad took her out shortly after her normal time. She tugged
extra hard on the way and took an extra-large poop. I'd say it was
coincidence, but she even gave me a *look* after to seal the deal.
Once she'd made her point, she took off to see her best friend
Bingley, an adorable Westie who I was pretty sure was one of
Pond's many crushes. I watched them play until my phone rang
a minute later.

Casey.

I wasn't used to my brother calling since, until recently, we'd
lived together my entire life, and we usually just texted if we
needed to talk. We also didn't have a friendship kind of relationship. We'd always done our own things and had different
friends and interests. The only friend we'd shared was Mack,
but they'd become friends after she ghosted me.

Not that I thought about that ever.

Not that it had bothered me for two years.

"What's up, Casey?" I said, my eyes fixed on Pond just in case she needed me.

"Hey, JoJo," he said, his tone as positive as always. "Not much, just thought I'd call and check in. It's been a while."

"Uh, yeah," I laughed quietly, confused more than anything. It wasn't terrible to hear from him, but it wasn't normal either. "School started. I'm at the dog park with Pond. Same old, same old."

"Cool, cool. How's newspaper going?"

Now it all made sense. "Dad told you." It wasn't a question.

"Yeah. He thought I could help."

So much for letting me handle my own life. Thanks, Dad. A pause filled the phone as I thought about how to respond. "I mean, thanks for calling, but I don't know what you can do, you know? I agreed to cover the volleyball beat. And it sucks that I have to write a feature story on your friend Mackenzie West of all people, but I'll get over it."

"You're writing about Mackenzie?"

Shit. I hadn't meant to tell him all that. He vaguely knew about what had happened the first week of freshman year, and he probably overheard me complain about it several times since, but still. This wasn't something I wanted to get into now. "Yeah. She made captain, so naturally I'll have to write about her."

There was another pause—this time because of Casey. "Maybe it'll give you two a chance to reconnect and put the past behind you," he said.

If that was the great advice Dad was hinting at, I didn't want it. "She's had two years to reconnect, not to mention apologize. I wasn't the one who messed up."

"I know, I know. I'm just saying you could be the bigger person. Maybe she wants to be friends but doesn't know how."

I snorted a laugh. "I seriously doubt that. But don't worry, I've got it handled."

"If you say so." Another pause. "Everything else okay?"

"What do you mean?"

"I don't know, just . . . life, or whatever? You good?"

I smiled a little at Casey's attempt to have a conversation. "Yeah, I'm good. What about you? What's new?" He'd left for Minneapolis shortly after graduation so he could get settled and start a job, so I hadn't seen him since July. Even though we weren't close, I missed having him around the apartment for family meals and random movie nights. I cared about him—I just didn't need him to know that.

"I met a girl last month," he said after a reluctant pause. "She's pretty great."

I laughed again. "Pretty great? That's all I get?"

"I mean, I could give you the complimentary list about how she's smart and funny and beautiful and probably too good for me, but I thought leaving it at 'pretty great' would keep me from getting my hopes up."

That was . . . kind of adorable. "Wow, so you're, like, in love and shit," I teased, tilting my head back to look up at the drifting clouds.

He scoffed. "Shut up. It's not *that* intense, but I like her. What about you? Got your eye on any smart, funny, beautiful girls?"

"No," I said slowly, thrown off by his sudden interest. I'd dated a girl last year who'd since gone off to college, and another the year before whose parents didn't know she was queer—which, no pressure, but it got too hard being someone's secret. But even with two exes, the question felt foreign to me. Dating wasn't a priority. "There's no one."

"Well, maybe that'll change this year," Casey said. "You never know."

He had a way of making it sound like he'd just willed his words into existence, but that only ever seemed to work for him. He'd gotten straight As with minimal effort while I did well after working my ass off. He played multiple sports over the years and was on homecoming court while I had newspaper and zero homecoming plans. He was attending the University of Minnesota in Minneapolis, and I'd probably end up at a mediocre-at-best state school . . . no offense to state schools.

"You never know," I said instead of getting into a rant about how nothing happened for me like it did for him. I was going to circle back to the girl—was she a girlfriend?—when I faced forward again and saw Pond barreling toward me with something in her mouth. "Sorry, gotta go. Pond is being a menace. Thanks for the talk."

Casey chuckled, knowing that Pond had her moments of chaos. "You got it. Good luck with Pond."

"Thanks, bye!" I hung up and stood in time for Pond to drop a baseball hat at my feet like it was a bone. Of course she looked proud of herself.

"You know better," I scolded her as I picked up the hat and was instantly transferred to the past. Looking up confirmed why.

As far as I knew, Mack hadn't been to the dog park since her family moved into their new house a couple of months after our friendship breakup. I wasn't able to face the park until I knew she'd moved across town. But there she was, slowing her run as she neared me with Sabrina, her dachshund. Of all the people I wanted to deal with right now, she was at the bottom of the list.

"I think she remembers us," Mack said with a light laugh as Pond started circling and sniffing Sabrina excitedly. Traitor.

"If that were true, she would've done worse than take your hat," I said before I could help it. If I was going to get a good story, I'd need to learn how to calm my biting remarks around her. "Sorry."

"No, I deserved that."

I remembered my brother's advice and quickly shook it off. That kind of stuff only worked out for him. "Look, I know we're being forced into a situation that we don't want to be in, so let's just get through it and move on, okay?"

Mack looked taken aback at my response, which made me realize I'd said it out of nowhere. "Yeah, sure," she said. "Okay."

I thought she'd be relieved that we could be civil without

having to pretend, but her face held a different expression. Hurt? No, she wasn't allowed to be hurt. I could pretend to get over her deception for the sake of solid journalism, but I wouldn't let her pull me back in. I brushed off the hat before handing it to her. "Sorry about Pond," I said.

"It's fine, thanks," she said as she took the hat, her eyes still on me. "Listen, don't feel forced to come on Friday, but it was a real invitation. I'm sure it's unconventional and more of a commitment than what you're used to for journalism—"

"What's that supposed to mean?" I asked. "You think I'm not committed to the paper?"

"No," Mack said quickly. "That's not what I meant. I'm just saying that we both care a lot about our passions, and if getting to know the team better will help you with your stories, we'd love to have you there. A lot of people think we're some bitchy cult or whatever, but most of the team is really nice. Count me as the exception if you want." She smiled sheepishly.

An unwilling laugh escaped me. "Maybe I will," I said. "And I'll be there. Audrey and Isaac, too."

"Cool," Mack said, and it sounded like she meant it.

"Cool," I echoed, looking at her for a moment before leaning down to attach Pond's leash to her collar. "Well, we better get home, but I'll see you Friday."

"Yeah, great, see you Friday!" Mack said, grinning at the confirmation.

Had she really driven miles out of the way to talk to me for a minute? She could've called or texted. Or did she still come here and I'd never noticed? That was unlikely. Whatever her agenda, she was going all in.

Walking off, I was no longer confident Pond had stolen the hat.

CHAPTER SIX

BY THE TIME Isaac and I parked in front of Audrey's house Friday night, I was ready to bail on the whole thing and drive us to The Diner instead. But Audrey hadn't stopped talking about it the last couple of days, and I *knew* Isaac wanted to see Olivia, so it was worth suffering for a couple of hours if it meant making their dreams come true.

Also, Operation Mack Attack would officially commence. I needed to work on a better name—no offense, Audrey—but that was future Jordan's problem. Tonight was all about getting on Mack's good side in a genuine, believable way and having that trickle down to the rest of the team. I didn't *know* that they had a bad opinion of me, but I also didn't know if the "summer stalker" story was a recurring joke among them—if *I* was a recurring joke. I needed them to take me seriously and not think of me as someone who'd asked for the beat so I could follow Mack around.

Easy.

"Okay, so here's the plan," I said as we walked toward Mack's house, which was only a couple of blocks from Audrey's. "If we drink too much, we'll have a sleepover at Audrey's. If not, let's have one anyway."

"Yes to drinking!" Audrey added a little skip to her step, as if any of us were drinkers—but hey, when in the lion's den. "Love it. What else?"

"Um, good question," I said, not thinking that far ahead. "Let's not stay for more than two hours? But if anyone is having a shitty time, then we all leave. No one gets left behind."

Isaac groaned. "You act like we're going into battle."

"Aren't we? This is an elite high school party that we'd *never* be invited to if Mack didn't want to make a great impression in the paper. It's basically a fake invite." I looked over at him. "And you want to impress Olivia, right?"

"Honestly, at this point I just want to survive high school," he said. "But yeah, I want to impress her. Or just hang out with her as myself and have her like me naturally."

"I second that!" Audrey said, practically giddy as she bounce-walked.

"Thirded," I said, letting out a nervous breath. "So we're all set."

I turned to them. Audrey had curled her long black hair and had on more makeup than usual, including winged eyeliner, and she wore a black skirt and white crop top. My look was similar but with straight hair, a regular white shirt, dark jeans, and a lightweight camo jacket. And Isaac was giving Nick Miller from *New Girl* vibes in his flannel. We were all pretty on brand,

and I loved that for us. We didn't turn into different people just because we were going to a party. And good thing, too, because we looked hot.

And then there was Isaac.

I grinned as I rang the doorbell. "Nick Miller."

"No, come on!" Isaac groaned. "You can't Nick Miller me right as we're about to enter a party."

"Too late, Nick Miller," Audrey said, giggling. When no one answered the door, she opened it herself to reveal a world of chaos. "Oh. My. God."

We laughed in unison, likely due to how out of our element we were. I'd half expected the invitation to be a prank to fuck with me, but there really was a party inside. Music blasted overhead as several groups of people gathered in various parts of Mack's house. Depending on where I looked, people were dancing, talking, eating, making out, playing drinking games, or just drinking in general.

I was entering my brother's world. He used to attend Mack's parties. It was one of the reasons our relationship was complicated. I'd been kicked out of her orbit and he'd drifted in—as if there could only be one of us. And here I was, back in—even if only temporarily—and I couldn't help but wish Casey was here to guide me through it. He'd know what to say, how to act, and have ten new friends by the end of it. I'd be lucky to survive the agreed upon two hours.

I snapped out of it when I heard my name.

"Jordan, you came!" Mack said, her wide smile giving away

an excitement that made me question her more than if she'd looked neutral. Was she actually happy that we were here? That *I* was here? "Find the place okay?"

Audrey snorted a laugh. "Considering we're basically neighbors, yes."

"Right," Mack said slowly as if she'd had no idea, then looked at Isaac. "Olivia's in the kitchen."

Isaac's eyes immediately found the route. "Do you mind?" he asked us.

"Not at all. Have fun!" Audrey said in a singsong voice before grinning at me. "I'm going to get a drink. Find me later?"

I'd thought the point of having my friends here was so I wouldn't have to be alone with Mack, but maybe this would help her open up more, be more vulnerable. Or having no backup would make it easier for this whole night to go wrong. Either way, I was on my own. "Yeah, happy drinking!" I said, feigning enthusiasm.

"Come on," Mack said once we were alone. "Most of the team is out back by the pool."

I'd never understood people who had outdoor pools in northern Minnesota. Then again, I was middle class and lived in an apartment. Even though they could afford a house, my parents would never put money in for a pool that we could only use four months out of the year, max. I pushed my rich-people judgments aside and nodded. "Sounds good."

After Mack found us two fruit beers in her kitchen, we wandered outside to where more people were gathered, cups littering the grass and the edge of the long in-ground pool. It seemed like half the school was here, but that wasn't realistic. Parties like Mack's had always been selective, so it was likely that "cool" kids from *other* schools were here. That would explain why I didn't recognize a lot of the crowd.

"Look who made it!" Mack said as we approached the volleyball team, who were lounging on cushioned furniture under a twinkle-light-lined pergola.

I'd never seen a sight like it in my entire life. As if on cue, most of the team stopped what they were doing and focused on me with matching expressions. Whether their small smiles were genuine or not, it was clear that Mack had asked them to be nice. Outside of school assignments, I'd never spoken to most of them my entire life.

Brie Carlson, a senior, was the only one who didn't follow suit. Like most of the team, she was blonde, tanned from the summer months, and strikingly pretty. She looked me up and down the way people in movies sized up a project—or an enemy. We'd been in homeroom together since I started high school, and she was friends with my brother. Ever since she'd huffed into homeroom last year and asked—no, *demanded*—that I tell my brother to text her back, I kept my distance. I'd also overheard her complaining to someone this week about how she was supposed to be captain. Was that true, or was it like how I was supposed to have an editor position? Regardless, I'd saved the info to my brain palace.

"Join us," she said, patting the spot next to her. "We were just talking about the match schedule for the season."

Her expression made my skin crawl, like a wolf who had found its latest prey. But I didn't dare start the night by intentionally sitting somewhere else, so I took her up on the offer. "What about it?" I asked, trying to hide both my nerves and my amusement. For them to be discussing volleyball at a rowdy party either made them committed or boring. And I doubted they were boring.

"Olivia had an interesting idea," Brie's best friend, Marissa, said before raising a brow at Mack.

"Oh, right," Mack said, shifting in the seat she'd taken across from me. "Olivia thought it would be nice if you joined us on the bus for the away games, to get the full picture of things. And obviously we don't go anywhere far, but there's a big tournament in Minneapolis later in the season. Could be fun, right?"

Was she rambling? Was this really that big of a deal? And why was it Olivia's idea? Did she really care that much about Mack's feature story or how well I covered volleyball? Or was this Mack's idea and Olivia wasn't here to say otherwise?

Before I could ask any of these questions, Brie chimed in. "And your brother lives in Minneapolis, so if he came to the game, you could hang out with him." Her grin grew. "You know, if you need convincing."

"Is that your way of trying to get Casey to come to the tournament?" I asked, seeing through her immediately. They'd never dated, but she used to hang around the apartment a lot with

Casey's other friends. In the very least, I knew she'd had a crush on him. "I'm pretty sure he has a girlfriend now."

"Technicalities," Brie said, shrugging. "And yes, maybe I do want to see him, but I don't *need you* to make that happen. We just need you there to write about us. Your brother would be a bonus."

No doubt.

"I'm Isaac's ride," I said, knowing it was a weak excuse. I didn't even know yet if he'd join for a game hours from home, send someone else, or have me take pictures.

"There's plenty of room on the bus for him, too," Mack said.

"And Olivia would *love* it," Marissa added, getting chuckles from the group.

Damn, also that. Seeing the team's reaction to whatever was happening between Olivia and Isaac made me nervous. The last thing I wanted was to be around Mack so much that it reminded anyone of what she used to say about me *trying* to be around her so much. Getting through high school without hearing the words "summer stalker" again was the goal, and this plan was getting in the way. But I couldn't say that without making the entire semester uncomfortable for all of us. "I don't know. I'll have to ask my parents."

That answer seemed to work for everyone except Mack. "If you don't want to, it's okay to say that," she said. "It's not a requirement, just a suggestion. But we'd all love to have you join us."

My eyes fixed on her. She hadn't called me out unkindly, but knowing she'd seen right through my BS so easily put me on edge. I hated how well she knew me after all this time, even if I didn't know her as well as I'd thought.

Her last statement was an opening, a peace offering. Whether genuine or not, she'd put it out there that they *all* wanted me there. And given how I'd be around them a lot this semester, I'd regret turning it down. "Well, I do hate driving in Minneapolis, so you can at least count me in for the tournament."

"Perfect," Brie said, flashing me a wink before looking at Mack. "See? I told you she'd be down. She's an Elliot."

Mack smiled sheepishly. "I didn't know if you'd say yes if I asked you myself," she said, shrugging.

Well, that was one question answered. Olivia had nothing to do with it, or at least she wasn't alone in the idea. "Give me a little credit," I said. "I'm a professional. If you think joining on the bus will help me get a better sense of the team, I'm in."

"Good. So am I."

She held her beer toward me, and I tapped mine to hers in a cheers before taking a sip. Everything was coming together easier than I'd imagined. I still wasn't thrilled about spending my semester in volleyball world, but at least the team was welcoming. Time would tell if it was real.

The feeling ended abruptly when a few of the girls turned from me and started talking about the football team, and a couple more got called to the pool. It felt like a cue that I should leave as well, but Mack's eyes lingered on me. No matter how much I disliked her, it was hard looking away from the face of someone who used to really see me. I opened my mouth to ask why she was staring when Olivia and Isaac appeared.

"Having fun?" Isaac asked as he sat beside me, Olivia moving across from us to sit with Mack. "Where's Audrey?"

"Inside somewhere," I said, instantly noticing that *I have something to tell you* look on his face. I nudged him. *Tell me.*

Isaac shrugged, his grin widening as he looked at Olivia, who was whispering something to Mack. He managed to be chill for, like, three more seconds before leaning in to whisper his news. "I asked Olivia out, and she said yes."

I couldn't hide the massive smile filling my face. As much as I loved embarrassing him, I wouldn't do it directly in front of the girl he was into. At least not until they got serious—if they ended up getting serious. I hoped they got serious. Isaac deserved to be happy, and Olivia was genuinely nice. The only strike against her as far as I knew was having the misfortune of being Mack's best friend. "I require details later, but congrats," I said before pulling back to drink more.

And then Olivia and Mack were staring at us. Of course Olivia was looking at Isaac like she might kiss him right then and there, but Mack's expression was less obvious. There was a softness that I hadn't seen in years. Maybe our best friends dating would make this semester easier. Maybe I didn't need to have some kind of scheme in mind to survive. But no matter how tonight was going, I didn't trust her yet. Part of this still felt like a game, or at least too easy to be real.

Mack's attention snapped back to Olivia, who nudged her and whispered something else in Mack's ear. Mack nudged back before getting up and stepping over to us. "Isaac, your presence is requested at my chair so you can low-key flirt with my best friend. Switch seats?"

Isaac sputtered a laugh, trying hard to hide his flushed cheeks. It didn't work. "Yeah, of course." He smiled apologetically in my direction before moving to sit with his crush, leaving me with Mack. I'd call him a traitor, but this was too adorable.

Audrey was going to be so mad for missing this.

"So, that's a thing," I said after a beat, having no idea what to say to Mack when we weren't focused on the safe subject of sports. And I really didn't want to talk sports.

"Seems like it, yeah," she said, pausing. "I wanted to talk to you anyway, so it kind of worked out."

I snorted. Of course there was a hidden agenda. "How convenient."

Mack's smile quickly disappeared. "Can we have a normal conversation without you coming at me?"

Our recent moment in the school bathroom came to mind. At first, I was sure she was trying to get under my skin, but maybe there was something else to it. But I had cut her off before I could find out. And I was doing it again.

"Doesn't seem like it," I said, glancing at her. "Sorry."

"It's fine." Mack looked around for a moment before turning back to me. "Can we talk somewhere without an audience?"

I didn't want to go anywhere alone with her. I didn't want

people to talk, or for her to have an excuse to make it look like it was my idea and further her "stalker" agenda. But whatever was on her mind, we needed to have it out. "Yeah, okay," I said.

We stood, Mack saying something about needing more beer, and I followed her back into the house. Followed her through the crowd of partygoers to the nearest closed-off room. Her dad's office was a clear sign that our lives were so vastly different. My dad owned a comic store, hers was a CEO. I took in the awards and photos and expensive furniture before sitting next to Mack on his couch. "What's up?" I asked, needing to break the silence after a few wordless moments passed between us.

Mack shifted to look at me better while maintaining a distance. "Look, I know we're in a weird spot. And I know we agreed to be civil and get through this, but we don't have to force it. We used to be friends, you know?"

I blinked at her words. When things ended freshman year, she'd made it clear she thought I was a stalker who she'd hung out with out of pity. She'd never acknowledged the friendship in front of people, which was probably why we were in a secluded room now and not with the team. Still, her words surprised me.

"I do know," I said, pushing a hand through my hair with a sigh. "But that stopped, thanks to you. And the only reason you're anywhere near me now is because you want me to write nice things about you."

"You're right," she said. "I mean, who doesn't want nice things written about them? But you have to know it's more than

62

that. I've been thinking a lot more about that summer lately, how much fun we'd had. And I want another chance to be your friend."

Was she for real? After everything that happened, she wanted to be friends again just like that? There had to be something else to it that she wasn't saying. "I'm going to need a little more than that."

"What do you mean?"

I laughed quietly. "This isn't just a simple *my bad* situation, Mack. You completely gutted me and walked away. So if this isn't about glowing volleyball articles, what *is* it about? Do you not care about being the cool girl like you did freshman year? Is it socially acceptable to be friends with a fat girl now? A lesbian? Do you need a token gay friend?"

"Oh my god," Mack groaned. "I can't talk to you when you're like this. Just forget it." She was off the couch and with the rest of the party before I could register what I'd said.

I don't know how long I sat there, but by the time I looked up, Olivia and Brie were standing in the doorway. Great, this was exactly what I needed. "What?" I asked, wishing I was anywhere else right now.

Olivia frowned. "Mackenzie doesn't care about any of that stuff," she said, her voice gentler despite the music overhead. "We're not in ninth grade, and she's not that person anymore. You should try talking to her—*really* talking to her."

"Yeah, for all of our sakes," Brie said, giving me a pointed look. "I have college scholarships on the line, and I can't afford the team playing like shit because our captain is a mess over old drama with our reporter."

"This isn't about your scholarships," Olivia said. She wasn't one to be annoyed, but it became more evident the more Brie spoke.

"Whatever. I said what I said." Brie rolled her eyes before heading back outside.

Olivia watched her go before focusing on me again. "I know it's hard to believe given everything that's happened, but I promise Mackenzie is coming from a good place."

Olivia had always been a kind person, a good friend, so I took her words to heart. Isaac having heart eyes for her may have had something to do with it, too. "Fine. I'll talk to her."

"Amazing, thank you!" Olivia said, looking genuinely excited. "She's probably upstairs in her room, but don't tell her I said that. She doesn't know about this conversation."

I snorted. Of course she didn't. Such a best friend move. I'd do the same for mine.

Once she was gone, I left to find Mack. Weaving through a couple duos making out on the stairs, I found her after only having to try two doors. Inside, I spotted a massive collage on a light-mint accent wall, covered with pictures of various people as well as volleyball medals. The entire room was clean with the exception of her desk. On it was her laptop, a few books, what I'd guess to be a poetry notebook that people probably thought was a journal, and a few other scattered items. She was lying in bed, faced away from me, her dog Sabrina curled up beside her. I stared at her back, having no idea what to say.

She turned toward me before I could figure it out. "What do you want?" she asked, sitting up and wiping under her eyes. Sabrina let out a single bark before wagging her tail in recognition.

I smiled a little before looking at Mack. Had she been crying? Ugh.

"I don't know how to be nice to you," I said. Maybe it wasn't what I should've said, but at least it was the truth. The whole fake-nice-for-a-good-story scheme was impossible when all I wanted to do was scream at her over years of unresolved pain.

"Yeah, I figured that out." Mack paused before patting the space next to her.

Reluctantly, I sat, staying several inches apart as if getting too close would end in death. Sabrina took it upon herself to wiggle her little body between us, and I immediately started petting her to help calm my jumbled thoughts.

"I don't give a shit about you being a lesbian or fat," she said after another pause. "I've never cared about that."

"And somewhere in my head, I know that," I said. "But you ghosted me a week after I came out to you. There had to be a reason."

"I know."

"And you have to admit it's pretty fucked up to go from acting like enemies for two years to wanting to be friends the moment you find out your image is in my hands."

"I *know*," Mack said again. "And I don't know how to explain it, but I meant what I said. Ninth grade was hard for me. We'd just moved here, and I was trying to figure myself out, and my place in the world. I clicked with people the first day of school and, I don't know . . . people are assholes. *I'm* an asshole. But that didn't mean I hated you or thought less of you for anything. I just . . . I got wrapped up in my new world and what all fit together."

I snorted. "Right, so not me."

"I didn't say that."

"You didn't have to—it's a fact." I turned toward her and let Sabrina climb onto my lap, my hand never leaving her. "But I like who I am. I always have. And that's not easy for a fat lesbian teen in northern Minnesota. People suck, but I don't care because I have *good* people in my life who care more about me than how being around me might make them look."

Mack blinked like I'd slapped her in the face. But I refused to feel bad about it. I wasn't ashamed of who I was, and I didn't want someone around who'd let outside judgment get in the way of a friendship—even if it didn't have to do with my size or sexuality.

"I'm really glad you know yourself and have people who love you no matter what," Mack said, staring down at her hands. "I know I make it look like I've got it all figured out and that I'm some badass volleyball star, but that's not me. And you know that. The person you were friends with that summer still exists.

I just didn't know how to be both when school started. And once I'd figured it out . . . I don't know, it was just easier letting you go on hating me." She looked back to me. "But if we're going to be spending all this time together, I don't want it to feel forced or painful. I get it if you don't want to be friends again, but I promise I'm not messing with you for a good story or any other reason you might be thinking."

My head spun as I took in her words, and I was grateful I'd only had one beer. I was torn between believing her and calling her out again. The timing was too convenient, even if she'd wanted to be friends for a while. But I also remembered the person I'd gotten close to that summer. We shared our writing with each other. She got me interested in hiking. I got her interested in nerdy stuff. We played with our dogs at the park. We shared our favorite music, movies, and books. The day she humiliated me freshman year made me feel certain that the summer had all been for nothing, but now I wasn't so sure. Maybe there was room for Mack to be in my life again, but I wasn't convinced yet. I'd need time to feel secure in her words.

"I don't know if we can be friends," I said honestly, keeping my eyes on her. "Spending more time together doesn't mean we can go back and be the people we were two years ago. No matter what the reasons were, you really hurt me, and you can't expect me to automatically take your word for it that you've changed. But we can work together and be civil . . . and have our best friends be into each other, apparently."

Mack laughed despite looking like she might be sick. "Yeah, that threw me off, too." She sighed. "And you're right, I can't expect you to believe me, but I can hope you will eventually."

"Yeah," I said, not sure how else to respond to that. I shifted Sabrina onto the bed before standing. "I'm going to check on Audrey, but thanks for the chat, and the invite. You throw a good party."

"You're welcome," Mack said, smiling weakly. "And thanks. I have the biggest house on the team and parents who are out of town often, so."

Her words hung in the air. Maybe she wasn't as in charge as I'd thought. Even if I didn't fall for it, I understood that peer pressure could be a bitch. And being the new girl freshman year had probably made Mack feel like she had to work extra hard to find a place on the team. Especially with girls who were either already on it or who'd played together in middle school. It didn't excuse how she'd treated me, but it helped me understand her a little better. "See you at school," I said, leaving before I could allow my empathetic side to ask if she wanted to elaborate.

I returned downstairs to find Audrey dancing in the middle of Mack's living room with a bunch of people I was sure we didn't know. As much as I wanted to leave her to her moment, I needed advice.

"Hey, girl!" she yelled as I got up to her. "This party is the best!"

"Yeah, it's pretty cool," I said, forcing a laugh. Clearly *some-one* had drunk more than one beer. "Can we talk for a minute?"

"Totally!"

After saying goodbye to her pals, we stepped outside and sat on the front steps. "What's up?" she asked.

"Mackenzie said she wants to be friends," I said. "Oh, and Isaac and Olivia are going on a date sometime in the future, so that's cool."

"So cool! Yay Nick Miller!" Audrey laughed a little before her face fell at the rest of my words. "And wait, she said that? For real?"

"Yes, for real."

"What a bitch."

I blinked, unable to hold back my laugh this time. "I don't know, maybe she means it?"

"I mean, yeah, *maybe*, but do you think she really wants to be friends after being horrible for years?"

I groaned, resting my head on her shoulder. "I don't know what's real anymore. It's so confusing. *She's* confusing."

"Don't let her get to you," Audrey said, moving her hand over my hair like she was petting me. "What are you going to do? Is our scheme off? And what about Isaac? Do you think he told Olivia about our scheme and she told Mackenzie, and now Mackenzie knows everything and is playing the long game to destroy your life?"

My head shot up as I burst out laughing. "Okay, *clearly* alcohol and Audrey don't mix. You're acting more paranoid than me, and that's saying something."

Audrey pouted, this time resting her head on my shoulder. "I'm just worried about you."

"I know, I know," I said, kissing the top of her head. "You're a good friend. And so is Isaac. He didn't out our possible scheme to Olivia or Mackenzie. He would never do that, not even on accident."

"Fine, but I'm still worried that Mackenzie is onto you."

"You might be right. I'm not going to just instantly be her friend again, and I told her that. We'll keep being civil to each other and spend the necessary amount of time together for me to get my story. If she ends up being a lying bitch, I'll find a subtle angle for a slam piece—"

"Slam piece," Audrey giggled.

I nudged her before continuing. "Okay, not a slam piece, but something she wouldn't want others knowing about her. And if she ends up being genuine about everything, I'll put out the feature story she's expecting. Either way, I'll write something Shannon will never forget."

"That's my girl," Audrey said, wrapping her arms around me. "Can we leave? I want Pizza Rolls."

"I thought you were having fun," I said, grinning. "And it hasn't been two hours . . . I don't think. Wait, what is time?"

"I don't know, but now that I'm not dancing, I'm sleepy."

"I thought you were hungry?"

"Both can be true," she mumbled. "Please?"

"Fine," I said, having no problem with bailing early. The volleyball girls had mostly been nice, but the idea of having a sleepover with my friends sounded better. "Let me text Isaac."

Jordan: Audrey is drunk, hungry, and sleepy. Ready to leave?

I scrolled through Instagram until he texted back.

Isaac: I'm going to stay. C u tomorrow?
Jordan: What about the sleepover?
Isaac: Sorry! I really like her. Have fun!

I sighed. Isaac having crushes was normal, but Isaac *succeeding* with a crush wasn't. This was new territory, and I didn't want to make him feel bad for it. Even if we'd all agreed to leave together. Even if we'd had plans.

Jordan: You too! ;)

"Come on," I said, moving an arm around Audrey and helping her up.

We walked back to her house in silence, but I couldn't put Mack's words out of my head. If she really meant everything she'd said and proved it over time, did I even *want* to be friends with her?

CHAPTER SEVEN

I SPENT THE rest of the weekend hanging out with Dad, watching Netflix, suffering through homework, and planning for Monday.

Whether or not Mack had told the truth about wanting to be friends, everything had changed. She'd put the words into the universe, and I could no longer treat her like an enemy without looking like the asshole. And I was better than that. I needed to keep her on my good side without slipping into a friendship that involved putting my heart on the line and risking getting hurt again. And that wasn't easy for a Cancer.

At least I wasn't alone in racking my brain over where my life stood with a volleyball player. Isaac texted me Sunday night after dinner, and it was clear he was entering new territory with Olivia.

Isaac: Don't need a ride tomorrow, Olivia is picking me up

Jordan: You're alive! I was thinking about coming over to make sure the cool kids hadn't kidnapped you

Isaac: lol nah just got busy with homework, temple, and
texting some girl

Jordan: Cuuuuute!!!

Jordan: And fine, all good reasons, I forgive you, but you owe
me Olivia deets soon!

Isaac: Tomorrow after school?

Jordan: Deal

Being the photography editor meant Isaac would need to attend a lot of school events as activities picked up for the semester. Between that and the occasional bar mitzvah photography gig and family time, it sounded like most of his remaining minimal free time would go to Olivia. As much as I didn't love that Audrey and I would see even less of Isaac now, I was happy for him.

I looked up from my phone as Dad came into the living room with a smile on his face. "Hey, Casey's on the phone and wants to talk to you."

I forced down a groan, already knowing what this was about. But I didn't want Dad to know, so I took the phone without complaint. "Hey, what's up?"

"Did it take me leaving town for you to finally go to a real high school party?"

Dad continued to stand there expectantly, and I laughed. "Hang on, Dad's creeping."

"I'm not creeping!" Dad said, holding his hands up. "Just bring the phone back when you're done."

I saluted him, waiting until he was out of the room before giving my brother a real response. "Who told on me?"

"Brie," he chuckled. "She also said you're going to visit me later this year. Glad to hear that news from someone else."

I groaned for real this time. "I was going to talk to you about that. You obviously don't have to go to the tournament if you don't want to. And if you're busy, I'll see you during the holidays."

"You're really selling me on wanting to get together," Casey said dryly. "Nice try, but I'm not missing a chance to hang with you *and* watch Brie try to get my attention."

I rolled my eyes. "Don't you have a girlfriend?"

"No? Oh! Yeah, no. We're just hanging out."

"Okay," I said slowly. "But if you like her, you should focus on her and not old high school hookups or whatever."

"I'll focus on what makes me happy until I decide to be in a committed relationship."

I rolled my eyes. Again. "Oh, to be a straight white male in America. Must be tough."

"Gets tougher every day," Casey said followed by a deep, dramatic sigh. "But come on, tell me about the party. Did you talk to Mackenzie?"

"We talked, but don't give yourself credit. We aren't instant friends again. I'm trying to be a professional journalist."

"Cut the shit, JoJo. You're sixteen. If you want to be friends again, be friends."

"Easy for you to say. Everyone loves you—even teachers I don't know talk to me about you. I don't have that. And I'm not going to risk my shot at a top editor position next year because I wrote some mediocre stories about volleyball all semester. I'm going to be civil with Mackenzie to make sure I get an incredible story."

Casey snorted a laugh. "You really think you'll achieve that writing about her?"

"I do. She's like you. Best at everything she does. Super smart. Good-looking. Everyone loves her. Can probably get two people to fawn over her at once."

"Okay, to be fair, the college girl I'm into doesn't *want* to be my girlfriend, but I understand the dig."

I sighed. "I'm not trying to dig at you. I'm sorry. I'm just saying that life is easier for people like you and Mackenzie. Things work out for you."

"But we're not perfect," he said, his voice softening. "And I know it was fucked up how she stopped being your friend and gravitated to my group, but you can't blame me for that forever. I didn't invite her in personally, and none of that was done to hurt you. I'm sorry it went down that way, you know I am, but it was just . . ."

"High school?" I said.

He sighed. "Yeah."

He was right. Once he'd realized everything that had gone down and where things had landed, he *was* truly sorry. But I was never going to ask him to abandon his friend group or get everyone to turn on Mack for my sake, so I let it go, let it bother me internally.

The silence hung in the air for a moment before Dad's phone beeped. A text came in from one of his employees about a rare edition of a Spider-Man comic, and as funny as it sounded, I knew Dad would take it *very* seriously. "I gotta go. I'll send you the details about the Minneapolis tournament."

"Cool, I'll be there," Casey said. "Have a good night. And don't write off Mackenzie. She's not a bad person, especially now."

I frowned, not knowing what that meant, but there wasn't time to dive back in. Spider-Man wouldn't wait forever. "Okay. Good night."

"Good night, JoJo."

I clutched the phone to my chest as I walked it back to Dad, then held it out to him. "Comic emergency."

"What kind?" Dad asked as he took his phone and unlocked it.

"The friendly neighborhood Spider-Man kind, of course."

"That's what I'm talking about!" Dad said, practically gleeful as he jumped out of the chair to call the employee back.

I couldn't fight the grin on my face. Dad's shameless nerdiness was enviable. I whistled for Pond to follow, and we retreated to my room to dive into my own nerdy pleasure—fan fiction reading. I made it through five chapters before my brain shifted to thoughts of Mackenzie West. My journalism future was in her hands this semester, not to mention my sanity.

No big deal.

By the time I entered school on Monday, I'd put together a list of how to write the best feature story of my life:

1. Interview Coach Pavek.
2. Interview the rest of the volleyball team.
3. Stop verbally attacking Mack every time she says something I don't like.
4. Get Mack to open up about real-life things without making it obvious that I'd use it against her if she hasn't actually changed.
5. Ride on the bus to the Minneapolis tournament.
6. Don't let Mack ~~hurt me again~~ ruin my life.

Most of the list was easy enough, but three and four would be my biggest challenges. No matter what anyone said, the past wounds ran deep. If I was going to get through this, I needed to be nicer but still on guard. At least Shannon was giving me all semester to get it right.

I scheduled feature interview times with Coach Pavek and some of the team, but Mack would need a different treatment. And it would have to start with me making an effort. Once practice ended, I waited by her car for her to come out. Someone could see this and file it away in the "summer stalker" category, but maybe that was the point. I'd swallow my fear of people's opinions and a repeat of freshman year for the sake of this story. Thinking back on Shannon's advice to be a real journalist, I'd do what needed to be done.

I got distracted scrolling through social media while waiting, and before I could think of how to actually approach the conversation, Mack was standing in front of me.

"Hey," I said, laughing a little to hide my shock. "You scared me."

"You're the one standing by my car," Mack said, an amused expression on her face. "What's up?"

Right. The plan. "I think we should hang out."

Amusement turned to confusion as Mack stared at me. "*Friends* hang out, and you've already made it clear that we aren't friends."

"Not *yet*," I said, grasping at words to turn the conversation around. "But I don't, like, hate you forever or anything. I'm just trying to focus on our related goals before thinking about friendship, you know?"

"Right," Mack said after a pause. "Well, what do you want to do?"

"I don't know," I admitted, not thinking that far ahead. "Maybe we could go to the Quilted Bean? Or The Diner if you're hungry?"

Mack shrugged, quiet for a moment. "I'm always hungry."

I grinned, and I hated that it wasn't forced. "Yeah, I remember . . ." Mack held my gaze. "So The Diner?" I asked after an awkward silence. Not knowing what she was thinking bothered me more than anything else. She'd just *look at me* like the answer was supposed to appear, but I'd never been good at reading faces unless it was obvious—and sometimes not even then.

"Yeah," she said, snapping out of whatever thought vortex she'd gotten sucked into. "I need to call my mom first, but I'll head over after that."

"I'll get us a booth," I said, trying to remain chill when I really wanted to ask what she was actually thinking. But I also didn't want to know the answer. I didn't want to care.

What was I doing here?

I never hung out at The Diner without Audrey and Isaac, but there I was waiting for Mack at my usual booth as if everything was normal. At least it was a common-ground location and not her house or somewhere full of her friends. I could do this. I was a professional.

Mack arrived several minutes later, sliding into the booth across from me. "Sorry about that. Had to make sure someone would be around to let Sabrina out."

"No worries," I said, understanding that life. After a waitress took our order, I set my notebook and a small recorder the parents bought me for my birthday last year on the table.

"I thought we were hanging out," Mack said.

Shit. I realized I'd forgotten to add the part about interviewing her when suggesting we spend time together. "We are," I said, hoping to salvage the situation. "I just thought it might be good to talk about some basic volleyball stuff. Not for the whole time, obviously, but just so I can start thinking about how to write your article. If that's okay?"

"Yeah, sure," Mack said slowly, her posture deflating. "I thought I'd have some time to prepare . . . maybe be sent the questions beforehand?"

"I don't really work like that," I said, not sure why she'd need to prepare to talk about a sport she knew well, or herself. "We're just going to cover the basics. And don't worry about how exactly it sounds. I won't write down every 'like' or 'whatever' you say."

"Whatever."

I opened my mouth to apologize for not preparing her better, but Mack was smiling. Right, she was joking. Or being cute.

No. She *wasn't* being cute. None of this was cute.

"Exactly," I said, laughing a little. "Anyway, sorry again for not mentioning this. I just take feature stories very seriously, so the more time I have with it, the better." I don't add the *for me* that lingered on the tip of my tongue.

"I appreciate that," Mack said after a pause, her posture straightening again. "I could talk volleyball for hours, so whatever you want to ask, I'm in."

I'd hoped she'd say that. The questions would be pretty simple, like I'd said, but eventually I'd have to find the big angle. *Popular, straight white girl making captain because she's talented* was fine and all, but it wasn't the story I wanted to tell. There was more to Mackenzie West, and I'd find out what it was—even if it took the entire semester.

"Okay, so we can freestyle things," I said, diving in to how I normally explained the process. "If you don't know how to answer a question, we can circle back later. And if you want to add anything outside of a question as you think of it, go for it. We'll probably do this in a few sessions, so not everything needs to be talked about today."

"I can't believe you're willing to spend time with me on multiple occasions," Mack said, biting back a smirk. "I'm honored."

"I'm a giver, what can I say." I chuckled and opened the notebook to a page where I'd written down a list of questions. After starting the recorder, I looked back at Mack. "So, why volleyball? What first drew you to the sport?"

Mack smiled at the question, and I shut down all notions that it was fake since I wasn't recording video or taking pictures. "My parents were in a volleyball league back in Arizona," she said. "It was a local thing, but they were really into it, and I'd go to their practices and matches when I was little. There are pictures of me holding a volleyball during their events, and I'd try running out to join the games. It was one of those cheesy things where people said I was born to play because of all that. And I *did* technically take my first steps because my mom was holding a volleyball out to me, knowing I'd want it bad enough to walk. Before long, I'd learned how to hit the ball and jump for it. My dad even made me a smaller version of a net so I could play with a few of the other kids in the neighborhood. My skills developed over time, and eventually I was old enough to play for real."

It was a moderately interesting story, and it amused me how she'd said she needed to prepare, then managed to weave a coherent answer. But from a journalist perspective, I was bored. "Did your parents push volleyball on you then?" I asked on impulse, knowing the question wasn't on my list.

I'd struck a nerve somewhere, because Mack's smile faltered. "I wouldn't say 'push,' but they've always been supportive of me pursuing it competitively," she said, her tone somewhat defensive. "We don't have a lot in common, but we all love volleyball. It's something we share, and that's really special to me."

I nodded, jotting down a note about that. "So, you all share a love of volleyball. Do you think you've stayed interested in it over the years because it's the only thing connecting you with them?"

Instead of answering, Mack grabbed my recorder, pushing the "pause" button.

"What are you doing?" I reached for the recorder, but I was no match for her long arms.

"That's my question," Mack said. "What does my relationship with my parents have to do with playing volleyball?"

"Maybe nothing," I said, shrugging in an attempt to stay casual. I couldn't fish for a real story if I showed my cards. "I've heard a lot of stories about parents putting a lot of pressure on their athletic kids. I was just curious if you experienced that at all."

"This isn't one of those stories," Mack said firmly.

"Are you sure about that?"

She looked at me for a moment, and I almost thought she was going to give me something. "There's no hidden dramatic journey or whatever else you're trying to get at. Maybe it's just as simple as me being really good at something. Or maybe I'm not a worthy story."

"I don't believe that," I said before I could stop myself.

Mack raised an eyebrow. "Then what *do* you believe?"

"I don't know." I glanced at the table, trying to find the right words. We had time. There was no reason to rush through this. Looking back at her, I went with the truth. "I think you have a story to tell, whether or not you agree. And there's more to you than volleyball. You're a great poet. You love and respect nature. And even if we aren't friends anymore, you're a good friend to Olivia and my brother and loads of other people. Those things matter."

"Then ask about those things," Mack said. "Don't dig into my parents like there's a scandal to uncover. There isn't."

"If that's true, why did you react like that?"

"Because you were acting like a gossip columnist, and it's beneath you."

I opened my mouth to respond but was cut off by the waitress. "I always come at the worst times," she said with an apologetic laugh as she set down cheeseburgers, fries, and shakes—mine chocolate, Mack's strawberry. "Enjoy."

I was more than okay with the interruption. "Thanks, it looks perfect," I said, forcing a smile. My gaze returned to Mack once the waitress left. Focus. "I'm sorry. I got carried away. If your parents are off-limits, they're off-limits. I can work with the story of your volleyball-playing parents and the cute toddler-sized net, etcetera."

"Thank you," Mack said, sliding the recorder back to me. "Can we stop for today and eat?"

"Yeah, sure," I said despite wanting to keep going. "We'll

take it slow. You can get in more hangout sessions with me that way."

Mack snorted and rolled her eyes. "My dream come true," she said dryly, but I caught a small smile as she took a bite of her cheeseburger.

As we ate in silence for several minutes, it sunk in more that I'd fucked up. No matter what Mack had done to me in the past, I needed to do the article justice. I needed to do the paper justice. I'd likely uncover something worth focusing on, but I was better than probing questions to get the truth. Mack would open up when she was ready. I could wait, but I also needed to help her get there.

"So, I was thinking . . ." I said after getting through most of my meal. "The leaves are going to start turning soon. What if our next interview was during a hike? I never get outside anymore other than walking Pond."

Mack huffed a laugh. "You hate hiking."

"I don't *hate* hiking," I said quickly, but she wasn't wrong. "I hate hiking through muddy trails and falling on a slippery murder rock and cutting my knee open. It hasn't felt the same since."

"You're such a baby," Mack said.

"I was wounded!" I said, a hint of a whine in my voice. Did my knee have a little scar from one of our hikes that summer? Yes. Did it get sore sometimes? Yes. Did I regret it? No. Even now, no. "But what do you think? Hiking interview?"

"I say yes," Mack said after a pause. "Let's go to Jay Cooke."

I frowned at the mention of a nearby state park. "The one with the death bridge? Are you *trying* to get me killed?"

"Oh my god, you really are a baby," Mack said. "Yes, the one with the bridge that's perfectly safe. You'll be fine."

"They call it a *swinging* bridge!" I narrowed my eyes. "Is this payback for my 'gossip columnist' questions?"

"I mean, obviously," she said, grinning. "But also, I haven't been there in a while and miss it. And it has trails that you won't break your knee open on. In theory."

"That makes me feel so much better," I groaned. "But fine, Jay Cooke it is."

"Perfect," Mack said, looking excited by our growing plan. "Next weekend should be good for fall colors. We could go on Sunday?"

"Sunday works," I said, knowing there was a match on Saturday. I also had very little going on outside school and friends, and I could hang with Audrey and Isaac Friday if they were free. "I'll pack a bunch of snacks so you don't starve."

"So generous," Mack laughed. "I'll do the same, just in case you don't pack enough. And I'll drive. We can do the interview on the way and enjoy nature distraction-free during the hike."

"Works for me," I said, knowing the trail was no place for a recorder, especially if I fell again. "Sunday at nine?"

"Can't wait," Mack said, smiling a little more.

"Me too," I said, realizing I actually meant it.

CHAPTER EIGHT

AUDREY FOUND ME at my locker the next morning, curiosity written all over her face. Or she was scheming. Sometimes it was hard to tell the difference. "I heard you and Mackenzie were being all cute at The Diner in *our* booth last night."

"Good morning to you, too," I said, laughing quietly at her accusation. "And please don't ever use the words 'cute' and 'Mackenzie' in the same sentence again. I was interviewing her . . . you know, for the article I have to write?"

"Whatever," Audrey said, waving her hand dismissively. "Please be careful with her, Jo. I don't want you two getting chummy again only for her to hurt you. How can I help?" She snapped her fingers. "Oh! I could chaperone future interviews? Read between the lines of her answers, figure out what she's *really* thinking?"

"Yes, nothing says totally chill like having my best friend facilitate," I said, rolling my eyes as I closed my locker. "Anything else?"

"You could keep interviews to school hours?"

"No, I mean—is there anything else on your mind, or just Mackenzie? Because I promise you have nothing to worry about there. She's not going to hurt me." I wouldn't let her, because that was totally in my control.

"If you say so. And yes, I actually do! Walk you to homeroom?" Audrey linked our arms before I could answer, steering us in the direction of my room. "I've been thinking about Isaac. Did you hear from him this weekend? I texted a few times, and nothing. Then yesterday he rushed off with Olivia after school to go to the QB. It's, like, their *place* now. Do we think Olivia possessed him? And she's going to sacrifice him to the popularity gods?"

"Yes, that's exactly what I think happened," I said, grinning at the image. "But come on, we've both dated people before. You know how new relationships are in the beginning. So let's focus on being happy for Isaac. If Olivia turns into a legit witch, we can reassess."

"Okay, fine," Audrey said, pouting her lips. "But I didn't say 'witch.' She could easily be an evil Whovian Time Lord. Or a vampire like in *First Kill*—rest in peace, sapphic television."

"RIP," I said solemnly. Audrey wasn't an unreasonable person, but she was incredibly protective of her people. Of course, we had Mack to thank for that since Audrey and Isaac were the first people I'd gone to after *that* disaster. And I loved her for wanting to protect us, but we all needed space to make our own decisions and mistakes.

"I just don't want to lose you both to the volleyball team," Audrey said, nudging me gently. "I know you're doing your job, but y'all have history. And I don't trust her after what she did to you."

"Don't worry about me," I said, forcing away the ache I still felt every time I thought about Mack. "And don't forget how much fun you had at her party. If Isaac and I are sucked into the volleyball vortex, you're right there with us."

"Yeah, yeah," Audrey laughed, nudging me again. "It *was* a fun party, but I'm not eager to get that drunk again anytime soon. Or ever."

"Good, because that was strictly business for me," I said. "I don't want to spend every weekend of my junior year at a party."

"Agreed. From now on, it's all movie nights and dinners and comic shop shenanigans."

"Perfect," I said, stopping in front of my homeroom door. "That reminds me, I have a volleyball match on Saturday and an interview Sunday, not to mention inevitable homework. Want to hang on Friday?"

"Can't," Audrey said. "I'm going to my aunt's fancy-ass cabin. Mom told me this morning because, quote, *we never do anything together*. As if I'm so busy all the time. But my cousins promised a K-drama marathon and snacks, so it could be worse—unless they decide to rewatch all of *Crash Landing on You* again." She scrunched her nose.

I laughed, knowing Audrey loved saving her weekends for friend time. But also, eating dinner with her family most nights wasn't the same as quality time with the whole family. "Next weekend, then," I confirmed before tapping her nose and walking into my homeroom.

Brie was at my side before I could close the door.

"Hey, girl," she said, a borderline-terrifying smile on her lips. "Sit by me?"

"Uh, sure," I said, laughing under my breath as I followed her to her normal spot in the back. "What's up?"

"Nothing, just thought we could get to know each other better now that you're an honorary team member for the season."

"You know you don't have to be nice to me, right?" I said, groaning quietly as I squeezed into the too-small desk. The school had some work to do in the accessibility department. "Like, I'm obviously not against it, but I'll write the truth about the matches no matter what."

"Of course, of course," Brie said. "But I still want to know you better. You were always locked away in your room when I used to hang with Casey, but it was cool seeing you at the party. I hope we'll see more of you?"

"I guess that depends on how often you party," I said, shrugging. "It's not really my scene, but I did have fun."

"Great! Well, you're welcome anytime as far as I'm concerned."

Did she mean that? Genuinely? I smiled regardless, taking what I could get. The last thing I needed was to get on her bad side. "Thanks. If I don't have stuff going on next time y'all hang out, count me in."

"Perfect, I'll let the team know."

So much for no more parties. Stellar restraint, Jordan. Our homeroom teacher started to drone on about the usual morning bullshit, and Brie flashed me another smile before turning forward to pretend to pay attention.

I didn't know what was happening in my life anymore, but despite how I *should* feel, I didn't hate it.

No matter how many times I'd imagined what junior year would be like, spending a Saturday watching girls play volleyball never made the list.

I sat a few rows behind the team so I'd have a good view of the court and sidelines, and Isaac was nearby with his camera. Technically, I could've borrowed it for the day since there aren't enough photographers to be at every single event, but try telling Isaac that with Olivia on the team. I hadn't had time to ask about their date, but him showing up today told me it hadn't been a disaster.

"Hey, paper girl."

I looked up from my notebook to see Mack smiling, a water bottle in hand. "Hey, volleyball girl," I said, cringing at my response.

But apparently it was funny because she laughed. "Are you going to drag me in the paper if we lose?"

"Probably," I said, completely straight-faced. "I report the truth and nothing but the truth, West. It can't be helped." Then a small grin came through.

"Right, right, of course," she said, her smile growing. "Question everything. Assume nothing. Learn the truth."

I blinked at her words, racking my brain to resurface a memory that never came. Those seven words were engrained in my head since freshman year when my dad bought me a framed sign of the quote. I said it to myself—and others when they'd get annoyed—to justify all the questions I'd ask for the paper. Not that it happened often. But I couldn't think of a time when I'd said that around Mack. "How do you know about that?"

Mack didn't reply and instead raised her hand, tapping her temple with her pointer finger as if saying she remembered everything. Even though there was nothing to remember. Then she winked at me. Mackenzie West *winked* at me.

Why was life so cruel? I was on a serious, future-altering mission this semester to make a name for myself on the paper. I couldn't have it all blow up because Mack winked at me and confused me with her quote stealing.

"Don't fuck up the match and you'll get a positive story," I said after snapping out of it. By the time the words were out, she had set her bottle down and was walking toward her team, but she acknowledged my response by waving a hand in my direction.

I sighed and looked at Isaac, who was staring at me with an expression that was best friend speak for *what the hell was that*. I shrugged and returned my focus to my notebook, writing the date and *First Volleyball Match* at the top.

The match started a few minutes later. Mack, Olivia, and Brie were on the court with three other players I didn't know as well—Brie's best friend, Marissa, and two sophomores named Emily and Kalie. I didn't know anyone from the opposing team, but I'd looked them up ahead of time in case I needed their names for the story. After researching volleyball on several sites and watching dozens of YouTube videos, I'd written down basic rules, positions, and names of different hits to feel more prepared.

The other team served first. The sounds of squeaking shoes, crowd cheers, and groans became the soundtrack as they racked up a couple of points. Then Olivia spiked the ball to gain possession, and I swear I saw Isaac fumble the camera. Olivia and Mack, the setter, high-fived before quickly getting back into position. Emily, who I was told was the team's best server next to Mack, sent the ball flying over the net. After a little back-and-forth, we earned another point.

As the set carried on, I found myself more engrossed than expected. It wasn't even that a lot of the girls were cute—I was genuinely enjoying myself. Glancing at Isaac between the first two sets, I could tell he felt the same. But his reason might have been 100 percent related to Olivia. He yelled louder every time she did something cheer-worthy. He was a goner.

Our team won the first two sets, but the visiting team came back and won the third. An hour had already passed, but it felt like no time. During the interval before the fourth, I moved to sit next to Isaac. "Have you managed to take any pictures?" I teased.

"Shut up," he laughed, leaning over to show me the camera. "I've gotten a ton of amazing shots, thanks very much. And not all of Olivia."

"Good, I was concerned." My eyes moved from the camera

back to him, and I smiled more when I noticed his cheeks darken. "You really like her, huh?"

Isaac scoffed, then looked toward Olivia and his face broke out in a wide smile. "Yeah, I really like her," he said quietly.

"And I take it she likes you, too, since you're here and looking all giddy?"

"You're not the only professional," Isaac said, the smile unwavering as his posture straightened. "I could handle being here if she'd stomped all over my heart. But yes, she likes me, too."

The team returned to the court, and I caught Olivia flash a wide grin in our—well, *Isaac's*—direction. "Wow," I said after seeing him do the same.

"Shut up," he said again, clearly forcing his face to calm down. It kind of worked.

"I won't say a word." I chuckled and looked to the court, seeing Mack give me a questioning look. No doubt she was asking if I was ready to write a positive story about the team, so I gave her a thumbs-up in response. She laughed and shook her head before calling the team together to start the next set.

Watching Mackenzie West lead her team was like watching the waves trickle onto the beach at Lake Superior. She was natural, effortless, and moved with a grace you could get lost in. But I had other things to focus on. I took in the entirety of the two teams, adding notes as big moves occurred and players rotated, not wanting to miss any of it.

The fourth set ended up being the last one when Kalie spiked the ball to score the match-winning point. Our team had won three out of the four sets, which according to my research meant they didn't have to play the fifth.

A part of me had wanted the team to lose, as if that would make it easier for Mack and me to dislike each other again. But now I had a winning match to write about, which would make me look better in the eyes of the team, especially Coach Pavek, who made her way over to me after talking to the team.

"Good to see you, Elliot," she said, her proud, elated smile taking over her face at the first win of the season. "What did you think?"

"Great match, Coach," I said, moving to stand with my notebook and bag. "You have an impressive team. I'll make sure the school reads all about it."

"That's what I like to hear." Her gaze shifted to Isaac. "Berman! Did you get some good shots of the girls?"

Isaac blanched. "Y-yes, Coach," he forced out, nodding fervently.

I had to force myself not to laugh as Isaac looked like he was an inch from death. "He's the paper's best photographer," I said helpfully. "You won't get better pictures than his. He's won awards."

"Good," Coach said, looking between us. "See you on Monday. Behave yourselves."

I snorted once she'd walked far enough away. "Behave yourself, Berman," I said in a mocking tone.

"I hate everything," he groaned. "Her question sounded so accusatory."

I giggled more and shook my head, taking my phone out to find multiple texts from Audrey in our group chat.

Audrey: So the cabin isn't terrible, but I miss u goofs
Audrey: How's the volleyball game?
Audrey: Are u in love yet, Isaac? I need a report!
Audrey: Wish u were both here

"Audrey misses us," I said, showing Isaac the texts before responding.

Jordan: The game was surprisingly fun. TBD on Isaac's love rating, but they're def into each other!

"Want to grab a bite?" I asked after sending the text. "Watching other people burn hundreds of calories made me hungry."

Isaac laughed, shaking his head. "I'd love to, but I'm hanging out with Olivia later and need to get the camera home. But I could use a ride?"

"Wow, is that who I've become?" I asked, my eyebrows lifting. "Your driver?"

"You've been my driver since you could drive . . . at your insistence, in fact."

"Yeah, yeah, technicalities," I said, grinning. "Come on."

We were halfway to the car when my phone buzzed again. I expected it to be Audrey chiming in with an Isaac joke, but I was far off.

Mack: Hope you enjoyed the match. Still on for tomorrow?

"What are you grinning at?" Isaac asked, reaching for his phone. "What did she say now? Is she making fun of me? Because she should be happy for me, you know."

"It's not that," I said, stepping away from him so he didn't try reading my screen. "And she's totally happy for you. We both are."

"Thanks, Jo."

"Always, my boy." I bit my lip as I read the message again, thinking too much about her words before responding.

Jordan: Pick me up at 9. I'll share my opinions then.
Mack: You're a cruel human, paper girl. See you at 9.

I chuckled at her response before putting the phone in my bag and getting in my car. All I could think about during the drive was those two words.

Paper girl.

CHAPTER NINE

MACK PULLED UP to my apartment building at almost exactly nine the next morning. Not wanting to come off as too eager, I waited until she texted to go outside. I walked to her SUV, wearing hiking clothes and carrying a small pack. Mack had insisted I buy one the summer we hung out, and I hadn't used it since.

"I assumed you'd be in for coffee and donuts," she said as I opened the door.

"Aren't donuts an after-hiking thing?" I asked. "Trying to slow me down with a sugar crash?"

"Crash away. You know we'll go at your pace anyway. It's not a race." She held out the pastry bag to me. "Just enjoy the damn donut."

"Fine, fine." I set my pack at my feet and buckled my seat belt before taking the bag. "Thanks."

"You got it." Mack drank back a little of her iced coffee

before starting to drive, glancing at me after a beat. "I'm glad we're doing this."

"Me too," I said, smiling a little, trying not to read into anything. I was a professional journalist, and the story came first. "I'm sure you could've done something better with your Sunday, so I appreciate you taking the time."

Mack laughed, shaking her head. "Don't make this sound like a business transaction. You can admit you wanted to hang out. No one's listening."

"Speak for yourself," I said, pulling out my recorder, notebook, and pen from my pack. "Let's get the business part over with, then."

"Works for me. Ask away. And if I don't want to answer something, move on, okay?"

Shame filled me as I took in her words. But she wasn't looking for another apology, so I didn't give her one. "Yes, that's fair." I opened my notebook to a new page of questions before starting the recorder. "So, other than your family connection to volleyball, what draws you to the sport?"

"It keeps me active," Mack said after a pause, her fingers drumming on the steering wheel. "I was always running around as a kid, always curious and trying new things. Volleyball came naturally because of my parents, but I also loved it on my own."

"What do you love about it?" I asked.

"So many things," she said, a fond smile peeking out. "I love the feeling of smacking the ball over the net, the uncertainty of where it'll land but knowing it'll land *somewhere*. I love having something I can depend on and improve on. I love feeling in control of myself, feeling grounded."

"Being captain must help, too," I said as I jotted down a list of key points to remind myself where to focus later. *Something to depend on. Feeling in control.*

"Sure," she said as she turned onto the highway. "But it's not really about that. It's about helping other people improve their game and working together. I don't carry the team. We all do, and I love that. You can't win without everyone giving it their all."

I nodded, letting the recorder do its job. It was refreshing hearing her speak about volleyball as more than something that made her look good. The team had an incredible reputation, and she was part of that. But hearing everything that mattered to her was inspiring.

I wouldn't tell her that.

"Can you talk about your relationships to the other team members?" I asked, moving down the list of questions. "Like, how close are y'all? Is it like a sisterhood kind of thing, or just a professional relationship?"

"It's definitely like a sisterhood, but it's also something you have to collectively earn," Mack said. "It doesn't just happen the moment you make the team. You have to go through several practices to get to know how everyone works together before you can truly call yourselves a team. It can be a tough transition for new players, but once you're in, you're in. Unlike some aspects of high school, it doesn't matter if you're popular or how much money you have or how smart you are. All that matters is every player is committed to doing their best and working together. That's where we're all equals, and that carries to life off the court."

"What do you mean?" I asked, pausing from note-taking to look at her.

Mack pursed her lips, then continued. "Sometimes a player joins the team but can't afford the equipment and fees, so we all work together to fundraise to make sure it's not a problem. We don't want anyone to be excluded for things outside of their control. If they're good, they're good, and we're committed to helping them succeed."

I'd covered a couple of other sports over the years and had never heard about anything like that. "That's really cool," I said, genuinely impressed. I couldn't think of an opinion outside that to add for the purpose of the interview, so I carried on. "So you'd say you're all friends?"

"Was that what you were getting at when you let me ramble?" Mack laughed, shaking her head. "Yes, we're all friends. We have disagreements sometimes, but at the end of the day we're like family."

"That's really cool," I said before realizing I'd *just* said that. I cleared my throat and looked back to my notebook, adding *team is like a family*. "So other than volleyball, what do you want to pursue at college?"

"Undecided."

The long pause before her answer was noted, and of course

I didn't believe her. "Is that the answer you're sticking with? Really?"

Mack sighed. "It's going to sound stupid, but the only things I'm interested in are volleyball and writing."

"Okay, so your answer is creative writing, or maybe English?"

"What would I do with that?"

"Um, be a writer? A poet? Teach? Whatever you want." I chuckled. "I mean, I'm going for journalism, which people think is a dying trade. But I'd rather chase my passion than something I don't like that has more of a guarantee."

"Can we keep this off the record?" Mack asked after another pause.

"Of course," I said, knowing she wouldn't continue otherwise. And I genuinely wanted to know. I wrote *writing off limits* in my notes and underlined it twice before pausing the recording.

"Writing is very personal to me," Mack said. "No one but my parents know about it, and that's only because they found some of my poems once. But they think it's just something I dabbled in and gave up."

"No one else knows?" I asked, raising my brows. "Not even your friends?"

"*No one*," Mack said.

My heartbeat quickened at the memory from two years ago. The vulnerability spread across her face as she let me read lines depicting her most personal thoughts at the time. Poems about being an only child, about her parents being gone a lot or too busy for her. A poem about losing her grandma to cancer. A poem about her fear of moving to a new place. A poem about making her first real friend in Davenport—me—and never feeling so connected to someone until then. That's what made everything that came after hurt so much.

For a brief time, I'd wondered if her poem about us had some kind of romantic meaning. But when I came out to her and she ghosted me not even a week later . . . well, I couldn't help but think my sexuality was enough to break everything. Whether it was that or the pressure to be popular, I'd quickly let go of the idea of a budding romance.

I didn't need to remind her of the obvious, but I did it anyway. "But you shared your poems with me."

Mack's knuckles whitened as she gripped the steering wheel. "It's different with you."

"Why?" I asked. "We'd only been friends for a month when I got to read them."

"What's your point?"

"My point is that *no one* knows, but I do. Why?"

Mack groaned. "I don't know! Maybe because you're also a writer, and we have more in common than I do with my other friends."

I blinked, finding it hard to believe she'd never spoken with another writer but me. But she wasn't going to budge on revealing any more, so I dropped it. "Are you calling me your *friend* now?"

"I'd like to, yeah." She glanced at me finally. Our eyes locked for a single second before she returned her focus to the road, her grip on the wheel loosening. "I'd really like to."

I couldn't help the smile that formed. "You're relentless."

She grinned. "Not sorry."

I needed to make a decision. Being nice while fighting her on the friends front sounded exhausting. If she was going to let me in more, I needed to at least give her an inch. "If I don't die falling off the Swinging Bridge, we can be friends."

"Yeah?" Her eyes met mine again, but then the car swerved and she had to quickly adjust. "Shit, I'm sorry. But yeah?"

"Yeah," I said, laughing quietly. My heart wasn't racing or anything—from the car swerving, of course. "Can I go back to my questions, on the record? I just have two more for this session."

"So professional," Mack said, grinning again. "Go for it."

I resumed the recording. "Do you have your eyes on any specific colleges?"

"Yes, but I don't want that in the article. I'm sure recruiters don't care about my article, no offense, but I don't want to risk offending anyone if they happen to come across it. Can't risk someone not making an offer out of spite or something."

I laughed at her answer, understanding spite all too well. "Fair enough."

"Last question?"

I stared at the notebook for a moment, debating asking it. But I'd been curious about something for . . . well, over two years. "Do you have your eye on any specific people? Like, to date?"

"What?" Mack laughed so hard that I jumped. "That can't be a real question!"

"Oh, it totally is," I said, glad I had a real reason prepared. "The theater feature story I wrote my freshman year was all about Stacy Ward growing old with her boyfriend of three years and planning on moving to New York to do Broadway together."

"Okay, that's kind of ador—Wait, didn't they break up?"

"Before graduation."

Mack cringed. "Ouch. Imagine that article reminding you how naive you were for the rest of your life."

"Harsh, Mackenzie West," I said as her words sunk in. "And don't divert! The readers will want to know why one of the most popular girls in school has been single since moving to Minnesota. Don't think I forgot about your eighth-grade boyfriend."

"Oh, Steve Rogers, not the superhero," Mack said with faux fondness. "Boy of my dreams."

"You're diverting again."

"So pushy," Mack said. "Yes, I've had my eye on specific people before, but I'm single because I want to be. I have a lot going on between school, volleyball, friend stuff, family stuff, Sabrina, and writing. Having a relationship is a lot to add, you know?"

"I mean, no judgment, but I *don't* know. I have all those things, except replace volleyball with journalism and Sabrina with Pond. And I've had a couple of girlfriends. They didn't last very long, but we didn't break up because the relationship got in the way of our lives."

"And that's cool for you, but dating isn't a priority for me. I'd rather have fun until something feels right with someone."

"And that hasn't happened yet?"

"I really hope you aren't going to write about my sad lack of a dating life for my *volleyball* feature story."

She was diverting again, but I didn't blame her. Apparently, there wasn't much of a story there, or at least not one that she wanted to share. I had to respect that. "Okay, fine. That's the end of my questions. I'll now chug this drink in silence and keep my nosy questions to myself."

"Appreciate it," Mack said, turning on a playlist as I worked my way through the donut and drink she'd bought.

It wasn't lost on me that she'd remembered iced soy dirty chai was my favorite drink and that I was obsessed with the band MUNA.

My eyes widened at the Swinging Bridge in front of us as groups of people passed to walk across it. The trail we were taking was on the other side, because of course it was. "Why did I think this was a good idea? I hate hiking!"

Mack laughed. "I thought you just hated mud and injuries . . . oh, and the energy involved in going uphill—your words, not mine." She flashed me a grin. "And make sure not to mock the woods or they'll hear you. Trees have feelings, you know."

"You're so strange," I said, unable to hide my growing smile. But another look at the bridge made it drop just as quickly. "Also, we should've brought the dogs."

"Sabrina would've made me carry her half the time, so I have no regrets over it being just the two of us," Mack said. "Plus, you look like *you* want to be carried, and I can't be responsible for both of you."

"I don't look like I want to be carried," I grumbled defensively.

"Your knuckles are white."

"Okay, but you don't need to comment on it." I sighed, unclenching my fists. "Let's just get this over with. You first."

Mack nodded and effortlessly approached the bridge, apparently confident we wouldn't fall to our deaths. I followed reluctantly, my hand finding the railing the moment I stepped onto the long bridge, the St. Louis River barreling below us. It was the kind of river people whitewater rafted on, and that was enough knowledge to keep me from focusing on it.

"Look at the water."

Clearly, Mack didn't understand.

"I'd rather not, thanks."

"Oh, come on!" she said. "It's beautiful. Looking down won't make us die. And if it does, at least you'll know I died, too. What a treat for you."

"Shut up," I laughed, fighting against my growing nerves as we stopped at the center of the bridge. Truly, I was amazed we'd made it that far after how long it took me last time. Mack shifted to rest her hands on my shoulders, steering me toward the side to face the river.

The water flowed beneath us, but it didn't rage as aggressively as I'd told myself. I mean, we'd still probably die if we fell in, or at least get seriously injured, but I was able to look past that slight possibility in favor of the view. A small island with a copse of trees separated the river into two parts that rejoined before the bridge. I wondered what it would be like to be that water—splitting yourself in two and not knowing where your other half was, then suddenly coming together again. There was a metaphor in there somewhere that I didn't want to think about. Fortunately, Mack redirected my thoughts before my brain could go too far.

"Isn't it beautiful?"

I took in the walled rocks and tall trees of varying colors on both sides of the river, the island that refused to be buried, and the bright blue sky above us. The scent was pure nature—leaves and bark and dirt and water. In that moment, my heartbeat steadied. "It's beautiful," I confirmed, smiling a little more and looking at her. "Thank you."

Mack didn't ask why, and her nod told me she didn't have to. Even if she teased me for my fear, she'd also helped me overcome it. I'd never been able to appreciate the view from the middle before, and doing it now was all thanks to her.

And then a small gust of wind swept by, causing the bridge to sway a little, and I gripped the rail again. "Okay, that's good. Let's move on." I was off before Mack could respond, and I didn't stop until our shoes touched the dirt.

We didn't say anything as we entered the trail and were soon surrounded by tall trees. The clean air filled my lungs, and I regretted how long it had been since my last hike. Mack was right—I didn't hate hiking. I just hated hiking without her. She knew exactly how much gear and supplies to pack. She knew the best trails, even on our first hike shortly after she'd moved to Davenport. She made sure we drank enough water and stopped for snack breaks. It was like exploring the world with a professional guide.

Being here with her made me wonder about the future. Would I ever trust her like I did that summer? A part of me wanted to, but I wasn't there yet. This swimming back and forth between trust and trauma was exhausting, as was digging up her betrayal all over again. A Cancer never forgets, but for the most part I'd at least moved on. Every moment of silence drove me back to this internal dilemma, and I needed to shut it off—at least for now.

"So, off the record, where *do* you want to go to college?"

"Off the record, Columbia," Mack said, and she laughed when I stopped walking. "What's wrong with Columbia?"

"Nothing," I said, shaking my head. "That's just . . . I want to go there, too. I'm not confident I'll get in, but I'd like to think I can get in *somewhere* in New York with a decent journalism program."

"I'm sure you have a good shot of getting in," Mack said, nudging me before starting to walk again. "You're really smart."

"I do fine," I said, knowing I wasn't being modest. Casey was naturally smart. He didn't even have to try, which made it even more annoying. But I worked my ass off and did *fine*. "I'm not great at test-taking, so I'm kind of relying on crushing journalism to make up for it. I figure since I want to go to college for that, it should be my best class, right?"

"Yeah, that makes sense," Mack said, smiling a little. "Is that why you're trying too hard with volleyball?"

I scoffed, rolling my eyes. "I'm not *trying too hard*. It's called dedication. Like you and volleyball, journalism is my focus. And yeah, maybe I wanted a bigger role this year than a sports beat, no offense, but I've already learned a lot, and that's essential in journalism. Get outside of your comfort zone. No story is irrelevant. Etcetera."

"I'm glad you think I'm not irrelevant."

I opened my mouth to confirm, but the knowing smirk was enough. I nudged her instead and focused on the trail. "So, why Columbia for you? Good volleyball team?"

"*Great* volleyball team," Mack said, pausing as if torn between the truth and putting on another Mackenzie West front. "They also have a good creative writing program, as I'm sure you already know. But I think NYU would be just as good for different reasons, so I'll apply there, too. I'm not set on Columbia, but I'm set on New York."

I nodded, feeling that in my soul. And even if she didn't end up a millionaire from multiple best-selling novels, I liked hearing her talk about writing as a real possibility. It was a big deal for her, and she was trusting me with it. "Me too. We went there after Casey graduated, and I was in love almost immediately."

"Yeah, he mentioned that, and I saw pictures on Instagram," she said. "It looked like you all had a lot of fun."

It'll never not be weird that Mack and Casey were friends. Another thing I had to let go in order to do my job. "Yeah, it was amazing. We saw *Six* on Broadway and hung out in Brooklyn and Central Park and all over the place." I paused. "There was a poetry reading at the Strand. It made me think of you."

"You thought about me on your fancy New York trip?"

Smugness stretched across her face, and I rolled my eyes. "Only because we watched *Dash & Lily* twice that summer. And because you're a poet, even if you pretend otherwise. If you go to college for writing, you'll have to share your work with strangers and participate in readings and all that stuff you shy away from now. Are you sure you want to do that?"

"Okay, first, I'm still obsessed with *Dash & Lily* and watch it every December, sometimes more, and ended up reading all the books," Mack said, her eyes lingering on me as her smile grew. "And second, if I can do all of those things away from here, then yes, I'm sure I want to do that."

Her lips drew me in, bringing me back to that summer. Each and every one of her smiles felt like they were just for me, like we were sharing a secret between friends. And when I'd come out to her and her mouth didn't curve the way I'd hoped . . . why did I still feel crushed to this day? Yes, I'd lost a friend, but why did it feel like more? Why did it feel so intense?

I shut my inner monologue down and cleared my throat. I could not, *would not*, focus on her lips. "Why can't you do that here?" I asked instead.

Mack shrugged, looking forward again. "I'm not saying I

suffer here, because I don't. I have great friends, and my parents are fine most of the time, and of course there's Sabrina. But I feel like there's a different life waiting for me. Maybe it'll be in New York, or maybe it'll be somewhere else, but I know it's not here."

I couldn't force away the dreams and stories we shared and memories we made that instantly came flooding back. As she spoke, it felt like we were those people again—just two girls preparing to take on the world. "It's not here for me either," I said. "I feel the same about my family and friends and Pond, but I want to forge my own path. I want to see more and do more and feel more and taste all the incredible foods that we just don't have here."

"You get it, then," Mack said. "A lot of people here would never dream of leaving. And it has its charms, obviously, but it's not the entire world. It's just a sliver of a massive planet of possibilities. I need to see it for myself outside of short vacations and from the privilege of nice hotel views. I want to *live* in it and drink it all in."

"Totally," I agreed in earnest, having no other words to add.

"I just remembered why we first clicked," Mack said after a pause. "I was so mad we were moving to a town that was freezing almost half the year. And when we'd met, you said something like *Welcome to Davenport—you'll probably hate it here*."

I laughed with her because that sounded exactly like me, even if I didn't remember it word for word. "And I bet I was right for the most part."

"For the most part, yeah."

"But it's not the entire world," I added, using her words from a minute ago.

"Nope." Her walk slowed a little as she reached into her pack. "Grab your water. We need to hydrate."

I followed suit, not realizing I was already somewhat winded from the talking-and-walking combo. Of course, Mack looked flawlessly at ease, but she made no comment about my appearance. She never did. That was something I'd always appreciated about her, which made me realize how ridiculous I'd been to think she'd ever ghosted me because of my weight. She had imperfections, but she wasn't *that* person.

We spent the rest of the hike talking about New York and writing, stopping for a snack midway. She agreed to let me read some of her more recent poetry sometime, even a couple of short stories she'd toyed with over the summer break. I talked about some of the random story ideas I wanted to cover, like the dangers of the new Caging trend of TikTok and how out of touch the older generations were. We also agreed to have our next interview at the dog park where our friendship had started.

Maybe by then I'd be ready for our friendship to continue for real.

CHAPTER TEN

TODAY WAS A writing day. I sat in the newspaper's adjoining computer lab to work on my first volleyball story for the monthly edition. The team had two games left this week, so I wouldn't finalize it until after that, but I wanted to at least make sense of all my notes.

Audrey plopped down in the open seat next to me before I could get far. "The cabin had nothing on a movie night with you and Isaac," she said as she signed in to the computer next to mine. "How was your interview?"

"It was actually really good," I said, thinking back on the drive and hike with Mack. "The leaves were at peak color change, so it was fun getting outside for it."

"Where was this interview?"

"Jay Cooke."

"What?" Audrey laughed, turning toward me. "You didn't say anything about a big nature adventure."

"I figured it would help having Mackenzie in her *natural*

environment, you know? I need her to trust me if I'm going to get a good story."

Audrey stared at me for several seconds. "Are you sure this isn't about you *wanting* to trust her again?" she asked, her tone sounding careful.

My brows raised. "What do you mean?"

"I mean you're not the kind of person who's going to actually manipulate someone to get what you want, even with bad blood there." She smiled, resting a hand over mine. "And that's obviously a good thing! We don't have to get revenge or use her or any of that if it doesn't feel right. I just thought you *wanted* to, but if you don't, then I'll drop it. Promise."

There was more she wasn't saying. And Audrey usually had no problem saying what she was thinking. "Are you worried I'm going to let her back in?" I asked, trying to understand. "That we'll become good friends again?"

Audrey sighed and moved her hand away, focusing on her computer. She clicked on different programs and screens as she talked. "I'm worried you'll get hurt again. You were a mess after what she did, and it killed me seeing you like that. Do you think I'd forget that just because she's acting nice now? She was nice two years ago, too. And then she wasn't."

I took in her words, knowing she was right. But that didn't help my reality. "I love you being worried about me, but you have no reason to be. I'm hanging out with her for the paper." My fingers started playing with the hem of my shirt, my voice quieting. "And if we happen to reconnect and talk through our past issues, so what? It's not like she's going to be my new best friend."

"Obviously, because I'm not going anywhere," Audrey said. "I'm a delight."

"Exactly." I glanced at her again, leaning in a little closer. "And I don't think this is just about me. I know Isaac having a girlfriend is bothering you."

"It's not the girlfriend part that's bothering me," Audrey said, scrunching her face.

"What then?"

She focused on the screen for a few more seconds before facing me again. "Everything is changing. I know we all have new and different obligations this year, but you both have new people, and those people are best friends. And I'm just . . . here."

I frowned. Olivia had only been around for a couple of weeks, and I was just starting to get into the volleyball stuff. Neither of those things were going anywhere anytime soon, but Isaac and I could try a little harder. "Want to come over for dinner tonight? I think my dad is making tuna noodle casserole."

"As much as I love your dad's cooking, I can't," Audrey said. "I'm expected at family dinner through Thursday because my dad is traveling for a couple of weeks after that. But let's hang this weekend?"

"For sure," I said, smiling a little. At least she didn't look mad. I wouldn't allow that. Our friendship meant too much to me to let the volleyball situation come between us. Isaac would feel the same—if he'd been here. I felt confident we could add these new things to our lives without ruining our friendship with Audrey. "The volleyball games are Wednesday and Friday this week, and homework shouldn't be too intense. So whatever you want to do, I'm in."

"Let's see if Isaac is around, too," Audrey said, taking out her phone to text him. "I know it hasn't been *that* long, but I miss our trio hangs."

"Me too." Having solo time with Audrey and Isaac was fun, but we had even more fun as a group—probably because it was easier to lovingly tease Isaac together. Even with Isaac and me knowing each other since birth, Audrey had blended in with us so effortlessly years ago that it felt like she'd been there the entire time.

I took out my phone to read Audrey's text to the group before adding to it.

Audrey: Come to the lab Isaac
Jordan: It's very important!!!

Audrey snorted. "Nice," she said, nudging my knee with hers before looking back to her computer.

"He responds best to emergencies." I shrugged, grinning as I saw him hustle into the room a minute later. "There he is!"

"Our knight has come to rescue us!" Audrey added with enthusiasm, which of course resulted in Isaac blushing.

"I hate you both," he said as he walked over. We were too used to those words to take them seriously, like, ever. "What's up?"

"We request your presence on Saturday for a friendship hang," I said, shifting toward him. "It's been too long."

"Yes, we hardly recognize you anymore," Audrey said, reaching up to pinch his cheek.

Isaac rolled his eyes, but he couldn't hide his smile. "We skipped one weekend of hanging out, and I see you both in this room five days a week."

"School time doesn't count," Audrey said. "And we barely hung out at Mackenzie's party. *And* you bailed on the sleepover."

"Yeah, so you owe us," I said. "Olivia can have after the game Friday and Sunday, but give us your Saturday."

"Please?" Audrey sounded like she was a child begging for a cupcake, or a teenager begging for a cupcake. Either way, it totally worked.

"Don't make it sound like a chore," Isaac laughed. "Of course I want to hang out. I'll just . . . rearrange my Olivia plans. She'll understand."

"Of course she will, because she's a decent human who seems to really like you for some unknown reason," Audrey said, grinning.

"Wow, guess I'm suddenly busy Saturday. Damn." Isaac grinned at me before ruffling Audrey's hair. He jogged out of the room before Audrey could swat him.

"Why are we friends with him?" she grumbled as she fixed her hair.

"Because we also like him for some unknown reason," I said, using her words. Her part was still off, so I brought my hand up to fix it. "You're a mess."

"Ugh, don't I know it," Audrey said, her smile returning quickly. "But yay! Best friend time! I'll think of something extra special for us to do."

I figured extra special meant a new movie for once or food other than The Diner, but I didn't say anything. It didn't matter what we did as long as we were together. Whatever Audrey planned, it would be better than homework or a volleyball match or hanging out with Mack—even if the last two things were growing on me.

The Wednesday volleyball game was brutal—if you were the other team. Mack, Olivia, Brie, and the others dominated while also making it look like they'd given minimal effort. I knew this about them, that some of the other teams weren't exactly competition—more like a stepping stone to the finals.

Maybe that's what made them so exciting to watch. Mack could land over a dozen serves in a row without batting an eye, and Olivia could spike the ball over the net in such a way that made the opposing team jump away instead of hitting back. The Wildcats were intense, and I couldn't help but admire them.

The next day after practice, I met Coach Pavek in her office for her interview. The team winning the first two games made me confident I'd be writing a glowing review, which would make this interview easier than if Coach was in a mood.

"The team is crushing it," I complimented as I sat across from her and pulled out my interview supplies. "I'm sure your leadership skills have a lot to do with it."

Coach practically barked a laugh. "You don't have to butter me up, Elliot. I'm happy to give an interview about West. And I'm even happier about it considering you haven't missed a game yet."

"There have only been two," I said, not following.

"Usually after one game the student covering volleyball is ready to write some fluffy garbage about the basics of team sports and call it a day."

"I told you I'd report the truth," I said, shrugging. "Can't do that if I'm not around to see it for myself."

"Good point." Coach clasped her hands together before leaning back in her chair. "All right, I'm ready when you are."

I nodded, opening my notebook and starting the recorder. "Tell me about your first experience with Mackenzie. What was the interaction like? How was her tryout?"

Coach nodded, diving right in with ease. "Well, I knew she was special from day one. You get that feeling about kids like her. They just have the kind of raw talent and confidence that falls off of them and latches onto you. I didn't know anything about her going into the tryout, but by the end of it, I knew we needed her. She skipped right through the junior level and on to varsity day one."

"That's impressive," I said in a professional journalist way, but it really was. That was like a freshman getting an editor position on the paper, which to my knowledge had never happened. "Can you be more specific about what made you decide to put her on varsity?"

"Of course," Coach said. "She was faster than the other girls. She had greater intuition about where and how to move for the ball, and she never missed or failed to deliver her hits. And she served as well as the captain at the time, who was our best server. Outside of how she played, she radiated positivity. She'd give pointers to the other girls trying out and encourage them like a natural leader."

The Jordan who'd met Mackenzie West before high school would've agreed, and the Jordan who'd gotten ghosted by her would've laughed. Current Jordan wasn't so sure how to feel. "So you saw a leadership quality in her early on," I said, smiling a little and jotting down *radiated positivity* and *natural leader*. "Did you know back then that she'd be the captain her junior year? I mean, that's also pretty impressive, right?"

"It is." Coach nodded. "I didn't know that first day that she'd be where she is now, mainly because there's so much uncertainty in sports, but I was confident that she'd go far as long as she kept at it and didn't get injured. But you don't get junior captains often, so she's certainly an exception."

"You must be really proud of her," I said. No matter where my head was at with Mack, I could tell she had a special relationship with Coach and the rest of the team. I couldn't hate her for that. "Is there anything that's really impressed you with her outside of how she plays?"

Coach nodded again, letting silence fill the room for a moment. "The main thing that comes to mind is her dedication to the team. Last year, she learned about a couple of girls who were really talented but couldn't afford the necessary fees and equipment, so she organized a fundraiser to help them. But she didn't make it look like a charity, she just positioned it as doing what was best for the team. Since then, we've done a lot of work to make sure anyone who has the talent but lacks the funding is able to play. That wasn't something we'd had before, which I'm honestly a little ashamed about. But money shouldn't be a barrier when you have talent like these girls."

I'd known about the story, but not that Mack had initiated it. Why had she left that part out when it easily made her even more likable and interesting? Maybe she just didn't want to sound like she was bragging. Either way, I wrote *Why didn't M mention fundraiser was her idea?* in my notebook and circled it. "That's really cool. She seems like a major asset to the team."

"She really is," Coach said, beaming proudly. "We'll miss her after she graduates. Fortunately, we have time to build on the work she and the other girls have done to strengthen the team. As long as the talent shows up, we'll be in good position to make it to the finals every year."

"Thanks to your guidance and training, too, of course."

"Of course," Coach said easily, chuckling. "But this isn't about me."

"Maybe not, but there's no harm in me giving you a little plug here and there," I said, looking at my questions again as a smile lingered on my lips. I reminded myself to thank Mx. Shannon for putting me in this role. They had a strange way of understanding me, just as Coach likely understood her team and their strengths. "So, how did the rest of the team take the news of a junior captain? I assume they were all happy for Mackenzie since her position sounds more than earned."

"It was, absolutely. And most of the team was ecstatic by the news and didn't seem surprised. There's always the lone girl or two who thinks they deserve something they don't get, but that's life. Sports aren't personal. It's about who would do the best job, and that was West. They all understand that."

She hadn't intended it, but her words hit me. Like with volleyball, it wasn't personal that Shannon hadn't given me the position I'd wanted. Yes, I'd worked hard, but they didn't owe me anything if someone else was better for the job at the time. Even if I was still salty about my fate, Elle Kuehn *did* deserve editor in chief. "That's great," I said, shifting back to the article. "I've been around some of them together outside of practice and games, and they seem really close for the most part."

"Yeah, they are. They have little spats here and there, but nothing worth writing about."

My thoughts went to Brie immediately, knowing she'd wanted to be captain. "Are you sure about that?"

Coach snorted, shaking her head. "You're more trouble than you've ever let on, Elliot. It's a shame you didn't get to cover volleyball your entire high school career. At least I'd be able to depend on you for a solid story."

"To be fair, I haven't finished the first story yet, so for all you know I could be trash."

"I know that's not true," Coach said. "I read all your stories from the past couple of years to get a feel for your style."

I visibly cringed at that. "Even the lawn gnome story?"

Coach smirked. "Even the lawn gnome story, which, by the way, was hilarious. You really know how to make any subject feel important. I know you'll bring some flair to my team, even if it's the last thing you want to write about."

"I mean, yeah, I was hoping for some more hard-hitting journalism this year," I admitted, shrugging. "I wanted to get an editor position, but here I am."

"You're making the most of it, and that's honorable. You won't always get what you want in life, even if you work your ass off. The girls on the team know this, and it seems you do, too. But if you keep at it, you'll land where you're supposed to."

I smiled at her words, taking them to heart. I had no idea where I'd end up after covering volleyball, let alone after graduation and college, but I felt more and more optimistic about it the longer I covered the sport. "To be honest, volleyball is growing on me, and so is the team. I've covered other sports and clubs, and none of them have been as welcoming. Not even the theater group, which I always thought I'd vibe with."

"Theater is a lot more elitist than volleyball," Coach said. "It's practically a cult, all that singing and twirling they do in the halls."

I laughed at that. Loud. No shame. Coach was legit funny

sometimes. "No doubt. And I have a couple more questions, if that's cool."

"It's cool."

I paused again to look at my list, feeling less and less comfortable about the idea of writing something that would expose Mack in a way she wouldn't want to be exposed. And if things shifted again, and I ended up doing that, I wouldn't use Coach in the process. "How are you feeling about the team in general, and the rest of the season?" I asked.

"I try not to get into that too much, but generally I feel optimistic," Coach said. "We have a strong team with a great captain. We have a shot at going to the finals and coming home with a trophy."

I nodded at the positive vibes. "I love that. Anything else you want to add about Mackenzie or anything?"

Coach looked thoughtful for a moment as a smile formed. "Find a way to write this that isn't cheesy, but I'm really proud of her. She has impressed me since day one, but she has still come a long way. And wherever she ends up after high school, she'll succeed."

My face almost hurt from the growing smile that wouldn't seem to calm down. Coach believed in Mack the way Mx. Shannon believed in me. They were willing to go on a limb for us and do what was best for the group as well as the individual. They saw our potential and ran with it, *trusted* it. I'd always been grateful to Shannon for that, but now I felt grateful to Coach, too. "I can make sure that doesn't sound cheesy," I said, closing my notebook and turning off the recorder. "Thanks for your time. Looking forward to the next match."

"Your dedication continues," Coach said, chuckling as she stood and held out her hand. "Good talk, Elliot. See you tomorrow."

I shook her hand before grabbing my things and leaving, feeling a whole new sense of respect for the volleyball coach.

CHAPTER ELEVEN

THE MATCH ON Friday started out much like the one on Wednesday. Everyone on our team was in sync and moving effortlessly. Isaac hadn't attended the previous game due to another photography commitment, but he was back today and looking like a fool in love a la *Pride and Prejudice*. But, also, he was taking pictures.

"So, what do we think Audrey has planned for tomorrow's festivities?" I asked him as the third set kicked off. We were at two wins, so with any luck we'd be done soon, and I could get home earlier than planned.

"Shit," Isaac muttered. "I forgot to update you about that."

"What do you mean?" I asked, looking at him. "What's there to update me on?"

"Don't make fun of me."

"No promises. Go on."

He nudged me. "Okay, so it wasn't something I *needed* to

go to, but a family friend's kid is having his bar mitzvah that day, and Olivia wanted to go with to experience my culture and deepen our bond."

I listened for the part that would make me want to make fun of him. "And I'm laughing at you because?"

"Because you're always teasing me over Olivia and, I don't know, thought you'd think it was ridiculous or too soon or something."

I snorted. "I'm by no means an expert on relationships, Isaac. And actually, it's really sweet that she wants to know you and your world better." I looked at him. "But Audrey is still going to be pissed, even if she'll agree that it's sweet."

"She'll be fine," Isaac said, but he *did* look sorry. "She'll have you. And I technically had this planned first. And it's a new relationship. I don't want Olivia to feel like she's not important to me."

"Yeah, I get that," I said, knowing from past relationships that it *would* be rude to cancel plans unless it was an emergency. "But I can't speak for Audrey."

Isaac opened his mouth to respond, but gasps sounded from the audience, and we whipped our heads forward in unison to see what had happened.

Mack was on the ground with a few girls hovering over her.

"Oh shit," Isaac said at the same time as I stood.

Everything stilled. I felt like I was running in slow motion as people around us disappeared from view and my eyes locked on Mack. Whatever had happened, all I could think about was that she needed to be okay. I wasn't done overthinking our situation yet.

Chaos returned to the gym as I stopped next to Brie, who looked horrified. The entire team did. "What happened?" I asked, but Coach ushered us away before she could respond. A referee knelt beside Mack, and Coach was quickly at her other side.

"Someone on the other team spiked the ball, and it hit her in the head," Brie said after a moment, our eyes still glued to the scene. "She probably has a concussion."

"Don't say that," Olivia hissed. "What's wrong with you?"

Seconds ticked by that felt like hours, but eventually Mack was helped up and escorted off the court. The other coach followed them out with their phone in hand, likely calling for assistance. I felt an urge to go with, but I knew no one would allow it.

"You okay?" Isaac asked.

We all turned to see him, and Olivia practically leapt into his arms. "I'm so glad you're here," she said as she buried her face in his shoulder.

Isaac held her close to him, giving me a look that clearly told me he'd seen everything I'd just done, and we'd definitely be talking about it later.

I didn't care. All I cared about right now was Mack.

The match continued after Mack was taken to the hospital. Even without her there to lead, we won against the visiting team. But there was little excitement over it. I overheard the team talking about going to the hospital after the match. It wasn't my place, but I wanted to be there, too. I'd only been around the team for about a month, but I already felt like a part of it. A couple of girls had even hinted as much after their second win.

"I just got off the phone with Coach," Brie said a handful of minutes after the game ended. "Mackenzie is up for company, but we need to visit in small groups so she's not overwhelmed. She has a concussion, and it sounds like she'll be able to play after a week or two off."

As expected, Brie had assumed the captain role after Mack was injured. And she'd done a good job from what I could tell. But she wasn't Mack.

Olivia whimpered and walked over to me and Isaac, who had stayed behind with me. "I'm going to drive some of the team to the hospital," she said, her eyes moving to me. "Meet us there?"

"Yeah," I said easily, forcing a small smile. "Should I bring this one with me?" I nodded toward Isaac, who looked border-line sick at the appearance of his sad girlfriend.

"Please," Olivia said. She gave Isaac's hand a brief squeeze before leaving with some of the team.

We followed them out and got in my car. My phone beeped in my purse, but I couldn't think about whoever was messaging me. I could barely focus on the road. Isaac had to yell at me about a stop sign I'd almost blown past.

"Do you want to talk about it?" he asked after I'd stopped.

"There's nothing to talk about," I said, gripping the steering wheel and letting out a breath before starting to drive again.

"You ran onto the court pretty fast."

"So what?" I snapped.

"So nothing," Isaac said, his voice still calm. "It's just . . . do you want to talk about it?"

I let the question sink in and find a home in my head where the answer lived. Part of me wanted to keep these confusing thoughts to myself, but a stronger part knew I could talk to Isaac about anything. "How can I cover volleyball for the entire semester when I already want to let her back in after a month?"

I didn't need to say who *her* was. He knew. "Maybe letting her back in isn't the problem," he said, his tone careful. "Maybe what happens when you do is what's bothering you."

"What are you talking about?" I asked.

"I remember how you talked about her after I got home from summer vacation," Isaac said. "I was *sure* we'd be welcoming a fourth person into our group."

"But we didn't."

"That doesn't change the fact that you had a major crush on her."

"No, I didn't," I said too quickly, defensively. A lie so obvious it was laughable.

"I've been in your life since diapers, Jo. You knew I was into Olivia before I did, and I'm telling you now that you were totally into Mackenzie that summer. That's why her ghosting was so hard. You didn't just lose a friend. You really liked her."

I swallowed hard, trying not to think about Mack on the floor of the court. Mack introducing herself to me at the dog park. Mack walking away from me in the hall that first day of high school. "She doesn't know," I said quietly. "And I don't want her to know."

"Why not?"

"Because it hurts," I said, my voice starting to shake. "She was the first person I ever felt that way about. I knew I liked girls before then, but I'd never been around one I liked the way I liked her. And then she just . . . stomped all over my heart." I sighed, wiping away a few rogue tears that had been rude enough to fall. "And now we're inching back to friend territory, but a part of me still doesn't trust it."

Isaac's hand took my free one, giving it a squeeze. "I don't blame you," he said. "But for what it's worth, Olivia mentioned that Mackenzie told her all about the Jay Cooke hike and how much fun she'd had hanging out with you. That wasn't fake."

I didn't know if his words comforted me or made me feel worse. "It would be easier if she'd had a terrible time or made fun of me or *something*. I just don't know if I can ever fully trust her again, you know? And Audrey was so excited to help me with this so-called revenge plot. I don't know how to tell her it's off no matter what happens next."

"So, it's for sure off, then?" Isaac asked.

"Yeah," I said, squeezing his hand before pulling it away to drive better. "Yeah, it's off. I don't want to hurt her just because she'd hurt me. Even if she ends up being shitty again, I'm not like that."

"You're definitely not," Isaac agreed. "You're better than that. And Audrey will understand. She can have a flair for the dramatic sometimes, but her heart is in the right place. She just wants you to be happy. We both do. But telling her about your true feelings is your call. No one will hear about it from me."

"Thank you." I let out another deep breath and focused on the rest of the drive. Canceling Operation Mack Attack on Audrey wouldn't go over as perfectly as Isaac wanted to believe, but we'd be okay. If having Mack as a friend again made me happy, Audrey would let go of the scheme. She had no reason not to.

We waited in the lobby until the whole team had a chance to see Mack. Honorary member or not, I wouldn't butt in on their moment. Olivia came out last after seeing her a second time. "Your turn," she said to me as she took Isaac's hand. "Thanks for bringing this one with you. I can get him home."

I nodded, knowing I'd only brought him with so she could see him after checking on Mack. "Thanks for the chat," I said to Isaac. "See you on Monday."

After they left, I went to Mack's room. The light was dimmed, but I could make out her body propped up on the bed. If I didn't know she'd been hit with a volleyball, I would've assumed she didn't need to be here. Still, I hated seeing her like this. It could've been worse than a concussion. Life-threatening injuries were possible in any sport. She could be in a coma, or worse . . .

"You going to just keep standing there, paper girl?"

I blinked, seeing her looking at me from across the room. "No," I said, laughing quietly as I moved farther into the room. "You really like attention, don't you?"

"You know me," she said, a weak grin on her face. "Seems it worked. Here you are."

"And your entire team." I sat in the chair that was pulled up next to the bed, ignoring how tight it felt. I could endure a shitty seat for this. "How are you feeling?"

"I've felt better," she said. "Sounds like I'll be out for two weeks."

"That sucks." I was quiet for a moment as I thought about the timeline of things. "Will you be able to go to the Minneapolis game?"

"I think so, yeah. But I'm going regardless, even if just to watch. A concussion won't keep me away."

"Such dedication."

"Something like that."

I watched her shift to get more comfortable, suddenly feeling out of place. "I can let you rest, if you want."

"I doubt I'll be able to for a while, but my parents should be here any minute. They were at a retirement party out of town."

I nodded, vaguely remembering them. They were gone a lot

for random reasons, and I'd only met them a couple of times in passing the summer we were friends. "Well then, I should definitely go—give you a little quiet time before having more company."

"I'm going home in the morning if you want to come over," she said. "We can make it a spontaneous interview if that will help you justify the time away from your busy schedule."

I chuckled, knowing the comment was a mixture of a jab and a tease. "I'm fresh out of questions for now, but I guess I can come over anyway. Your friends won't mind?"

"No, I told them all I wanted a quiet weekend," Mack said, her eyes fixed on mine despite how exhausted she looked. "And you're my friend, Jo. Even if you don't want to be."

I smiled a little more at her words, taking them to heart despite my growing nerves. "Well, you know what they say. Forced friendships are the best friendships."

"No one says that," Mack said, rolling her eyes before cracking a smirk. "See you tomorrow?"

"Yeah, see you." I looked at her for a moment before giving her hand a little pat. Her expression was hard to read, but I was pretty sure she was laughing on the inside.

I bolted before she could make fun of me for showing an ounce of decency.

By the time I got home from the hospital, the parents had eaten and were watching one of the *Star Wars* movies in the living room. "How was the match?" Dad asked after pausing it. The scene he'd stopped on confirmed it was *The Empire Strikes Back*—his favorite. They took turns choosing what to watch when they were kid free for a night and Mom didn't have to work late.

"We won," I said, petting Pond when she arrived at my side. "But one of the girls got a concussion. I'm going to her house tomorrow to keep her company, if that's okay?"

"What about Audrey and Isaac?" Mom asked. "It's in my calendar that you're all doing something. Or did I mess up the date?"

Shit.

"No," I said slowly. "This obviously wasn't planned, but it sounds like this girl needs someone there for her, and I want to help."

"That's thoughtful of you," Dad said.

"What about the other girls on the team?" Mom asked, going straight to logic.

I shrugged. "She wants to hang out with me."

"Ah," Dad said, grinning. "I see."

"Shut up," I laughed, walking over to steal some Twizzlers from them. "It's not like that."

"Whatever you say," he said, his tone teasing.

"Oh, leave her alone, Clark," Mom said, swatting Dad before looking at me. "I'm sure your friends will understand. Want to watch with us?"

"I'd never dream of interrupting date night," I said, smiling a little. They could be disgustingly romantic sometimes, but I was grateful for them. No matter what was going on at school or with friends or Casey, they were my constant, even if Mom didn't always get it. "I should call Audrey anyway, update her on things."

"Makes sense," Dad said. "There's lasagna and salad in the fridge."

"Love you," Mom said.

"I know," Dad and I replied in unison, a very common exchange in our household considering the *Star Wars* nerds who resided in it. Thanks, Han Solo.

After eating leftovers, I settled in with Pond and took out my phone to call Audrey. My stomach dropped at the flood of texts in our group chat with Isaac.

Audrey: I know I just saw you both like an hour ago, but I can't wait for tomorrow!

Audrey: I have the perfect day planned. Be here at noon?

Audrey: And pizza or barbecue for dinner?

Audrey: How was the game?

Audrey: Hello???

I groaned after reading the texts a couple of times, annoyed that Isaac hadn't taken a moment to tell her about what had happened tonight, let alone that he'd planned on bailing even before that. I curled up in bed with Pond and called Audrey, not even sure where to start.

"Hey! You've alive!"

She sounded relieved but still excited. No one hated me more than I hated myself in this moment. "Hey, you. Yeah, I'm alive."

"What's wrong?" she asked.

I let out a slow breath, not wanting to get teary-eyed thinking about how scared I'd been. "Mackenzie was hit with a volleyball at the game, and she got a concussion."

"Oh my god," Audrey said, sounding genuinely concerned. "I didn't know that was a thing that could happen. Is she okay?"

"I think so," I said, letting out a breath before continuing. "She had to go to the hospital, but it sounds like she'll be out in the morning."

"Well, that's good at least."

"Yeah," I said, quiet for a moment. "Is it okay if we move our plans to next weekend? I want to check on her tomorrow. And I know Isaac is worried about Olivia because she was shaken up over what happened today."

"Can't you check on her and still come over?" Audrey asked. "Can't Isaac?"

"She asked me to hang out with her," I said, bracing for Audrey's reaction to that since it went beyond a quick check-in. And Isaac . . . I was annoyed that he clearly hadn't talked to Audrey yet. "And maybe you should call Isaac? I don't want to answer for him."

"If you're telling me to call him, that means you know something I don't."

Sometimes it was spooky how well my friends knew me. "You're right, I do. And I shouldn't be the one telling you this. He either forgot or is being a coward, I don't know, but he wasn't able to get out of his plans with Olivia for tomorrow. He's taking her to a bar mitzvah. But you should ask him for details."

Silence.

"Hello?"

"It's happening again."

"What do you mean?" I asked, confused.

"I mean Mackenzie, only this time it's Olivia, too. When you told us about her that summer and how amazing she was and how we were going to love her, I knew something had changed. And when she humiliated you the day we were supposed to finally meet her, a part of me was relieved. And I know that makes me a terrible person, but at least I still had my best friends and nothing had to change. But now you're both being sucked in by these people. It's like . . . I don't know, some fucking volleyball conspiracy."

Normally, I'd joke about Audrey's many conspiracy theories, but now wasn't the time. "There's no conspiracy, Audrey. Isaac got a girlfriend who he wants to share his culture with, and I'm deciding to put a shitty situation from two years ago behind me for the sake of my sanity. I'm sorry that we won't be enacting our grand revenge plot, but no one is taking us away from you. We're just growing our circle a little, that's all."

"Right, growing it so the only person who loses is me," Audrey said, groaning. "This is bullshit, Jo. I'd planned something really cool for us, and you're acting like I'm ridiculous for being upset that you're bailing."

"I get that you're upset," I said, struggling to find a solution that worked for everyone. "And I could still come over for a while. I don't need to be with Mackenzie all day. But Isaac made it sound pretty clear that he wouldn't be coming over. I can't change that."

"Don't bother coming over," Audrey said. "I was invited back to the family cabin anyway, so I'll do that. But I hope you take a second out of your busy life to think about the fact that you're letting someone in who only started giving a shit about you again because it benefitted her. No matter how nice she's being or how you feel, that fact doesn't just disappear."

"Audrey—"

"I'll see you on Monday."

She hung up before I could get in another word, and calling her back would result in a redirect to voice mail, so I texted Isaac instead.

Jordan: I had to tell Audrey about your plans since u failed to do it yourself
Jordan: Start thinking of ways to make it up to her bc she's pissed
Jordan: Have fun with your gf, love u

I set my phone on my nightstand before opening my laptop to watch *Doctor Who*. I held my goofy dog close as I fell asleep to adventures of the Eleventh Doctor and the Ponds.

CHAPTER TWELVE

GUILT CONSUMED ME as I rang the doorbell at Mack's house the next day. Knowing Audrey was upset made me feel less enthusiastic about being there, but it sounded like I was the only one showing up for her today. And even if I changed my mind, Audrey would probably still ignore me until school on Monday. So there I was face-to-face with Mack's mom. She didn't seem to like me in the *before* times, but I couldn't remember why.

"You must be Jordan," she said, forcing a polite smile as I walked in. "It's nice to meet you."

Okay, apparently she didn't remember meeting me. Solid. "Nice to meet you, too, Mrs. West," I said, not wanting to call her out. It didn't matter enough to make it weird.

She had a Cate Blanchett look to her that was both mesmerizing and terrifying. Her blonde hair stopped at her shoulders, and her flawless makeup and blue-and-white dress made it look like she was off to a fancy garden party.

The longer she stared at me, the more her smile faded. "Mackenzie is in her room upstairs. Second door on the right."

I was dressed in black leggings with an old-school *Doctor Who* T-shirt, because last night's mood lingered. My hair was up in a ponytail, and I didn't have any makeup on since I didn't wear it daily. Whatever the reason, my look was clearly unacceptable to her. "Thanks," I said, taking off my green Adidas before heading upstairs, glad to be free of the woman.

I stood outside Mack's door, suddenly hit with the feeling that I was doing something huge. Even if it was just a visit, today would change things. Showing up without a volleyball-related agenda meant I wanted to be friends.

Part of me wished I'd come with an agenda.

After knocking and being told to come in, I opened the door. Sabrina was at my heels within seconds, whining excitedly as her little tail wagged. "Hi, sweet girl," I said, bending to pick her up before focusing on Mack, who was lying on her side, looking at me. "How are you feeling?"

"Okay," Mack said, moving slowly to sit up. "Thanks for coming."

"Sure thing," I said as if my being there made perfect sense. "I brought you a few things. I was going to get you a get-well-soon latte, but I researched concussions and learned that would be a bad idea because of the caffeine."

I felt her eyes follow my movements as I set Sabrina on the bed and opened my backpack. I'd read that concussed patients

141

should avoid technology, reading, light, music, sports, caffeine, and unhealthy foods. Pretty much all good things were off-limits. So instead, I pulled out a few bottled fruit smoothies, a bag of mixed nuts, and a stuffed animal black cat.

Mack's smile grew as she took it all in. "Did you really get me a Salem to go with my Sabrina?" she asked.

"I did," I laughed, wanting to cheer her up beyond my glowing presence. "Also, research told me you should basically be in a dark solitude for at least a couple of days, so if you want to just sleep more, I can go."

"I slept for almost twelve hours and have sat in a mostly dark room since getting home," she said as she opened a smoothie bottle. "I can risk a snack and a little conversation. Unless you have plans or something. I guess I never asked that last night. Sorry."

"Don't be sorry," I said, knowing she wasn't trying to steal me away from my friends. And there was no volleyball conspiracy, *Audrey*. "But if you do need to take a little nap or something, I could read until you wake up."

"I'm good for now, but thanks." Mack drank a little before setting the bottle down and opening the nuts. "I checked my phone on the drive home. There were . . . a lot of messages, because of course people had to talk about what happened." She smiled a little. "But your brother texted, and he mentioned being excited to see you at the Minneapolis tournament. Is it weird not having him at home anymore?"

"Yes and no." I shrugged. "We didn't hang out much, and we had different activities and friend groups." I considered her words. "You two still talk a lot?"

"Not often, but after Brie told him about yesterday, he reached out. We didn't chat long since I'm not supposed to be on technology. I can't do much of anything right now, but I guess you know that from all your fancy research."

"Ha-ha," I said dryly, smiling a little at the tease. "Should've brought you a donut."

"I would've greatly appreciated that." Mack shifted her pillows so she could rest against them. She cuddled the new stuffed animal under one arm and ate a few nuts before continuing. "Which parent let you in?"

"Your mom. She's a delight."

Mack groaned, her nose scrunching. "I'm sorry about her. She can be a lot."

"It's fine." I zipped my backpack and set it on the floor before sitting on the edge of the bed to pet Sabrina, who was giving me cute eyes. "My mom's that way, too, so I get it."

"What makes yours a lot?"

"You already know about my mom," I said. A perfect summer with someone I'd thought I could tell anything to resulted in a lot of personal stories and venting.

"I know, I know," Mack said. "But maybe I just like listening to you ramble, so answer the question."

I rolled my eyes and bit my cheek, mainly to cover my

growing urge to beam at her words. "Okay, fine. My mom is one of those people who needs to be number one at everything, and she wants that for her family, too. And she cares a lot about her appearance, so the fact that I don't disappoints her. She never says the words 'I'm disappointed in you,' but it's one of those things you can know without being told, if that makes sense."

"It does."

"Yeah, so that can be hard. She's never, like, scolded me for being fat or tried to get me to diet or anything like that, but I can tell she wishes I'd 'try harder,' as if that's how it works. And I just . . . I don't hate my body. I never have, even when kids made fun of me constantly in middle school. I had my friends and other people who cared about me, and that was always enough."

"I don't hate your body either."

I looked over at her, allowing a small smile that time. "No?"

"No," she said, smiling back at me. "If people judge you by your size, that's their problem. I'm not going to call you perfect because you'll get an even higher opinion of yourself, and that would be insufferable, but you're damn near perfect."

Considering I'd always thought of her as *damn near perfect*, it was hard not to laugh at her words. But I could tell she meant it, which hit me in a complicated way. I didn't know how to react, so I shrugged. "I'm really not, but I appreciate the compliment."

"See? It's already going to your head."

I narrowed my eyes, trying to keep my face calm. "I should take your gifts away."

"No," she said, her tone borderline whiny as she hugged Salem closer. "I love this cat too much. We can't be parted."

"Don't say that too loud. Your dog is right here."

"Sabrina knows she's number one."

At the mention of her name, Sabrina hustled her little hotdog body to Mack's lap and started kissing her. "It seems she does," I agreed, chuckling. I watched them for a moment before thinking on the earlier conversation. "So, what's *your* mom like? Again, pretend I don't know anything already." It was like we were starting over in a way. And two years could've changed things, so I was curious where they stood now.

"Well, we've already established that she's like yours. Loves being number one and wants that for me. And you saw her, so you know her appearance is a big deal." She paused. "You were right during that first interview. I mean, I have more in common with my dad, but I *did* stick with volleyball because of my mom. I love it, too, but I wanted something we could share, something that would make her proud of me."

"If she's not proud of you for being you then she wins Worst Parent award," I said, feeling immediately protective of Mack. My mom might get lost in her own thoughts and agenda sometimes, but she was still proud of me. Maybe not as proud as she was of Casey, so my brain told me, but still it was there.

"She's not all bad," Mack said, shrugging. "But it's hard

sometimes. You grow up thinking if you can make your parents proud of you, then they'll be around more, but that didn't happen. They're gone a lot, traveling for work or fun. That's why I have the parties and surround myself with friends. Being alone is . . . lonely." She shook her head. "Anyway, I could obviously have it a lot worse."

"Sure, but that doesn't mean you aren't allowed to feel lonely," I said. Of course we were privileged growing up in an admittedly decent town. We both had awesome friends and were involved in activities we loved. We had roofs over our heads and cars to drive and family members who loved us despite their imperfections. But that didn't mean we had to be happy all the time. "Your feelings are valid, Mack, no matter what's going on."

"Thanks," Mack said after a beat, smiling a little. She kissed the top of Salem's head before setting him aside and shifting to lie down again. "But you mentioned books. Would you mind reading to me for a bit?"

Her request made it clear that she didn't want to talk anymore, or at least about heavier subjects, so I retrieved my backpack from the floor and pulled out the books I'd brought. "Okay, so I have *Persuasion* by Jane Austen, a total classic that I highly recommend. But if you want something more modern, I have *Cute Mutants* by S. J. Whitby, which is basically queer X-Men. I'm addicted to it. Actually, it's the fourth book, so you'd be totally lost. But if it sounds interesting, I'll loan them all to you sometime."

"Of course you brought two books," Mack teased. "You

choose, but don't sit uncomfortably at the corner of my bed. Concussions aren't contagious."

My cheeks warmed, but I grabbed a pillow and situated myself up by Mack's headboard. I glanced down at her. "Better?"

"Better."

It was unlikely she'd stay awake long given the concussion and her tired eyes. "*Persuasion* it is," I said, figuring something less action-packed would help her sleep. I turned on the bedside lamp and started reading.

She was asleep by page two and curled against me by the end of the first chapter.

To avoid waking her, I carefully switched to reading *Cute Mutants* to myself, letting it fill me with queer feels while I tried not to get too comfortable with Mack so close.

I was over halfway through the book when I felt Mack shift, and I looked down to see she was awake. "Welcome back," I said somewhat quietly, not wanting to startle her brain.

"What time is it?" she asked, her voice groggy.

I checked my phone and saw that almost three hours had passed since she'd fallen asleep. "Just after two," I said, surprised. It hadn't felt like that long.

"You stayed." It sounded like a giant question mark.

"Yeah, of course. I mean, there's a dog and a comfortable reading spot. It's exactly what I'd be doing at home."

Mack considered my response. "Yeah, I guess you're right. But now that I'm awake, I should eat something more substantial. Are you hungry?"

"I could eat," I said. "Also, I really need to pee."

"You haven't peed since you got here?"

"I didn't want to wake you."

"Wow," Mack said slowly, staring at me for several seconds before giving me a light shove. "Go take care of that, and then we'll figure out food."

Shocked she didn't make fun of me, I nodded and got off the bed. I wasn't two steps out into the hall before nearly colliding with Mack's mom. "Oh god, I'm so sorry," I said, no doubt looking like I'd seen a ghost or—well, *her*.

"It's okay," Mrs. West said, her expression unreadable. "Are you on your way out?"

"No, just using the bathroom." I forced a smile before escaping down the hall without another word. Why was she so scary?

I spent an extra thirty seconds in the bathroom convincing myself I was being paranoid about Mrs. West hating me before heading back to Mack's room. My feet came to a stop outside the door at the sound of Mrs. West's voice.

"It's inappropriate, Mackenzie," she said in an annoyed tone. "You need to rest and not get distracted. You've worked too hard to let it all end."

I made out the smallest of sighs before Mack replied. "Nothing is ending, Mom. This was a small setback, but I'm focused. I promise."

"Good. Wouldn't want all this commitment and money to go to waste. Columbia won't settle for someone who spent their junior year in bed."

"This just happened yesterday." Mack's voice was quieter, borderline defeated.

"Exactly, so you should be treating this seriously and not having friend time." She paused. "Now, take it easy. I'll bring you up something to eat soon."

I tried to step back toward the bathroom, but the door opened before I could. Mrs. West looked me dead in the eye for a few seconds before walking to the stairs without a word. I took a couple of deep breaths, then continued to Mack's room. "Everything okay?" I asked, unable to help it. Journalist habit—or just nosy.

"Yeah, fine," Mack said, looking at me with a small smile. "My mom wants to spend some time with me. Do you mind if we call it early?"

"Oh." I couldn't hold in my surprise. The lie came so easily. I'm sure she had her reasons given how her mom could be, and what I'd just heard, but watching the words come out so effort-lessly stung. "Yeah, sure."

"I'm sorry."

At least the apology sounded real. "Will you be at school on Monday? My research didn't give me a solid answer."

"I'll be home all of next week," she said. "But seriously, thank you for coming over. Even if I was asleep for most of it, I had fun."

"Me too," I said, knowing I would've stayed all day if things had been different. But they weren't. I was clearly entering a world that, even years later, wasn't completely ready for me. But

I still didn't regret coming over. And maybe that was the problem. I grabbed my things and gave Sabrina a few pets. "I'll see you when you're back at school."

"Yeah, see you," she said quietly.

I left her room and nearly ran out of the house to avoid another moment with the panic-inducing Mrs. West.

CHAPTER THIRTEEN

I SPENT THE rest of the weekend doing homework and hanging out with Dad at the comic shop. Most of said homework involved writing my first volleyball story, which focused on the matches they'd played so far. I credited Coach's leadership and the team's ability to make the game appear effortless. Mack's injury was a tempting angle, but I left it at a simple footnote about how she'd been dominating up until that and that she'd be back before we knew it.

If I'd been able to get her out of my head, I probably wouldn't have mentioned the injury at all. We hadn't talked since I left her house, which was probably for the best. The stuff with her mom had been awkward and intense, but it wasn't my place to make it a big thing. Part of me had turned inward, but I also didn't want to overthink something that might have been nothing.

But it might have been *something*. Time would tell.

On top of everything else, Isaac and I had texted on Sunday and agreed that Operation Audrey Apology was aggressively needed, and making it up to her required thought. You couldn't just get someone like Audrey a coffee and hope for the best. She required a heartfelt apology and a side of groveling. *And* a coffee.

We arrived at school early and waited for her outside of the main entrance. Of course she noticed us a hundred feet away and did that faltering thing when she thought about turning around. To save us all the embarrassment, she carried on until standing a few feet away.

"Hey," she said, her head held high. She knew we had to work for it, and she was totally okay with that.

"We're really sorry, Audrey," Isaac said as he held out her favorite drink, smiling sheepishly.

"The most sorry," I added, doing the same but with a pastry bag that had a lemon poppy seed muffin in it. "No matter what we were doing, it was no excuse to bail on you."

"No excuse," Isaac agreed. "We have new people in our lives, and that's kind of weird for all of us, but you're still our number one. We're sorry for taking your time for granted."

I nodded at his words before looking back to Audrey. "Please let us make it up to you."

Audrey glanced between us for an agonizingly long pause before shrugging. "Fine, but only because that was a pretty decent apology."

I laughed as Isaac let out a deep breath. "That's the spirit," I said. "We thought about making a detailed plan, but really we'd rather do whatever you want. You can pick the day and the details. The only exception is if we have paper obligations, but no girlfriend will get in the way this time." I shot Isaac a pointed look.

"And neither will an ex-friend-turned-maybe-friend," he said, nudging me.

I rolled my eyes. "Okay, she had a concussion and asked me specifically to come over. How do you say no to that?"

"'No,'" Audrey said with a grin, and Isaac snorted.

"Now I remember why we're perfect together," I said. "We're all monsters."

"Love that for us. Never change," Audrey said, grinning. "But hey, I gotta get inside, besties. I have some editor shit to do before homeroom." She looked at me as she backed toward the door. "Is your volleyball article done?"

"I emailed it last night," I said, giving her a double thumbs-up. "Get ready to be amazed by sports writing for the first time in your life."

"That almost makes me jealous of the sports editor, but I can't wait to read it." She winked at us before walking off.

"That went better than I thought it would," I said, turning to Isaac. "But let that be a lesson. We can't fuck up again, or we'll owe her more than treats."

"Like what, my firstborn?" Isaac asked, letting out a dramatic gasp and clutching his shirt over his chest.

"And your second," I said, ruffling his hair. "But wait, how was the bar mitzvah?"

"So much fun," Isaac said, beaming instantly. "My family

adored Olivia, and she really got into it. She'd done her own research beforehand and asked a lot of great questions. Made me think of the first time I took you to one . . . you know, except there was making out after."

I wrinkled my nose at the thought of Isaac kissing anyone. "I love you, Isaac, but I don't need to know the details. Glad you two had fun, though, and I love that she was into it. That must've meant a lot to your family."

"Thanks. And yeah, it really did."

"Good."

We walked together lost in our own private thoughts until we had to split up to go our separate ways—me to my messy locker, Isaac to his adorable girlfriend.

Ever since our recent talk in homeroom, Brie had made a habit of acting like we'd always been friends. And today was apparently no exception.

"Oh my god, how intense was that game?" she said, standing and pulling me into a tight hug when I entered the room.

"Um, yeah, so intense," I said, giving her an awkward pat on the back and pulling away once she released her grip. "Does that kind of thing happen often?"

"Not really, at least not to us," Brie said, sitting back down. "One girl got a really bad concussion my sophomore year and had to be out for most of the season, but it sounds like Mackenzie's injury wasn't *that* bad, thank god."

"Thank god," I agreed. "Good thing you were there to help pick things up after she left."

"Yeah." A hint of a smile appeared before vanishing just as quickly. "I mean, obviously the entire team is *super* worried about her, including me, but someone had to do it."

I nodded despite feeling she was more focused on taking over than Mack's injury. It was a shitty thing to think, but the vibe was there. "Yeah, that makes sense."

Brie nodded, glancing across the room before focusing on me again. "So, how's she feeling? I heard you were going to hang out with her on Saturday."

"Yeah," I said slowly, trying to think of who would've told her. Olivia, probably. And it was likely an innocent mention because they were all really close, but coming from Brie it felt like gossip. And I didn't want to fixate on it or get her gears turning. "She just wanted someone to keep her company for a while."

"Oh." Brie pursed her lips. "I see. Huh."

"What?" I asked.

"Nothing. I just heard from Marissa that you stayed there for hours while she slept. Not sure who told her . . . Emily maybe? She talks to Olivia the most." She blinked at me. "Do people usually need to be kept company while sleeping?"

So much for that plan. "It's not a big deal. I just sat there and read like I would've done at home."

"You spend your Saturdays *reading*?" Brie asked, her eyebrows practically shooting up.

"Yes, and?" I asked, not liking where this interrogation was going.

"Nothing. It's cute. Fun activity, I'm sure." She shrugged. "Anyway, it was *so* nice of you to stay there all day with her. I'm sure she *really* appreciated that."

"I wasn't there *all* day."

"But you were still there while she was sleeping. Even if you were just reading, isn't that a little . . . I don't know, weird?"

My cheeks flushed, and I could feel my palms starting to sweat. It was becoming more and more clear what she was implying, and I didn't like it. Even if it had been mentioned casually by someone, the team had been talking about me. *Mack* had been talking about me. And if Brie thought it was creepy, maybe Mack did, too. Maybe her mom had been an excuse to get me out of the house. Maybe we were already going backward.

"Why does it matter?" I asked, my voice louder than normal. My heart was practically pounding now. "She asked me to come over, so I came over."

"There's no need to get so defensive," Brie said, her eyes narrowing. "Are you okay, Jordan? You look like you're going to cry."

"I'm fine," I said quickly, standing with my bag and leaving the room before she could say anything—before she could get into my head any further.

I locked myself in the last stall of the nearest bathroom, relying on people being in homeroom a while longer to give me privacy. I sat on the toilet, burying my head in my hands and breathing deeply, shakily, trying to force any tears from spilling.

It worked for the most part, but a few still made their way onto my cheeks.

One simple hangout at Mack's house, and the team was already talking. How was I going to survive the rest of the semester if everything I did was dissected? How could I keep writing about this team that apparently wanted to make me out to be some kind of . . . stalker?

Before I could overthink it even more, a couple of girls entered the bathroom cackling over some movie one of them had watched that weekend. Why weren't they in homeroom?

I waited until they were both in stalls before wiping under my eyes and leaving the silent sanctuary. I wanted to text Mack, ask her what was going on, but I couldn't bring myself to pull up my messages. And she should be focused on healing, not her phone.

Brie could be causing drama needlessly, or Mack could've really thought I was being creepy. If the former, I'd need to figure out a way to get Brie to back off. If the latter . . . what? There was no getting out of the volleyball beat now. I'd have to keep playing my role, write amazing stories, and move on— hopefully with my dignity and heart intact.

There was no answer, but I'd find one. I just needed to panic first.

Mx. Shannon called me into their office after class on Friday. The latest batch of articles had gone live that morning, and Shannon had alluded to there being many impressive pieces as well as a few writers who had "opportunities for improvement." While that likely meant the new writers, I couldn't help but worry they'd meant me.

Even if volleyball wasn't my strong suit, I felt good about my story. I'd covered the first few games like I was supposed to, but I'd also gone beyond that. If Shannon took issue with it, maybe they'd see I wasn't meant for the beat after all. And if they liked it, I was officially stuck with the volleyball team for the rest of the semester.

"What's up?" I said casually as I sat across from Shannon at their desk.

"I'd like to talk about your article," they said, as if I had no idea what I was doing there. Their eyes lingered on me for several seconds with an unreadable expression before it broke into a smile. "It was perfection."

A deep breath escaped me. I wasn't exactly sure how to feel. "Yeah? Okay. Wow. Thank you."

They laughed, shaking their head and turning their computer screen toward me. My story stood out with a photo Isaac had taken during the second match. Brie was spiking the ball over the net while the other players looked on, determination in their eyes. She'd love having a feature shot. "Seriously, I haven't read a sports article I wanted to stick with the whole way through for a long, long time."

"That means a lot to me," I said, feeling my cheeks warm as I focused on the photo. Up until talking to Brie earlier that week,

I'd felt like a part of the team as much as the rest of them, even if my job included sitting and watching . . . like a creep. Fuck, I needed to stop thinking.

"Coach Pavek came by over lunch to congratulate me on finally having a student do the team justice," Shannon said, unaware of my internal dilemma. I looked over to see their amused expression. "I think she's really looking forward to having you with them in Minneapolis during the tournament. It's a lot more competitive down there than with some of our usual opponents. She said something about being glad you'll be there to write about every tear shed from the opposing teams when they're scraped across the court."

I laughed as I imagined their conversation. I'd attended a couple more matches during the week and made sure Coach knew I'd focus on their win instead of their loss, but I couldn't pretend the loss hadn't happened. She respected my honesty and focus on the positive, which made me feel like I was doing the sport justice even more—doing her and the team justice. "Is it weird that she's growing on me?" I asked.

"Not weird, just unexpected," Shannon teased. "Anyway, great work. This was stellar journalism. I'm excited to read your next story. And I have to admit, I admire the lengths you're going to with this team. No promises, but you have a damn good shot of choosing your beat next semester."

"And next year?" I asked, eager for an answer. "How's next year looking?"

"Someone is getting ahead of themselves," Shannon said, turning their computer back to its usual position. "Let's just say you shouldn't be worried about next year."

Editor position. They didn't have to say it for me to know what they meant. "I'll do my best to follow that advice," I said, unable to hide my growing smile.

"Good. And I'm sorry Isaac won't be able to join you at the tournament. I know that would've been a fun friend adventure."

Being the photo editor and main photographer, Isaac had a lot of commitments. Shannon let him attend as much volleyball stuff as possible, but he was needed that weekend for other school events in town. Plus, I'd proven my photography skills enough over the last couple of years that I'd be able to borrow one of the cameras and do a good job.

"We understand," I said, shrugging. "It's business."

"Spoken like a true professional," they said. "Well, that's all I had, so I'll let you get out of here and enjoy your weekend."

"Thanks, Shannon."

I left the newspaper room feeling better than I had all week. If I stayed focused on volleyball and delivered more stories like the first one, nothing would stop me from becoming an editor next year.

CHAPTER FOURTEEN

AUDREY, ISAAC, AND I spent all day Sunday baking monster cookies and bungeoppang, dancing to her curated K-pop playlist that mostly consisted of Seventeen and Blackpink, and watching *Doctor Who* episodes featuring her favorite duo. I understood the appeal of the Tenth Doctor and Rose, but no one was better than the Raggedy Man, the girl who waited, and the Last Centurion.

The next week passed in a blur as most weeks did—school, a couple of volleyball wins, friend texts, Pond time, comic shop with Dad, reading fanfic. Mack returned to school that Monday, but we hadn't talked. She was trying to catch up on homework and volleyball stuff, and I was trying to focus on not letting myself read into what had happened at her house—or after. Especially after.

The Saturday morning of the Minneapolis trip, I drove to the school and parked in the lot near the volleyball bus. The sun wasn't up yet, which was honestly a crime, especially on a weekend. I grabbed my backpack and coffee thermos before getting out of the car and walking toward where a few team members were standing.

"Jordan! Good morning."

Olivia was far too peppy for my drowsy brain, and I was still a little on edge from Brie's gossip, but I smiled anyway. "Hey. Ready for the big tournament?"

"*So* ready," she said, pulling me close so she could wrap an arm across my shoulders. "We've never had a special guest on the bus. Hope you can hang with our singing and games."

"Seriously?" I asked as a couple of girls laughed. I couldn't force a smile that time. It really was *too* early. Not to mention every laugh around me made me wonder if they were laughing with or *at* me. Thanks, Brie.

"She's joking."

I looked behind me. Like the rest of the team, Mack was wearing a hoodie and sweatpants—both of which had the team name and logo on it and her last name and number on the back. Unlike the others, her hoodie had a *C* on the top left. She also had a large pair of headphones hooked around her neck, a duffel bag in her hand, hair up in a ponytail, and no makeup. The casual, effortless look was my favorite on a girl, and Mack rocked it.

Not that I was thinking about how Mack looked.

"Promise?" I asked, burying that thought.

"Yeah. I mean, we talk and stuff, but we mostly get hyped up quietly, especially when it's this early." She grinned. "It's *after* the game that you have to worry about."

"There it is." I chuckled and turned my focus to the rest of the team, shifting into pro mode. "I was hoping I could interview a couple of you either on the way down or back?"

"I'd love that!" Olivia said, moving her arm from me. "Count me in, but maybe on the way back?" The others murmured in agreement.

Did I want the interviews out of the way in case Brie wasn't just being dramatic and things got worse? Yes. Could I wait until the way home? Hopefully. But I didn't need them knowing I was nervous, so I nodded. "Cool, thanks."

I drank some coffee as two more players showed up, and Coach Pavek stepped out from the bus. "Okay, girls, let's go!" she called, shooting us all a final warning look as if she'd already told us. "The rest of the team is seated and waiting."

"I hate the bus," Brie groaned as she approached, one of the last teammates to arrive. "One perk of college volleyball will be getting a real coach bus, not these awful school buses." She looked at me, taking me in for a moment. "Sit with me?"

I blinked, half convinced I was still asleep. We had barely spoken since the homeroom debacle, and now she wanted to hang out? I'd planned on sucking it up and sitting with Mack to make sure things were okay between us, or get the truth out of her if things weren't, but she was already walking to the bus with her headphones over her ears. Everyone else was pairing up or already seated, and the last thing I needed was to make my Brie situation worse. Saying I wanted to sit alone would definitely do that. "Yeah, sounds good," I said, forcing a smile.

"Perfect," she said, linking her arm with mine. "I need your advice on something."

"Mine?" I sputtered, letting her steer us. "Are you sure?"

"Yes, silly. I'm seeing your brother in a few hours, and I don't want to make an ass of myself."

"You're friends," I said, moving my arm from hers so I could climb onto the bus. "What's there to worry about?"

She didn't respond until we found a spot near the back. "I'm going to U of M next year. He joined a really good frat and has already made a name for himself in the social scene, and I don't want him to see me as some girl he was friends with in high school."

Of course he'd already made a name for himself. I didn't know any of this, but that was the reality of him moving away. We didn't have to do the cool brother / nerd sister thing anymore. People weren't constantly trying to get my attention in the hopes of getting his—at least most people weren't. I was free to live my life without Casey around to attract the spotlight. Not that I wanted the spotlight, but I wanted the *option* of having it. I wanted to be Jordan—*just* Jordan.

"Honestly, you're asking the wrong person for help," I said, shifting uncomfortably. Brie didn't seem to notice I was partially off the seat. "We aren't super close, so."

"Really?" Her eyebrows rose. "Could've fooled me. He talked you up a lot in high school."

I snorted. Surely she was joking. Casey didn't hate me, and

the sibling awkwardness was likely one-sided, but still this was news to me. But when her expression didn't change, I cleared my throat. "Okay, um, how can I help?"

Brie was about to respond when Coach called our attention. "I don't know if anyone saw the forecast this morning, but there's a large band of snow hitting the Minneapolis area throughout the day," she said, and a round of groans echoed throughout the bus. "Don't worry, we aren't canceling the tournament, but there's a chance we'll need extra time getting back tonight, and we might get slowed down a little on the drive there. So, if anyone needs to call their parents, do it before the first game so you don't forget."

"Oh my god, I hope we get stuck," Brie said, looking like all her dreams were coming true. One guess as to why. Thanks a lot, Casey. Stop being so charming or whatever.

"Don't say that!" Olivia whined. "I have brunch plans with Isaac tomorrow. We're going to that cute new place on Pine."

"What's better, getting stuck in Minneapolis and staying at a hotel that will no doubt have a hot tub, or getting home in time for brunch?" Brie asked.

"I don't think you want her to answer that," I joked, smiling at Olivia. "I'm sure it'll be fine. Positive thoughts, yeah?"

Olivia smiled at my response and nodded. "At least *someone* is on my side."

"Whatever," Brie said, rolling her eyes before nudging me. "Anyway, back to your brother. Tell me everything. Does he talk about me? Is he dating anyone serious? Do you think I could convince him to stay at the hotel if we get stuck?"

"Oh my god," I laughed, shaking my head. "I don't want to think about that. And as far as I know, he doesn't have a girlfriend. And he doesn't really talk about you, but we don't talk much, so that's not really saying anything."

Brie huffed a sigh, but I didn't know what she'd expected. "Fine, be vague about it. But just know that I still like him. And it would benefit you to help me figure out how to make that work for me."

"What's the supposed to mean?" I asked, feeling a nervous jolt run through me.

"Oh, I don't know," Brie said, shrugging as a light smirk formed on her lips. "Your move, Jordan Elliot. I hope I'm not disappointed."

The bus was already in motion, but that didn't stop her from standing with her bag, climbing over me, and walking up a handful of rows to Marissa. She glanced back at me before sitting, leaving me with more confusion than ever.

Was there a secret *you help me, I help you* agenda hidden in her words? Or did my life just turn into a horror movie? Was I going to be sacrificed if I failed at playing matchmaker? For my *brother*?

I regretted not trying to join Mack. Sitting alone wasn't a problem—that's what books were for—but I wished I knew which songs were pulsing through her headphones right now so I could have something else to focus on.

* * *

The drive to Minneapolis was uneventful, at least until we reached the suburbs. According to the weather app, rain had turned to sleet early that morning, which was then followed by snow. We saw several cars in ditches, and the bus had slowed significantly to avoid ending up in the same position.

By the time we pulled up in front of the school, we had a little less than an hour before the first game started. Coach looked agitated by how slow the driver had gone, but I was personally happy we'd made it alive.

"Okay, girls, you don't have as much time as normal," Coach said. "Head to the locker room to get ready, and don't dawdle. I'll make sure the games are on schedule. With any luck, we'll get back on the road before dark."

Knowing the team had a long day ahead, I was already exhausted for them. As we filed out the bus, Coach told me to hang with her so I could get the full experience of this sort of event. I waited for her outside, smiling a little when she stepped out. "Great day for volleyball, Coach," I said, trying to stay optimistic.

The conditions outside weren't an omen—even though the first snowstorm of the year was happening weeks before it usually did.

Everything was going to be fine.

Coach chuckled, clapping me on the shoulder before heading toward the school's entrance. "Let's hope so, Elliot. Your first article was stellar. I'm sure Shannon sang your praises for it already."

"I heard you did, too," I said, grinning.

"Damn right I did. I've never been so impressed with a high school journalist. Better than some of the professionals, in fact."

My cheeks warmed. My dream to cover hard-hitting stories felt more real every time someone gave me a genuine compliment. "Thanks, Coach."

"Don't thank me—you earned it," she said. "And if you keep it up, I'll make sure you get your very own team sweats like the girls are wearing."

I laughed at that. The newspaper nerds didn't get that kind of swag. At best, we made T-shirts with some kind of journalism pun on it, but sweats were always reserved for the sports kids. "Will my last name be on it?" I asked, unable to hide my excitement.

"If you earn the sweats, your last name will be on them," Coach said.

"Wow, happy Christmas to me," I said, full-on nerding out at this point.

I followed Coach to the gym where a handful of people waited, but mostly it was empty. The referee confirmed that the games were still on, but he couldn't confirm that we'd be able to get home. Most of the teams lived in the area, but our two-hour-plus drive could be enough to keep us there.

"It'll be fine," Coach said confidently. "Everyone gets paranoid when the first snow hits, but the bus still works. We'll get home tonight."

I admired her confidence, but after looking at the weather

app again, I had my doubts. She walked off to talk to the other coach, and I took the break to text Dad that we'd made it safely but might have to stay overnight. I was going to call Casey next, but I looked up and saw him walking into the gym. "Casey!" I called to get his attention before heading toward him.

"What's up, JoJo?" he asked, pulling me in for a tight hug. "Good to see you!"

"You too," I said, actually meaning it. I was still getting used to him not being across the hall from me every day. "Thanks for coming, even if you have a hidden agenda."

"What?" he said, dragging out the *a* as he pulled back. A huge grin was on his face. "There are no hidden agendas. I came to hang out with you and watch an amazing team kick some ass."

"Uh-huh," I said. "Well, I know a certain volleyball player who's going to be really glad to see you. So if you're not into her even a little bit, don't mess with her."

"I think you're mistaking me for someone else, JoJo. I'm a *romantic*. I can't help it if it doesn't always work out."

"You're such a guy," I groaned. "And honestly, I'm surprised you came. It's madness out there!"

"It's not that bad," he said, shrugging. "And my place isn't far. Only slid through, like, four lights?"

"Casey, oh my god!"

"I'm kidding!" He laughed, shaking his head. "Just one. And don't worry about me. If anything, worry about getting home."

"Yeah, about that. We might be staying the night."

Casey nodded, looking thoughtful. "Well, if you get stuck

here, we should hang out tonight. I could come to wherever they put you up . . . unless you'll have to fend for yourself since you're not on the team? I could make my roommate stay with his girlfriend so you can crash with me."

I smiled a little at the offer. "Thanks, but I'm sure the parents would get me a hotel room if it came to it. And if we do get stuck here, you're welcome to hang out. But again, *someone* might want your time."

"I know, I know," Casey said, grinning. "Brie's cool, okay? Or are we talking about someone else on the team who's into me? Do I have a new fan?"

I rolled my eyes, shoving him. "I'm sure there's always someone else, but I meant Brie." I looked around for a moment before back to him. "She's kind of . . ."

"Terrifying?"

"You just said she was cool!"

"She is, but I know how she can come across."

It wasn't just that she came across a certain way—she *was* a certain way. And the worst part was how hot and cold it felt. There were times I thought she was nice or being a good friend to someone, but then a switch flipped and I couldn't tell her motives. I wanted to ask Casey if he'd ever noticed that, too, and ask for his advice, but he continued before I could.

"Anyway, forget about Brie. How are things going with Mackenzie? You two getting along?"

I'd never wanted to go back to talking about Brie more than

this moment. "Um, things are fine, I guess. We've had a couple of interview sessions so far." I paused. "And I hung out with her after she got a concussion."

"Yeah, I heard about that."

My stomach dropped. "From who? Brie?"

"Why would I hear about it from Brie?"

"No reason."

He shot me a look before letting it go. "Mackenzie told me."

Was that any better? "Then why ask how things are going if you already know?"

"I want to hear about it from you."

I scanned the gym, not wanting someone from the team to overhear and make things even more complicated. And I didn't know how much I should say. Casey wouldn't gossip like the team had apparently done, but he'd been a big Mackenzie defender these past few years. It would just be more of the same. "It's weird," I said, focusing on my hands so I wouldn't have to look at him. "We've mostly been around each other for volleyball reasons, and those times were good, but after I went to her house . . . I don't know, it almost felt like things went back to square one, like any progress I thought we'd made wasn't progress at all. It feels like a guessing game sometimes, but I don't want to question her or our friendship . . . if that's what's even going on."

Once I started talking, I couldn't stop. The words spilled out of me—and to a person I never spilled things to. I hesitated before looking over, expecting a look of pity or annoyance or something that wasn't there. Instead, Casey had a gentle smile on his lips, and the eyes of someone who saw me—truly saw me—and understood.

"Maybe she's being careful because of everything that happened," he said. "Like, she doesn't want to move too fast?"

I snorted at his answer, shaking my head. "How do you move too fast with a friend?"

Casey shrugged. "I don't know, JoJo, but don't write her off yet, okay? If she hurts you again, then obviously get rid of her, and I will, too. I mean it. But if she's just being selective about what she shares or whatever, don't hold that against her."

Casey being wise was on my shit list, even if I didn't know what he meant by her being selective about what she shares. But in the moment, it didn't matter. I was secretly glad there was something we could talk about that didn't involve Brie or end in an argument. "Yeah, okay," I said. "I'm going to find a bathroom, but if you want to sit with me, you have to promise not to distract me *too* much. I have to take pictures *and* notes."

"Damn, look at you being professional," Casey teased. "And deal, I'll grab us a seat."

"Good luck," I said dryly, grinning. "It's crowded."

"You're such a dork," Casey said fondly before jogging toward the almost-empty bleachers.

If the snowstorm *did* end up being an omen, it wasn't in reference to the team. As with almost every game so far this season, we dominated. Mack's absence the last two weeks had been felt, but we only lost one of the four games. And now that she was back, so was the team's power. They just played *better* together when she was there, even when she wasn't on the court. I suspected that was part of what made her the captain.

Casey managed to give me space to work during the game, and he cheered the team on loudly point after point. It wasn't lost on Brie, who'd flashed us—*him*—several grins throughout the day. I didn't bring that situation up again, feeling uncomfortable enough after the first time. If she wanted to keep his attention, that was her business. If she had been threatening me before, she'd have to realize that one comment to Casey would ruin her plans. Plus, I had the power of words.

Not that I'd actually use it, but she didn't need to know that.

When the final match ended in a win, the team had a celebratory moment before Brie jogged over to us, looking casual about it but no doubt having her own agenda.

"That was intense!" Casey said as he hopped off the stands, wrapping Brie in a hug.

"No, I'm sweaty!" Brie said in a fake-whine tone that made it obvious she was loving the attention.

"Wow, never been around sweat before, I'm scarred for life," Casey said, his voice dripping with sarcasm. "Seriously, incredible tournament. You all crushed it."

"Thank you, thank you," Brie said, stepping back from him to look at me. "Did you get some good pictures? I have preferred angles, you know."

I didn't know. "I'm sure your angles are just fine," I said.

Casey laughed and rested an arm across Brie's shoulders. "I told JoJo that I'm free to hang tonight if you end up getting stuck here."

"Good," Brie said, no doubt assuming he'd meant hang out with her.

Maybe that *was* what he meant?

There was no time to clarify because Coach gathered the team, and we walked over to join the group. "Sounds like our bus driver is afraid of a little ice, and he won't let me drive, so we'll be bunking down here tonight. Call your parents. I'll make arrangements with a hotel. You'll all need to double up, so have a buddy picked out by the time I'm off the phone."

A collection of reactions came from the team. Brie was beaming and stepped away to talk to Marissa, who said something about going shopping, as if that was a real option. Olivia groaned audibly, as did a few other girls. Emily and Kalie started making plans for the pool. And Mack was acting odd again, showing no special reaction to the news either way.

I took out my phone to update Dad. He'd be worried, but it was better than trying to drive home on ice in the dark.

"Tell Dad hi," Casey said as he looked over my shoulder. "And I guess that means we can hang tonight, huh?"

"You mean you can hang with Brie," I said, quiet enough so no one overheard us.

"That wasn't my plan, JoJo."

"It's cool." I shrugged. "I need to go through my notes and pictures anyway."

"Oh."

I glanced up to see the frown on Casey's face. Had I misread the situation again? "Not that I don't want to hang out! We obviously can, but I know you're friends with a few of these girls, so I assumed you'd want to hang with them."

"I mean, we could've all hung out," Casey said. "But it's cool. I should probably be smart and go home before the roads get even worse."

"I'm sorry," I said, kicking myself for acting like I'd rather work than spend time with my brother. I didn't know how to act around him sometimes, and not having the parents here to facilitate didn't help. And to be fair, historically, he *did* prefer to hang out with his friends rather than me. It was hard getting used to Casey taking an interest in me, just as it was hard for me to take an interest in him.

"All good," Casey said, pulling me in for a hug. "But hey, it was fun watching you in your element. Journalism suits you."

I hugged him back, my cheeks warming at the compliment, but I still hated myself for being so *me* toward him. I'd need to work harder on that. "Thank you, and thanks for coming. See you at Thanksgiving?"

"You know it." He ruffled my hair before stepping away to find Brie, likely to let her down gently. But honestly, nice try thinking you'd get to have a sleepover with a guy on a school trip. Coach was pretty cool, but I had no doubt she acted like a warden when it came to keeping the girls in line on her watch.

CHAPTER FIFTEEN

WE ENDED UP at a Holiday Inn Express near Mall of America. Much to Marissa's disappointment, it was too late and stormy outside to go shopping by the time we checked in.

Because the team had an even number of players, I was the odd girl out for sleeping arrangements. Fortunately for me, that meant having a room to myself with a king-sized bed. Coach put in a pizza order while we all went to our rooms to get settled. Since I had nothing to unpack, I sat down on the bed to check in with my friends.

Jordan: I'm sure Isaac already knows from Olivia, but we're stuck in Minneapolis for the night. HUGE snowstorm!

Jordan: Is it bad up there too?

Audrey: Worst luck!!! We've only gotten a couple inches here, if that.

Isaac: I HATE BLIZZARDS!!!

Jordan: Only because it ruined your brunch date

Audrey: Make sure to cuddle Olivia for him tonight ;)

Jordan: LOL! Yes we'll snuggle all night

Isaac: Rude Audrey! I was going to invite you to brunch since my date is STRANDED but never mind.

Audrey: Nooo ily so much, I take it back!

Isaac: Fine, but I'll need a ride.

Audrey: I know the drill!

I laughed at their banter and was about to reply when someone knocked on my door. My pathetic hope that it was Mack was shattered when Brie stood on the other side. "Hey, what's up?" I asked. "Is it time to eat?"

"In a few. They're setting up a room on the first floor," Brie said, moving past me.

"Come on in," I said dryly, closing the door before looking back at her expectantly. Her being here wasn't exactly a mystery.

"I can't believe you sent your brother away," she said, her eyes cutting into my soul. "Do you *realize* how much I wanted to hang out with him?"

"Okay, technically, we should be almost halfway home by now, so I don't know why you'd have that expectation in the first place," I said. "Also, I didn't *send him* anywhere. We're in a blizzard warning, so him getting home safe was kind of important."

She stared at me for several seconds before sitting on my bed, falling back on it with a heavy groan. "Ugh, you're right! I know you're right. I just like him so much, you know? But in high school one of us was always dating someone, sometimes each other's friends, so it never really worked out. And now he's here, and he's so funny and sweet and se—"

"I'm going to stop you there," I said quickly, not wanting to hear anyone call my brother sexy. And I empathized, kind of, but being a supporting character in Brie's romance-novel aspirations with my brother . . . nope, hard pass. But I had to say something, so I sat in the desk chair across from her, waiting for her to sit up and look at me. "My brother is great, but he's getting settled at college while you're wrapping up your last year of high school. Don't you want to enjoy the rest of your youth? I mean, you two could keep being friends and figure it out when you come here for college?" If she hadn't moved on by then, of course.

"Why are nerds so wise?" Brie wiped under her eyes as if she'd been crying. She hadn't. "Sorry if I've been a lot. Senior year has just been a real bitch. I'm ready to move on."

Considering I was a proud nerd, I took no offense to her question. "Don't blame you, but try to have fun with the time left anyway. Go celebrate the big win today. Eat some pizza. Scream into the void if it'll help."

"It will. All of it will. Thanks, Jordan."

"You got it."

She stood and went to the door, looking back after opening it. "Don't forget about the pizza, too. We need the whole team there."

Of all the people to suggest I was part of the team, Brie wasn't on my list. But after our brief conversation of me essentially talking her down from potentially embarrassing herself in front of my brother, we seemed to have reached a new under-standing. We weren't friends, but maybe she wasn't *so* bad—I just didn't know how to handle her strong emotions.

"Yeah, I'll be down soon. Need to write some notes about the tournament first."

"Your dedication is admirable," she said, winking before leaving the room.

I sat with her words after she left. *We need the whole team there.* Even though I wasn't actually on it, my heart warmed at the idea of being part of something that involved everyone doing their bit. Newspaper was the same, technically, but the writing was so solitary. With sports, you had to be working together at all times or you'd lose.

It made me appreciate the team's closeness and support of each other. More than that, I appreciated their invitation to be a part of it.

I didn't know how much time had passed between Brie leaving and hearing another knock at my door, but the disruption made me realize I was hungry. As if hearing my stomach grumble, Mack was holding up a pizza box and a bottle of water when I opened the door.

"What time is it?" I asked.

"Almost eight," Mack said, smiling a little. "Can I come in?"

"Yeah, sure." I walked over to the desk to clear away my tournament notes and make room. "But don't let me keep you from the party."

Mack followed, the door closing behind her. "It's not a party so much as half the room whining about not having time with boyfriends and half the room whining about not going shopping."

Getting sucked into my article notes had worked in my favor. "So you're not missing anything?"

"Exactly." She set the pizza box on the desk. "I figured I'd see what you were up to. That, and I know Olivia will be up late on the phone with Isaac, and when she does finally fall asleep, she snores."

"Ah, I see—you're using me."

"No!" Mack said, her eyes widening. "Oh my god, I'm sorry, that's not—"

"I'm kidding. You can use me," I said, instantly realizing my words. Why was being alone with her so mortifying for me? "I mean, you can hang out here. I was just going through my notes."

Mack's expression calmed as her lips turned into a grin. "Sounds riveting. I'm glad I came by to rescue you." She opened the box, revealing a variety of slices that she'd clearly arranged just for us. "Take your pick."

I added a slice of cheese and a slice of supreme to the paper plate she'd brought. Had she not shown up, I probably would've crashed without eating dinner, and that's basically a sin, so good on her for stopping by. "Want to watch something?" I asked as I sat on the bed.

"Sure," Mack said after a pause, leaving space between us as she joined me. "Ideas?"

I thought about it as I turned on the TV. "The hotel has Netflix, so we could just turn on something as background noise? I don't want to think too much."

"Good idea," Mack said. "Not thinking sounds perfect."

"How's your head?" I asked immediately, hoping her injury didn't worsen from playing all day.

"It's fine. I just meant because today has been a lot."

"Oh, right. Good. I'm glad it's over so you can relax." I took a bite of pizza to shut up and started going through the options after signing in. "What should we put on?"

"Hmm." Mack watched me scroll for several seconds. "*Dash & Lily*?"

Why hadn't I thought of that? Oh, right, because I tried not to think about that summer. It was easier to let go when watching it with my friends, but this . . . It was a lot. But maybe the suggestion meant something? Or she was really into Dash. Either way, it was just background noise.

"Yeah, sounds great," I said, finding it and pushing "play."

We got maybe five minutes into eating and TV time before Mack spoke again. "So, I actually wanted to talk to you about something, if that's okay?"

"Guess it depends on what you want to talk about," I said. We *needed* to talk, but that didn't mean I *wanted* to, especially after the long day.

Mack nodded, taking a moment to let it out. "I want to apologize about the other week. And my mom."

"And by that do you mean lying about spending time with

her when she really didn't want me there anymore?" I asked, not unkindly. Everyone had their shit, and I needed to let her have hers without thinking she owed me something just because of how freshman year had gone.

"Yeah," she said quietly, her cheeks warming. "I should've told her I wanted you to stay longer, because I did."

"But did you?" I asked, looking down at my plate. "I mean, obviously we have history, but even with trying to put that behind us, not hearing from you after made me feel like you didn't want me around. And if you have stuff going on with your mom, that's not my business, but if you're embarrassed to be my friend or think I'm some kind of stalker—"

"That's not it," Mack said quickly, her hand finding mine. "I promise. There's so much more to it, but it has nothing to do with not wanting you around."

I glanced at our hands, taking in the warmth of hers and how perfectly it fit in mine. And then I pulled it back and focused on her face, which didn't make it any easier. "Tell me?"

"Well, for one thing, I was embarrassed. My mom can be hard on me sometimes about prioritizing volleyball. She didn't want anyone coming over, but I knew I could get away with one person instead of the whole team. When she noticed you were still there, she wanted you to go, like you hanging out while I slept would somehow make my concussion worse." She sighed. "Her heart is in the right place, but . . ."

She stopped talking, and I gave her hand a gentle squeeze. "But?"

"But I don't love volleyball as much as I've let on, at least not lately, and she's picking up on that the longer I play. She even implied the other day that I somehow made that ball hit me so I could get a couple of weeks off."

"That's . . . Damn." I sighed, unable to imagine one of my parents saying something like that to me. "How did she find out?"

"My notebooks," she said. "I always bring the current one to school with me, but I'd left it out one day when running late, and she found it when gathering laundry. We got into it that night because I told her I wanted to go to school for English and wasn't sure I wanted to play volleyball after high school. I've been running ragged for years, not dating or making many friends outside of volleyball, or doing anything that might distract me from sports and straight As. The parties are my little rebellions, but even those aren't that much fun. Everyone partners off or gets into some drama, and I end up spending half the night in my room."

Whether or not Mack realized it, she was giving me dirt, a real story for the paper, but I wouldn't use any of it. Even if she'd told me she didn't want to be near me, I'd never sink that low. Her secret would live in my head. Right now, she needed a friend, not a reporter.

"If you don't want to play volleyball in college, then don't," I said.

"Easy for you to say," she said. "You get to write amazing stories. Everyone in your life knows about your college ambitions and supports you. They don't treat it like a hobby you'll

outgrow. Shit, they even cheer you on. And obviously I'm grateful for what my parents have given me, but I wish they'd see me
for me and not this volleyball star they want me to be. I mean,
they don't even go to my games very often, and my mom still
has the audacity to sometimes act like I'm ungrateful or not
committed enough." She sighed. "And I just . . . I wish they'd
believe in me."

"I believe in you," I said, squeezing her hand again.

"You do?"

Our eyes met, and I had to force myself not to gasp. We
hadn't looked at each other—really looked at each other—in so
long. Her eyes were practically sparkling. "Yeah, I do."

Mack's cheeks were flushed as I chanced a look at them.
One, two, three beats passed. Then she let go of my hand as the
softest of laughs escaped her lips. "Thanks, Jo."

"Yeah," I said, unable to look away from her. "So, what was
the other thing?"

"Other thing?"

"You said *for one thing* before talking about volleyball."

"Oh. Right." Another small laugh fell as she tucked loose
strands of hair behind her ear. "Um, remember when you came
out to me that summer?"

"Considering we talked about that not long ago, yes, I remember," I said.

"Right," she said, her eyes meeting mine again. "Well, I liked
you as more than a friend."

I blinked, taking in the meaning of her words. Every ridiculous reason I'd formed in my head over the years for her ghosting made more sense than this. "Why not just tell me that then?" I asked, going the logical route and forcing any old feelings aside. "I obviously would've understood."

"I know, but I didn't want to start at a new school as the lesbian on an all-girl sports team. I'd heard this part of the state wasn't always the most accepting, and I didn't want to risk anything messing with being on the volleyball team. And the whole thing with my parents not wanting me to shift focus . . ."

"But it's part of who you are," I said, frustrated that she felt like she couldn't be herself. Like, okay, it wasn't always easy being out, but it wasn't a complete nightmare either. But that was me, I had to remind myself. Not everyone had a family like mine. Not everyone had friends like mine. Those support systems were everything. "If people cared about you, they wouldn't care who you're attracted to. At least that's how it should be."

"You're right," Mack said, groaning. "And I know how it sounds. I hate myself for even saying it, but I had two goals when moving here. One was to crush it with volleyball so my parents would be proud of me, and the other was to survive. I didn't care about being popular or the party host or whatever. All of that stuff happened on its own, and I wasn't going to draw attention to myself by fighting it or explaining it. And it worked . . . at least until you got assigned the volleyball beat."

"What do *I* have to do with this?" I asked, not sure how it all lined up if she'd liked me back then and managed to get through two years without issue.

"I hated how much I'd hurt you," she said. "And I was able to ignore it all for a time, but after the universe brought us back together, it was like . . . I don't know, fate?" She laughed bitterly. "Staying away from you has been one of my biggest hurdles since high school started. It made you hate me, and it made me hate myself, but it didn't change how I felt. And I *knew* what letting you back in would do to me. But here we are, and I don't know what else to do about it except let it happen."

My eyes didn't leave hers as she talked. I used to think I knew everything there was to know about Mackenzie West, and then she dropped the biggest info bomb on me. "Let what happen?" I asked quietly, still trying to gather my thoughts.

Mack leaned toward me a little before stopping. "Can I kiss you?"

I should've seen this coming after the *I liked you* confession, but I was shocked in place. My brain short-circuited. The thing I used to dream about was actually happening when I'd finally thought I was over it—over *her*.

But I wasn't. I was so far from over her.

And then she pulled back before I could prove it. "I'm sorry," she said, her face a mess of emotions. "I shouldn't have assumed that me wanting to kiss you for over two years meant you'd wanted to kiss me, too."

"I did—I mean I *do*," I said, laughing at my own goofy words. "It was kind of all I thought about after meeting you. And now the shock of it is making me ruin a really romantic, swoon-worthy moment."

"You didn't ruin anything, Jordan," Mack said. "I should've waited for your brain to catch up."

I shook my head and moved the pizza box and plates to the nightstand. "I'm caught up now," I said before pulling her close and kissing her, completely prepared this time.

Fortunately, I hadn't ruined the moment. Mack's lips responded to mine as she kissed me with desperation, like we were making up for something that was long overdue. Like we'd finally indulged a craving. She moved to straddle my waist after an unknown amount of time, taking my face in her hands and deepening the kiss. I pulled her ponytail tie away so my hands could find home in her hair. The times I'd fought back an urge to comb my fingers through it—even after we'd become enemies—were finally being rewarded. And it was *so* worth the wait.

Our lips stayed together as our hands cautiously explored each other's bodies over our clothes. Despite the desperate kisses and lap straddling, Mack's hands were shy. Given her big secret, I doubted she had a lot of experience. And while I had a little, I was in no rush. I just wanted her here, whatever that looked like.

I'd lost track of time, but our lips eventually parted ways. We shifted to lie on our sides facing each other, and I looked over her face, remembering something she'd said earlier. "When you said Olivia snores . . . do you want to stay here tonight?"

"Yes," Mack said easily, her light grin returning as she inched closer to me. "I mean, earlier it was because of the snoring, but now I have other reasons for wanting to stay."

"Is that right?" I matched her movements, wanting to be as close as possible. "Tell me all about them. Details are good."

Mack rolled her eyes, her arm wrapping around my waist. "I really do like you, you know," she said, her voice soft. "The feeling calmed down a little over the years, but it still lingered, like it knew if I'd waited long enough, it would work out."

I played with her hair absently, feeling more content than I had in a long time. "It didn't hit me how much I'd liked you until you broke my heart." It wasn't fair to say it like that since we'd just been friends back then, but it was the truth. And I wanted to be honest with her. "I never thought I'd ever let you in again, but I guess all it took was spending time with you. But even then, I told myself those feelings were dead."

Mack frowned. "I'm so sorry for hurting you in such a big way. When you came out to me, I promise I didn't know you liked me like that. I'd say I would've handled everything better had I known, but I was fourteen. Really, it's shocking I'm handling this well at all now."

"Actually, you're doing terrible," I said, a small smile tugging my lips. "Three out of ten at best. A true nightmare."

"Shut up," she said, shoving me playfully.

I chuckled, taking her hand before she could move it back. "Do you regret any of it? Not just this right now, but everything?"

"I want to say yes, because I know how shitty I was, but no. If I'd walked into the first day of school as a lesbian with Jordan

Elliot as my girlfriend, we wouldn't be here. We would've probably broken up by now and hated each other for other reasons."

"You're such a romantic," I teased.

Mack laughed before shifting even closer to rest her forehead against mine. "You know what I mean, Jo," she said quietly. "Freshmen are immature and selfish and still figuring out how to be people. And maybe we aren't adults yet, but we're better off now than two years ago. Maybe we needed to go through all that drama first."

She was right, but it didn't make the last couple of years disappear. It would take time for me to feel fully secure with her outside this room, but I wanted to try. We could take it slow—go on a date and see what happened. But I was getting ahead of myself. Mack needed to come out to other people first, and I needed that to be her idea. "You're right," I said. "I'm just glad we got here eventually."

"Me too," Mack said, her hand moving to my cheek. "I'm going to keep kissing you until we fall asleep, okay?"

"Okay," I said quietly, my smile growing as I remembered Netflix. "But just know that Dash and Lily are watching."

"You're ridiculous." She laughed a little before her lips returned to mine.

True to her word, we stayed like that until falling asleep.

CHAPTER SIXTEEN

I JUMPED AWAKE to the sound of my phone's alarm going off the next morning. I'd set it the night before, knowing I didn't want to get left behind in Minneapolis. That was before Mack had shown up.

Mack.

I shifted onto my other side and saw her staring down at a notebook, deep in thought. I smiled at her focus, waiting until she noticed I was awake before saying anything. "Writing a masterpiece?" I asked.

"Yeah," she said, laughing quietly. "Just a little poem. Don't want to forget a single second of yesterday. Not that I ever could."

Her eyes moved down again, and the previous night returned as I took in her expression, my heart sinking. I didn't have to ask to know what she was thinking, but I needed to hear her say it. "What is it?"

"Last night was perfect," she started slowly. Her eyes moved to the space between us that now felt miles apart. "But I can't . . . People can't know about it, or us. Not right now."

Her words echoed in my ears as I stared at her. I still wanted coming out to be her idea, but I hadn't considered that last night wouldn't change anything for her. "Why didn't you lead with that instead of kissing me?" I asked, trying to stay calm. "I mean, why tell me at all?"

"Because I couldn't not tell you," Mack said. I could hear the regret in her voice, but I didn't know if it was because of last night or the reality of the morning. "And I don't *want* this to be a secret, but I'm not ready to be out yet. Please don't say anything to anyone."

"I won't," I said, borderline offended she had to even ask. No matter what happened, I'd never out someone. A person's sexuality was their business. Only Mack had the right to tell people she liked girls if and when she was ready. But that didn't mean this situation didn't suck. "I think you should go."

"Please don't be mad at me," Mack said, reaching for my hand, but I moved off the bed before she could take it. "I still want to be friends."

Those six words broke my heart, and I shook my head. "I need time to think. But I'm not going to tell anyone, so don't hang around just to make sure I stay silent."

Mack looked like I'd slapped her in the face, which, fair. After everything we'd been through, and now this, I kind of wanted to. "I wouldn't have told you the truth if I was actually worried about that."

"Maybe you shouldn't have told me," I said, my frustration inching toward anger. "Last night you acted like we were so much better off than two years ago, but clearly nothing's changed."

"That's not fair."

"You're right, it's *not*. It's not fair to pull me back in and then push me out again. I know you don't see it that way, but it's exactly what you're doing. Like, admitting you like me but then saying we can't do anything about it . . . it hurts."

"You deserved the truth, Jo," Mack said, her eyes watery as she walked up to me, resting her hands on my shoulders. "I'm sorry I'm not ready to come out yet, but it doesn't change how I feel about you or that I still want you in my life. I wish you'd believe me."

I looked at her face and saw the desperation in her eyes, the sadness, the regret. I should've known we wouldn't be going on a date anytime soon or holding hands in the hall at school or making out after volleyball practice. It was more complicated for Mack than that. And I understood, but I also hated it. "I know you're sorry," I said after a pause, deflating. "And I am too. It just really sucks."

"Yeah, I know," she said, squeezing my shoulders. "If it makes you feel any better, it's going to be torture being near you and not being able to do anything about it."

"Oh, that definitely makes me feel better," I said bitterly. Granted, I'd also feel tortured, but at least I wasn't alone this time.

Mack smiled a little and nodded. "Good. So, still friends?"

I groaned at the question before nodding. "Yeah, still friends," I said. "But try to keep your hands off me."

"No worries there, I've had years of practice." She winked at me before heading to the door. "See you on the bus."

I wanted to preserve the sound of her laugh in a music box. I wanted to make a drink that gave me the feeling of her lips on mine. I wanted a blanket that secured me like her arms. I wanted *her*.

"See you," I said quietly, but she was already gone.

The drive home was dicey and awkward. Dicey because sections of the road weren't completely cleared, and awkward because everyone had figured out where Mack had slept. Either someone saw her leave or Olivia mentioned it innocently to the wrong person, but at least they didn't seem to know *everything*. Not that that stopped them from taking turns looking back at me and whispering to their seatmate.

I needed to interview some of them for the feature story, but today no longer felt like the right time. Instead, I texted Isaac and Audrey. Keeping the full story from them would be hard since I told them almost everything, but it wasn't my thing to share, so I focused on them.

Jordan: How was the new brunch spot?

Audrey: OMG SO GOOD!!! Isaac moped about Olivia not being there, but I got to eat delicious pancakes so I didn't care

Isaac: A true friend

Isaac: How was the rest of your night?

Jordan: Uneventful, but we'll be back to town soon so you won't have to wait long to see your gf

Isaac: We've already made plans.:)

Jordan: Shocker! I have homework when I get home, but let's hang sometime this week?

Audrey: You know it! Can't wait

Isaac: Same. See you tomorrow.

Jordan: <3 <3

I looked up in time to see Olivia sit next to me, like she'd heard me texting about her. "Hey, can I ask you something kind of awkward?"

Oh god. Did Mack tell Olivia about last night? Maybe Olivia knew everything and had encouraged Mack to go to my room.

Okay, slow down, Jordan. She wouldn't bring that up on the bus . . . would she?

"Yeah, what's up?" I asked, trying not to panic.

"I know you're all friends, but does Isaac like Audrey? You know, like he likes me?"

Oh. I chuckled, unable to help it. The image alone gave me nightmares. "No, definitely not. Why?"

"We had brunch plans, and he went with her instead. I was really excited to check out this new place with him, and it's like he didn't even care."

"Trust me, that's definitely not it," I said, smiling in an attempt to keep myself from laughing again. I envied her relationship dilemma. "The three of us have always been close, but only as friends. We're basically siblings. And he's, like, annoyingly into you. The restaurant was him being a guy and not thinking about how it was going to be a special thing."

"Are you sure?" Olivia asked, her sweet eyes widening.

"A thousand percent sure," I said. "Seriously, you're pretty much all he talks about. Audrey can just get nervous when our friend group changes. She got like that when I had a girlfriend, too. So I promise it's friend stuff, not feelings."

"Okay," Olivia said after a beat, laughing a little. "Sorry if I sound like a paranoid weirdo. I just really like him, you know?"

"Oh, I know," I said, grinning. "And he likes you, too, *a lot*, so don't worry about that."

"Good," Olivia said, practically beaming now. "Thanks, Jordan. You're a good friend."

"I do what I can," I said, shrugging it off. Isaac would do the same for me in that position, so it wasn't a big deal.

Olivia looked away for a moment before back at me. "Speaking of you being a good friend, thanks for letting Mackenzie crash with you last night. She can be *very* dramatic about my snoring, which isn't even that loud, so it was good she ended up in your room."

"Yeah, it's no big," I said, trying to believe my words. "She brought me pizza, so it was the least I could do."

"For sure," she said, giggling now. "It's kind of funny how things work out, huh?"

"What do you mean?" I asked, instantly on high alert.

"Like, Isaac and I have gone to the same schools since kindergarten but didn't really *see* each other until this year. And then you and Mackenzie were friends, then not, and now are again. You *are* friends again, right?"

"Yeah, we're friends again." I needed to calm down.

"Good. And I hope we're friends, too," she added after a beat. "I love my alone time with Isaac, but it would be cool if we could all hang out and not have it feel like you're both being third wheels or something. And Audrey could hang with us, too, of course. I really do want to know her better."

Isaac and Olivia dating had thrown me for a loop at first, but the more I got to know her, the more it all made sense. She was a little needy, but then again so was he. And Olivia was a genuinely nice person, even before this year. If he was going to date anyone on the volleyball team, I was glad it was her. "Yeah, totally," I said. "I'd love to group hang sometime."

"Perfect, because Mackenzie is hosting a Halloween party soon and you're all invited!" Olivia said, grinning as she practically bounced with excitement.

I laughed at her stealth. "That was a clever lead-in, getting me to agree *before* telling me about a party that I *have to* go to. Genius."

"Right? But say you'll come! I want you all to be there."

I thought about it for a moment. "I assume this means I have to dress up?"

"Of course, silly! I mean, no pressure if you don't want to, but everyone always dresses up. And it's not like the movies where *everyone* looks sexy. People switch it up."

"Right, because we're high schoolers, not thirty-year-old actors playing high schoolers."

A laugh burst out of her. "Exactly! You get it."

I hadn't cared about Halloween since I was . . . eleven? I couldn't even remember when I'd stopped going trick-or-treating, and I'd definitely never been to a Halloween party as a teenager. The apartment complex didn't have a lot of trick-or-treaters, so I usually watched themed movies with Isaac and Audrey or went to the comic shop to help Dad hand out candy. I didn't hate Halloween, but I didn't make an effort either.

And dressing up would be . . . interesting. Of course fat-girl costumes existed, but they were usually either super corny or trying to be sexy. I'd probably have to figure out my own look. Fortunately, Audrey was really good at that kind of thing, and she wouldn't rest until we all had incredible costumes—hers being the best one, of course.

"Okay, count me in," I said. "I'll get Audrey on board, too."

"Yay!" Olivia took her phone out from her sweatshirt pocket. "I'm going to tell Isaac. He'll be so happy to have friends there, and I hope you're excited, too, because Mackenzie's Halloween party is always so much fun. Last year, the seniors even skipped out on their plans to attend. It was huge!"

"You're totally selling me on this party," I teased. "But seriously, it'll be great."

"So great!" she agreed, giving my hand a squeeze before standing. "Okay, talk to you later!"

"Yeah, later," I said, smiling at her enthusiasm.

Of course Isaac didn't *need* us in order to go to the party since he'd been surviving just fine around Olivia's friends the last several weeks, but it still felt nice being *wanted* there. And it was at Mack's house. And Mack would be there, no doubt looking hot in whatever costume she decided to wear . . .

Fuck.

I was *so* screwed.

CHAPTER SEVENTEEN

"WHAT DO YOU want to be for Halloween?"

I laughed at Audrey's question. We'd just gotten our food at The Diner, our best thinking spot. "If I knew the answer, I wouldn't have asked for your help."

"Fine, fine. I just hoped you had *some* idea." She ate a fry, thoughtful face on. "Let's start with what kind of costume you *don't* want, work from there."

"I don't want to be a sexy anything," I said. "Like, it could happen to look sexy, but I don't want the point of it to be sexy, if that makes sense."

"It does," Audrey said, nodding along and nudging Isaac when he snorted. "What else?"

"Um, I guess not a couple's costume?"

"What if you went in a costume that could have a pair, and then you meet the girl of your dreams wearing the other half? Like Amy and Rory!"

My heart sank at the idea of meeting the girl of my dreams.

I thought I already had, but after Minneapolis, I wasn't sure about anything anymore. And I didn't want to meet another girl of my dreams at Mack's house. "I appreciate the sentiment, but I doubt a girl is going to show up to Mackenzie West's party dressed as the Last Centurion."

"You don't know that," Audrey muttered.

"But the answer is obviously something *Doctor Who*, right?" Isaac chimed in. "I mean, you could still go as Amy Pond or one of the Doctors or Clara Oswald. You could easily pull off any of them."

"At this point, I feel like I should go as an Ood," I said before eating a fry. At least that kind of costume would help me be somewhat invisible. Or avoidable.

"No Ood costume!" Audrey said, her face scrunching. "You'd have to go around all night being extra polite and offering to help people with things. Ten out of ten do not recommend."

"I guess I could be Amy Pond." And then reality hit. "I'm going to Halloween as my dog. I've peaked."

"No, you're going as Karen Gillan as Amy Pond," Isaac said. "Super sexy."

"No!" Audrey yelled.

"Isaac!" I groaned.

"What?" Isaac asked. "She's—"

"You're not allowed to say 'sexy,'" I cut him off, cringing. "I feel like I need a shower."

"I hate you both," Isaac said, nudging Audrey and kicking me lightly under the table.

"You haven't told us who you're going as yet," Audrey said after nudging him back.

Isaac sat a little straighter. "That's because it's a surprise."

"It's totally a couple's costume," I said, grinning.

"Yaaaasss," Audrey clapped. "I wondered if Olivia would convert you to the dark side, and I think she's done it!"

"Just because I have someone to do a couple's costume with doesn't mean it's 'the dark side,'" Isaac said, pouting.

"Listen, my date would totally do a couple's costume if I asked her, so don't act like you're so special," Audrey said. "But I'm an independent woman who can pull off a look without the use of arm candy. Same goes for Jo."

"Damn right," I said, laughing a little before drinking from my shake. And then her words sank in. "Wait, what date?"

"Yeah, what date?" Isaac asked.

"You know Emma from the paper?" Audrey asked, unable to hide her smile at this point.

"The girl who talks over people?" I asked.

"The girl who critiques my photography because she's, and I quote, *just trying to help*?" Isaac added, his eyebrows shooting up.

"Oh my god, her having opinions doesn't mean she sucks," Audrey whined. "Anyway, I asked her to the party, and she said yes."

"Damn right she did!" I grinned, holding my hand up.

"Right?" She gave me a high five before slapping Isaac's arm. "Don't say anything. She's really nice, which you'd know if you actually talked to her during editors' meetings instead of being bitter about that one time she asked you about angles."

"It was a demand," Isaac mumbled before taking a large bite of his sandwich.

"Whatever," she said. "The point is that I have a date, but we're all going together. There's no fifth wheel situation."

"Cool, I didn't think there was until you said that," I said, my shoulders sinking. "Maybe you should all go and I can hang at the comic shop with my dad instead?"

"Nope!"

"Not happening!"

I groaned, wishing I could forget about the party. Olivia wanted us all to hang out, but I knew how parties worked. It started as a group thing, then eventually the couples and duos wandered off and the solo person got left alone in the dancing area holding an empty cup while people made out around them. Hard pass.

But Audrey wanted me there, and I'd done enough to disappoint her lately. I could survive one night.

"Promise me I won't be left alone, and I'll go," I said.

"Promise!" Audrey said easily. "Just because I'm bringing a date doesn't mean I don't want to hang out with you. And real talk, Emma will be a perfect backup when you inevitably find your new best friend and get lost hanging out with the volleyball crowd."

"That won't happen. I'm going for you two." I'd see them there, maybe chat a little, but best friend time came first.

"That's the spirit," Isaac said, tapping his shake cup to mine in cheers before drinking more.

I looked at the two of them, feeling certain everything would be fine as long as we stuck together. Historically, that move always worked in our favor. "Okay, I think you've convinced me to go as Amy Pond. Now I just need to figure out which specific look."

"You could convince two people to go with you as Amy's poncho boys," Audrey suggested. "Or there's the police officer look she had early on. Or that standard look she had in all of the promo materials."

"I'll probably do the standard look," I said, not wanting to think about asking two people to walk around in blankets all night. And the police look . . . No, just no. "I'll find a wig."

"Or you could dye your hair," Audrey said. "That would be so cool! All the wigs will be, like, super orange anyway. Dyeing it would make it look more legit."

I considered the idea. I'd never dyed my hair before, but the color wasn't aggressively dramatic like fire-hydrant red or lime green, so it could work. "Yeah, let's experiment with that next week. If it's a disaster, we can buy an emergency wig."

"Deal." Audrey grinned. She'd always wanted to dye our hair. Isaac was almost the first victim once, but he woke up before we could do it. Rude.

And just like that, I was going as my not-dog Amelia Pond for Halloween.

* * *

The next week at school passed with a couple more volleyball games, another article that mainly featured the Minneapolis tournament, and one daunting task: figuring out my last interview with Mack that Saturday.

We'd agreed to meet at the park so our dogs could play together and we could be somewhere public. It's a good thing we did, because I didn't trust us in a private space right now. And as much as I already missed having her lips on mine, I didn't want to think about kissing someone who wouldn't hold my hand in public or gush to her friends about me or go on a date with me.

This interview would be harder than the other two, but at least I had Pond if it got to be too much.

We entered the dog park from one side, and I saw her enter with Sabrina from the other. The smile on her face betrayed her, and I hated myself for smiling back just as widely. I leaned down to let Pond off her leash and watched as she barreled toward Sabrina.

The walk to meet Mack halfway at a picnic table was torture. It was set up like a slowed-down movie moment where the characters found the perfect words to say at the end. In reality, I was flailing inside, my heart was racing in a chaotic way, and I hoped the interview would end quickly. And even though I'd told her we could be friends, I wasn't sure about the *how* part. Especially when seeing her hair made me think about running my fingers through it again. And those lips . . .

"Hey," she said as we sat on opposite sides of the table. "How've you been?"

How have I been? Really?

"Um, okay," I said. "You?"

"Okay." She looked at me for a moment. "I didn't want this to be weird. Is it weird?"

"It is now. Congratulations."

A light grin that I knew all too well formed. "Shut up," she said fondly. "Should we just get to it, then?"

"Yeah, good idea," I said, knowing I didn't want to do small talk, and I definitely didn't want to do big talk. I opened my notebook to the new questions and started the recording. "So, it's been quite the season for you so far. You made captain, which is a huge accomplishment for a junior, then you got a concussion a few weeks in. How are you feeling today?"

Mack shifted, likely not wanting to focus on an imperfection such as a concussion that was completely out of her control, but it couldn't be ignored. "I feel good," she said. "That first week was rough, and I mostly had to rest in bed, but by the second week I was back at school and able to focus again. And since we won the Minneapolis tournament and I didn't get hit again or pass out, I'd say it was a success."

"It was definitely a success," I said, forcing myself not to think beyond the games. "The entire team crushed it, and having you back on the court gave them the extra spark they'd been missing while you were gone."

"Thanks," Mack said, her cheeks turning red. "I mean, they

won most of their games while I was gone, too, but it felt good being back."

"I'm sure," I said. "You're all very talented, but they needed their captain. I'm sure they were thrilled when you recovered."

"They were," Mack said, her voice quieting. "They're a stellar group. I'm lucky to be leading them, and I'm grateful Brie was there to step in while I was gone."

"Yeah, that was really helpful," I said to kill a couple of seconds as I looked back at previous notes. I saw the question about whether or not Mack had her eye on a special someone, and my stomach dropped. I knew the answer now, but I couldn't do anything about it. And I really, really wanted to do something about it.

"Are you okay?"

"Yep," I said quickly, shifting focus to the new page. "I want to circle back to the writing question from last time."

Mack groaned. "Seriously? I told you I don't want to talk about that."

"I'm not talking about everything you shared during the tournament, just the part about your writing interest. That wouldn't change anything about how the volleyball side comes across." I sighed. "And I'm not going to write a feature story that only talks about coming up with the fundraising idea to help the team afford the costs. As genius and considerate and wonderful as that was, it's not enough. There's so much more to you than that and an outstanding stats record."

Mack's eyes narrowed. "I never told you the fundraising was my idea."

"Coach told me, because she thought it was really special. She thinks *you* are really special. And I thought you wanted this amazing article written about you, but so far I've gotten more positive shit from other people."

"I don't want to come off as braggy, okay?" Mack sighed. "All that stuff could make it sound like I do it to look good, and I don't. It was just an idea I'd had to help the team."

"I'm in charge of how you come across, remember? I'm setting the tone for your story, but I can't do that properly if you don't give me the truth."

Mack groaned, moving to rest her head on the picnic table. "But what does writing have to do with volleyball?" she grumbled.

I looked at her, trying to figure out what was so terrible about being a writer. Sure, writers felt things differently and sometimes got into personal stuff, but I wasn't asking her to publish a poem. I just wanted everyone else to see the person I saw— minus the dreaded *feelings*, of course. "This story is a feature on Mackenzie West," I said gently. "You're more than just volleyball. You're thoughtful and caring and smart and talented in multiple ways. You're surprising." I lowered my voice even more. "You're special."

Mack stared at me for a few seconds. "You think I'm special?"

"Shut up, you know I do," I said, glancing quickly to my notes again.

Several more seconds passed before she replied. "Okay, we can talk about writing."

"Yeah?" I watched her sit up straight again. "Great. Share whatever you want about it. I just think it's relevant if that's what you'll go to school for. Maybe you could share why you started writing in the first place?"

"Sure," Mack said. She turned to check on Sabrina, who was happily chasing Pond, before focusing on the interview again. "I started writing more seriously in middle school, mostly poems but also short stories. I had a lot of jumbled thoughts and emotions—pretty typical for a teenager. I put them all into words on the page. It was therapeutic for me, I guess. An outlet."

"What kinds of things did you write about?"

"Oh god, *everything*. Teachers I enjoyed. Teachers who annoyed me. My parents. My friends. Other family members. People I had a crush on. Volleyball. Hiking. Nature. Strangers I'd watch at the park or library or wherever I was hanging out. Just . . . everything."

I nodded, smiling at the image of middle school Mack creeping on people's conversations in the park. But I guess I did the same thing here, minus the poems. Most of my ideas lived in my head, but sometimes I'd dabble in short stories. "What drew you to poetry specifically?"

"I loved reading it. I'd go to the library and check out as many poetry books as they'd let me. It wasn't a massive selection, but eventually I started going to the bookstore to read books there, and buy the ones I really loved. I studied how they wrote, which words drove the image or emotion."

"What's your style like?" I already knew, but her readers didn't.

"Chaotic," she laughed, shaking her head. "I guess you'd call it free verse. It doesn't have to rhyme or follow a certain beat. It just comes out as I feel it. You can't plan or order your life down to the second, so I don't want my poetry to feel like that. I want it to surprise people and hook them without a formed expectation. And I want to leave room for them to feel however they want based on their own experiences."

Seeing Mack's face light up talking about poetry moved me. It was something she'd found herself, not something her parents encouraged or people counted on her for. Maybe that was why it stayed private—making it public would add attention and expectations. She had something she could make her own without anyone telling her how to perform. And considering the secret she'd told me last weekend, I assumed her poetry was a place for her to express her secrets freely.

And I was trying to force all that out of her.

And she was letting me.

"We don't have to put all of this in the article," I said after she finished talking.

Mack's smile faded. "What? Why not?"

"I know it's really personal to you, and I'm sorry for trying to push you in a direction you didn't want to go." I shook my head and reached toward the recorder to turn it off.

Mack's hand took mine before I could get there. The hand that had wrapped around my waist. The hand that had touched my cheek. The hand that had *wandered*.

"Don't do that," she said, giving my hand a squeeze before

pulling away just as quickly. "It's fine. And you're right. If I'm going to go to college for writing, I should own up to that sooner than later. It's unlikely, but college recruiters could end up reading this article, and it would be good for them to know I have a plan for college other than volleyball."

Of course she had to find a logical answer. I thought that was my job.

"Yeah, that's exactly what I was getting at," I said. "No other reason like selfishly wanting to hear you talk about your passions."

Mack laughed. And then her foot was pressed against mine. "You're making this really hard for me, you know."

My heartbeat quickened, and I shifted so my foot was on top of hers. "I didn't mean to, but you're making it hard for me, so I guess we're even."

Her foot moved against mine for a moment before she pulled it back. "I'm really sorry about everything. You know that, right?"

"I know," I said, glancing at my notes, which were generally blank. Thank god for my recorder. And thank god no one else had access to it. "Doesn't make it any easier, though."

"I know," she said. "But it won't be like this forever. I just want to get through more life stuff first, maybe get accepted to college?"

I sighed, hating how she felt like some kind of agenda would change anything. "There's no convenient time to be gay. You just are."

"I know," she said again, more firmly this time.

"And you know colleges won't care that you're a lesbian, right?" I added. "I don't think they *can* care, like, legally. And Coach would never kick you off the team. She seems open-minded. Even if she wasn't, she'd never lose her star player."

"That makes me feel so much better," Mack said dryly. "It's not just all of that. It's my friends, my parents, and people in general. I've heard stories about parents losing their minds over queer girls on teams, like we're somehow taking advantage because we happen to be in the same locker room."

"That's so fucked up," I said. I wanted to tell her that would never happen, but I'd had my share of girls over the years telling me to stop checking them out when changing for gym class when I was actually looking for Audrey or just, you know, looking somewhere other than at my feet. I never hid in a bathroom stall to appease them because fuck that, but I didn't want that kind of hate for Mack—not in gym class or for volleyball or anywhere else. It infuriated me that that was one of her main concerns. "I hate people sometimes."

"Yeah, me too," Mack said. "But getting into college for volleyball means that I don't have anything else to prove here. And I'm not going to ask you to wait until then because we don't know what'll happen tomorrow let alone a year from now, but if you're still into me after college acceptance letters arrive next year . . ."

I laughed at her words. "I've had two girlfriends since I first realized I had a crush on you, and here we are. I'm not going to hold you to what you just said, but if you ever get to a point where you're ready, know that I probably will be, too. Unless some goddess comes along between now and then, of course. You might have to fight for me."

"I think you'd make me fight for you even if there was no goddess," Mack said in a teasing tone that I couldn't help but laugh at.

"Damn right I would," I said, full-on beaming at this point. There were zero guarantees, even if everything unfolded how she'd described, but at least she hadn't pushed me away again. At least we could be friends until a day came where we could talk about the possibility of more. Even if that in-between time would be torture. Even if it never came. I could be her friend. That could be enough.

"Good," Mack said, pressing her lips together and shifting to check on Sabrina.

My eyes stayed on her for a moment as my foot found hers again. "I'm proud of you, you know that?"

"What?" Mack laughed quietly. "Why?"

"You didn't just tell a girl you liked her. You came out to someone. And it means a lot that it was me you came out to, even if you had another reason for it. And I just . . . Whenever you're ready to tell people, I'll be right there with you, if you want. Because you deserve to have people supporting you and having your back. And maybe someone on the team or some girl in gym class will be a bitch to you, but your real friends will verbally destroy them. You have the support—you just have to be brave and take that first step. And I know you can be brave. I believe in you, and so does everyone else who gives a damn. I'm not saying it won't be hard or weird for a while, because I know it will be from experience, but you'll be able to do it because you succeed at everything you set your mind to. You just have to believe in yourself and trust that good people will be there for you to help you through it. *I'll* be there."

I hadn't planned on saying all that, and she clearly hadn't planned on hearing it. "Thanks, Jo," Mack said, turning back to me with a smile that didn't reach her eyes. "Should we continue the interview?"

My heart sank. I'd wanted to follow it up with asking if she had a date to her Halloween party. I'd wanted to ask if we could hang out there even if it was hard. And I'd really wanted to ask if we could make out in her room when no one was paying attention. Instead, I nodded. "Yeah, sure."

I glanced at my sparse notes again before returning to journalist mode. We spent the next twenty minutes talking about volleyball before calling it a day. In the end, she'd asked me to find another angle because maybe she wasn't comfortable talking about poetry so openly after all.

As I walked Pond home, I couldn't get it out of my head how lonely it must feel being Mackenzie West.

I spent the next few days preparing my costume for the Halloween party in between homework sessions and article writing. I'd submit my next team story shortly after Halloween, with the Mack feature story publishing just before winter break. The other team stories had been a success, so I had no concerns about writing another one. It was the Mack story that I was worried about. Okay, *panicking* over.

After trips to a few different stores, I had everything I needed to be Amelia Pond. Brown cowgirl boots. Black tights. Black shorts. Maroon camisole. Brown leather jacket. All that was left was to dye my hair, but I wouldn't do that until the night before in case it was a disaster. And because that was the night Audrey and I both had free between school and life obligations.

On Thursday, I reached peak panic over the party and decided to confide in someone outside my friend circle. Knowing Mom was working late, I brought pizza to Dad's comic shop where he was hosting Dungeons & Dragons night. As much as D&D tempted me, I never let myself get wrapped up in it at the shop because the players were dedicated in an addicted, took-it-very-serious way. Like, respect, but I couldn't commit to that life.

"Hey, JoJo!" Dad said as I walked in. "What a nice surprise. Have you finally decided to hang out with the cool kids?"

A few of the players laughed as one cheered and another chanted something I didn't understand. Nerds, am I right?

"Nice try, but I'll never be that cool," I said as I approached, holding out the box. "Do you think the group will survive without you for a bit? I need your brain."

"You better go, Clark," Monica said. She was by far my favorite regular and had an Instagram account dedicated to cosplay and LARPing. If my costume had been more involved, she would've been my go-to for putting it together. "If a girl needs to talk to her dad, you'd regret saying no."

"Oh no," Dad said, paling as he looked me over. "Is it serious? Are you okay?"

"I'm fine, Dad," I said before sticking my tongue out at Monica. "Nice try, wizard."

"I'm a ranger," Monica groaned, throwing her hands up.

"I know." I winked at her, and Dad chuckled before leading us to his office in the back.

"What's this about?" he asked after we sat. "You don't have to put on a show for the gang. It's okay if you're not okay."

"I know," I said. "And I love that you refer to them as a gang."

"Hey, if the game was real life, you'd be terrified."

"Oh, I'm already terrified," I teased, quiet for a beat. How did my life get to a place where I was going to ask my dad for romantic advice? "I'm . . . having girl trouble?"

"Oh. Oh!" Dad grinned at the news. "You came to the right parent. I happen to be an expert, after all, enchanting your mother like I did. Only a true wizard could pull that off."

"I don't think your magic is going to help with this one," I said, laughing despite wanting to take this seriously. But that was the cool thing about Dad—he could have a serious conversation without making it feel *too* serious. It was calming. Mom would've wanted to develop an agonizing strategy or call Mack's mom and chew her out because that was always her solution. Either way, this conversation needed Dad's touch. "I really like this girl, and she likes me, too, but she's not out to people, and she doesn't think she'll be ready for, like, a year."

"That's a long time to wait, JoJo," Dad said. "And you went

down this road once before with your first girlfriend. Is this one worth it?"

As if I needed the reminder. Amazing how this had already happened to me twice. "On the surface, totally. She's fun to be around. She's smart and funny and super talented and has this smile that's torture to look at. But we have a weird history, and I don't always know if I can trust her. She keeps a lot close to her chest, and I'm worried I'll be one of those things. I'm worried she won't come out until college or even later. And that's obviously her right, but it puts me in a weird position. I don't want to be someone's secret for years."

Fortunately, Dad didn't know the entire Mack history, and he didn't know enough about my day-to-day life to know who I was talking about. "And you shouldn't be," he said. "You deserve better than that. But honestly, I don't know how I can help. You seem to have a very mature take on all of this."

"I think I just need an adult's opinion. Like, would you wait for someone if you didn't know how it would all end up?" I sighed. "Or is it childish to think we could be together just because I waited?"

"First of all, you *are* still a child, so that's not a real question. And second, that's something you'll have to figure out for yourself. If she's as special as you make her sound, waiting won't feel like a huge sacrifice. But if you don't know if you can trust her, that's another issue you have to consider. I don't want you pining for someone who isn't good for you, but I also don't want you giving up on someone who feels right."

I'd walked into the shop hoping Dad would give me a solid answer, but that clearly wasn't going to happen. I was on my own. "She's going to be at the Halloween party I'm going to this weekend, and I've been thinking about talking to her again."

"What do you plan on saying?" Dad asked.

"I don't know, but I need sense of where we're at. I'm not going to ask her to come out for me, of course, but I don't want to get hurt again either. I don't know. Whatever I land on, I'll find a more romantic way of saying it."

"You must take after me," Dad said, chuckling. "I think you've got it figured out better than you think you do. I'm proud of you, JoJo."

"Thanks, Dad." I smiled and stood, stepping over to hug him. "You seem very busy here, so I'll just take this pizza and be on my way."

"Not a chance," he said, wrapping me in a tight hug. "I gave you my precious time, and I technically paid for the pizza, too. I've earned a few slices."

"Fine, fine," I said, letting out a dramatic sigh as I pulled back. "I guess I can stay and watch the nerds for a while and share my pizza that you so generously paid for. And thank you for your time. I know you're a very busy, very important man."

"Don't forget it," Dad said, winking before walking out, trailing behind me. Maybe he hadn't solved my dilemma, but at least he was around to listen. That alone made me feel grateful and fortunate. I just wished that Mack could do the same with her parents.

CHAPTER EIGHTEEN

I'D HAD AMELIA Pond hair for a full twenty-four hours and still didn't hate it. Audrey managed to find the perfect shade—ginger, but not *too* ginger. I sat in my car in front of her house wearing the outfit I'd scrapped together with her guidance. The plan was to walk to the party in case we drank too much. And I could act as her excuse to bail if she ended up hating Emma outside school. Fair.

Sitting there, I realized I'd never actually talked to Mack about the Halloween party. Olivia invited me, but obviously Mack knew I'd be there. Right?

Oh my god, what if she didn't know?

I jumped as my door swung open with Audrey standing there in her costume. She told me it was a surprise, and a part of me worried she would actually dress up as the Last Centurion. But no, she was something else entirely.

"Oh my god, are you Tina Belcher?" I asked, laughing. "That's genius!"

"Right?" Audrey laughed, looking down at her costume. "It's fucking cold out, so I figured if you'd be walking to Mackenzie's house in shorts, then I should suffer, too."

I laughed at her rationale. "What's the real reason?"

She rolled her eyes. "Okay, so Emma and I bonded over *Bob's Burgers* during the first editors' meeting. I obviously picked the costume for *me* because I love Tina, but also, I think she'll appreciate it."

Audrey wasn't the type to change herself for someone she was into, so I didn't need her to justify it. Regardless of the reason, it was perfect. "I love it," I said as I got out of my car. "Let's go, Tina."

Audrey let out a Tina-worthy groan in response as we headed toward Mack's house. Despite the cold, snow hadn't returned to the area since the Minneapolis tournament, so at least we weren't contending with cold *and* snow. It was a Minnesota miracle.

"Promise me you'll have fun tonight," Audrey said. "I know things have been weird lately, but obviously you and Isaac are allowed to have other people in your lives."

"Thanks for saying that," I said, taking her hand and squeezing it. "Who knows what will happen after this semester. The only thing I feel sure of is that Olivia isn't going anywhere, which I like. She's good for Isaac."

"She is," Audrey agreed. "What about Mackenzie? Do you think she might go somewhere?"

"I don't know," I said. I couldn't tell her about Minneapolis, and there wasn't a way to explain it without that key information.

"I mean, we're friends now, but the history still makes me a little paranoid." The whole we-have-feels-for-each-other-but-no-one-else-knows part was also a factor.

"I don't blame you. I mean, you went from wanting to get revenge to hanging out with her willingly. I'm forever going to tell you to be careful, but if your friendship stays strong, then I'm happy for you. As badass as Isaac and I am, *I guess* you're allowed to have other friends."

I laughed, choosing not to remind her that she'd wanted revenge more than me. "No doubt, no doubt. And hey, I'm excited about your date with Emma! I hope y'all have fun."

"Me too!" Audrey said, adding a little skip to her step at the mention of Emma. "You know I wouldn't ask just *anyone* out. I have very high standards."

"Girl, I know," I teased, nudging her. "And she should be so lucky, going on a date with Tina Belcher."

"Exactly," Audrey said. "It's the perfect test costume, too. Like, if she was hoping for something sexy, then she's not right for me. But if she thinks it's cool . . . game on."

"I'm crossing my crossables for you," I said, showing her my crossed fingers to prove it.

"You're the best," she said, smiling more. "Let's do this."

"Let's do this."

Learning from the last party, we didn't wait for anyone to let us in. We stepped into Mack's house to find an even more chaotic scene than the first party. A remake of the "Monster Mash" song played overhead, and the house was full of themed decorations like spiderwebs and ghosts hanging from the high ceiling. It was like a real Halloween party you saw in kids' movies, except the kids were older, making out, and drinking. So I guess it was like *Mean Girls*.

We found Isaac and Olivia hanging out by the fireplace with a few other people. "Love the costumes," I said, pausing. "What are they?"

"We're Bonnie and Clyde!" Olivia said, grinning as Isaac made finger guns.

"Love that!" Audrey said. "It's perfect."

"Did you pregame and not invite us?" Isaac asked, resting his hand over Audrey's forehead. "Got a fever?"

"Shut up," she said, swatting his hand away and smiling at Olivia. "I'm just happy you're happy, that's all."

"And because she has a date," Isaac told Olivia, who laughed.

"Well, *I'm* happy you were all able to come," she said. "And I love your costumes. Tina and . . . some adorable redhead?"

"Amelia Pond from *Doctor Who*," I clarified, not blaming her for having no idea, especially since the costume wasn't super obvious and the fandom wasn't as popular for my generation as my dad's. "Why Bonnie and Clyde?"

"I'm obsessed with their story, and the musical is *amazing*," Olivia said. "I had Isaac watch it on our second date and he . . . well, he didn't hate it."

"Give me a little credit," Isaac laughed, wrapping an arm around her. "We'd just started dating. It was impossible to focus with you sitting next to me."

"You are so cute!" Olivia kissed him quickly before looking at us. "Isn't he just so cute?"

"The cutest," I said, nudging Audrey. "And with that, we're getting drinks."

Audrey failed in her attempt to not giggle as she followed. We got two steps before hearing a voice bellow across the room.

"Tina!" it said in a loud, drawn-out way.

We turned in unison to see Emma walking toward us, dressed as a zombie. It took me a minute to piece together why this was the most perfect costume she could've chosen. "Okay, we might like her."

"Good, because I'm a goner," Audrey said, laughing before practically running up to meet her. And then they were making out. I was pretty sure it was their first kiss, and damn, they were really going for it.

With both my friends distracted by kisses and cuteness, I slipped away to grab a drink in the kitchen. The table had snacks like Rice Krispies pumpkins, witch guacamole, mummy hot dogs, and vampire teeth made out of apples, peanut butter, and marshmallows. The main drink labeled "Witch's Brew" was being served in a cauldron, and I opted for that instead of beer, hoping it tasted better. I drank back half the cup before refilling it and moving through the house to see if I could find Mack.

It didn't take long. I spotted her through the crowd talking to Isaac and Olivia, who'd stopped sucking face. Olivia pointed toward me and said something to Mack, who looked at me with one of those smiles that said I was in big trouble in a good way.

For once, it wasn't guarded because people were around. For once, she waved to prove she actually wanted me to come over. For once, I believed it.

And she was dressed as Sabrina.

Like, *hot* Sabrina.

Shit.

"Hey, friends," I said as I stopped in front of them, looking at Isaac. "Glad to see you could tear yourself away from each other for a minute."

"You try tearing yourself away from this girl," Isaac said, squeezing Olivia's side. "It's almost impossible, trust me."

"Are you telling me to put myself in a position where I'd have to tear myself away from her?" I asked, raising my eyebrows and grinning.

"What? N-no," Isaac stammered as the two girls laughed.

"I adore you," Olivia said, tapping my nose before looking at Mack. "You hear me? *Adore* her! I'm so glad we're all friends."

"Me too," Mack said, smiling a little more as her eyes met mine. "How's the brew?"

"That depends . . . Did Sabrina make it?"

"She did."

"Then I guess it's okay."

Mack broke out in a laugh, and I thought about how I'd wanted to bottle that laugh up forever. But really, I'd settle for just hearing it every day.

"You're ridiculous," she said, looking me over. "Amelia Pond?"

"You got it," I said, trying my best at a Scottish accent that didn't land. "Dyed hair and all, thanks very much. And legs for days, obviously."

Mack snorted. "Obviously. And I'm short just like Sabrina."

"The shortest," I said, rolling my eyes at the joke. "Also, love the wig. Super lifelike."

"Oh, this isn't a wig," Mack said. "I totally dyed and cut my hair."

Olivia gasped. "You didn't! Oh my god, Mackenzie!"

Right, our friends were still there. Cool.

"What?" Mack asked, messing with her hair to prove it wasn't a wig. She really had dyed her more natural-looking blonde hair to the platinum-white Sabrina shade. "It's not a big deal."

"I know, I know," Olivia said, smiling again. "I just had hair envy. You look amazing, seriously. *And* it'll be a killer look for the big tournament next month, especially if you wear this makeup, too."

As far as I knew, the team didn't wear makeup for games, but Olivia was right. The other teams would be too distracted by the haunting Sabrina look. *I'd* be too distracted.

"Thanks, lady," Mack said, her cheeks flushing as she looked at me. "What about you? Think I ruined my perfect hair?"

"No," I said too quickly, still picturing Sabrina-Mack playing volleyball. "It looks great. And you should absolutely play the tournament looking like Sabrina. Make it extra witchy." Better than great. Her hair was . . . Well, this just wasn't fair. I was in trouble.

Mack's smile grew. "Thanks, maybe I will." A loud noise

came from the other room, like something big had fallen over, and she groaned. "Okay, I need to see what that was, but let's talk after? Please?"

So, I wasn't the only one who wanted to talk. That was a good sign. Maybe she'd taken some of my words from the dog park to heart. Maybe she was ready for real.

Okay, calm down, Jordan. It was probably just a regular talk. Spend-time-together talk. Not make-out-because-people-are-around talk. It was fine. I was fine. Everything was fine.

"Yeah," I said, smiling hopefully because I hadn't calmed down. "Meet in your room?"

"Perfect." Her eyes fixated on mine for a beat before she turned to Isaac and Olivia. "Have fun, you two. But not so much fun that I find a naked Isaac in the guest room in the morning."

"Stop!" they said in unison, instantly mortified.

Mack winked at them and flashed me another smile before walking off. I watched her for a few seconds too long before glancing at the others. "Don't steal too much, Bonnie and Clyde," I said, setting my cup down, not wanting to have more alcohol if the talk was going to be even a little bit serious. Isaac and Olivia went back to kissing before I could turn away, making it even easier for me to disappear upstairs.

The door to Mack's room was cracked, but before I could open it more, I heard voices from the other side. I felt like an intruder, the same as the last time I was in Mack's house, but I couldn't move after hearing my name.

"I just can't believe she actually came. It's so embarrassing.

I mean, how isn't it obvious that the team just wants good press and to keep Coach happy? She needs to play her part like all the other newspaper nerds that came before her and accept that she'll never be one of us. Her obsession is . . . I don't even know."

I didn't have to look inside to know Brie's voice, and where there was Brie . . .

"But is it even *us* she's obsessed with?" Marissa asked, giggling. "Have you seen how she looks at Mackenzie? I thought she wanted to murder her at first. And maybe she still does, but there's something else there. There has to be."

"Oh, totally!" Brie agreed enthusiastically. "And Mackenzie is *obviously* using her. She just has to be more strategic than us since they used to be friends or whatever."

Marissa gasped. "I had no idea! Guess that explains why she was so pissed in the locker room after Jordan showed up to that first practice."

"Seriously, she probably thought her past was behind her. I guess Jordan was her first friend when she moved here . . . you know, before she could make *real* friends. They used to meet at the park and watch their dogs play like a bad teen romance movie. It must've gone to Jordan's head. She always looks like she'd melt if Mackenzie touched her. And then she went to Mackenzie's house and sat there while she was sleeping. Makes my skin crawl just thinking about it."

"It's pathetic," Marissa said. "So, you don't think she likes Jordan at all?"

"Oh, I *know* she doesn't. She's totally using her to get good stories written about her, and the fangirl attention is just a bonus. She makes it look so easy, too, but I guess it's not that hard to manipulate someone who's obsessed with you. Maybe that's why she's the captain. She can make anyone fall for her charms and lies."

"You're right, you're right," Marissa said. "She doesn't deserve captain. And Jordan doesn't deserve being dragged through the mud by her, even if she's a total weirdo. I mean, why did she ride with us on the Minneapolis trip? She should've known to say no."

"Why do you think?" Brie asked. I could hear the smirk in her voice as my stomach threatened to explode.

"Oh my god," Marissa said, practically cackling now. "That's so sad!"

"No shit. Honestly, I can't believe I tried being her friend. I guess she's not as cool as her brother." She sighed again. "Oh well, lesson learned."

I didn't register the footsteps until the door swung open, and I was standing face-to-face with Brie. My blood was boiling, but I couldn't form words.

"Oh, Jordan," Brie said, looking genuinely surprised, but she quickly covered it with a malicious grin. "It's rude to eavesdrop, you know. Even for a journalist . . . bad taste, girl."

Marissa's eyes trailed over my costume. "Who are you even supposed to be?"

"Amelia Pond from *Doctor Who*," I said quietly, too in shock to come up with a biting remark.

"Oh my god, what a *nerd*," Marissa said, laughing loudly before nudging Brie. "Let's go. This is too painful."

She walked off, but Brie remained. "Sorry, Jordan. If I were you, I'd let this go. You don't want to embarrass yourself, you know?" She gave my shoulder a pat. "I think you've done enough."

My skin was on fire. Of course I'd had my suspicions about the team, about Mack, but I'd been hoping it was all paranoia. But after all that . . . I had to get out of there.

I ran down the stairs, weaving through the dancers to get to the door, ignoring yells from Audrey and Isaac that I could always hear through a crowded room. Despite my hatred of running, especially in uncomfortable boots, I didn't stop until I was in my car in Audrey's driveway.

Everything sunk in as I tried breathing through it. I shouldn't have let Mack back in, shouldn't have trusted her with my honesty and my compassion and my heart. She was using me, just as I'd always worried. She even came out to me to hook me— if that part was even real. Did it need to be a secret *because* it wasn't real? Or did she tell me all those deep truths to make sure I wouldn't question her? Or had things changed between us, making her stop her scheming?

Whatever the truth was, she clearly thought she had so much power over me with her smiles and kisses and that damn costume that I'd never find out the truth. That I'd never confront her. That I'd never have the guts to write something terrible about her. Like I was too "obsessed" with her to be honest about who she really was.

Well, fuck that. I'd show her.

The apartment was quiet when I got home. Mom had a work event, and Dad was hosting a party at the comic shop, costume contest and all. The smart thing would've been to hang out there until I'd calmed down. At least my costume would've been appreciated. But no, I had business to attend to.

I changed out of my costume that I'd totally worn to impress Mack. After switching to pajamas and pulling my stupid Amy Pond hair into a messy bun, I opened my laptop and started writing fast and furious.

Have you ever met someone and immediately known they'd change your life forever? That's how I felt the day I met Mackenzie West.

Here's the truth: People like Mackenzie West are impossible.

People like Mackenzie West grow up having it all while expecting more. They look for ways to get exactly what they want while stepping over whoever it takes in the process. They have no regard for how their actions affect others. Their success is number one, and there is no number two.

Take volleyball, for example. You have a girl who grew up with parents who bullied her to stick with a sport that they seemed to love more than her. There's a level of sympathy there, sure, but there's no respect. Respect would be watching her forge her own path. Yes, she could play volleyball simply because she enjoyed it, but she could also chase her true passion. Writing is the great love of Mackenzie West's life, but her words remain in notebooks wrapped in a box under her bed to hide the fact that she found her own dream—a dream her parents won't praise her for.

And because being number one is still the ultimate goal, the dream is ignored.

Mackenzie West is a shoo-in at whatever college she wants to play volleyball for, but people like her never stop at being the best. They create charity events so everyone knows they are the most thoughtful. They throw parties so no one forgets how fun and cool they are. They make captain as a junior just to show everyone they can, taking the title away from other girls who'll never get another shot. They make their coach believe they're irreplaceable. They make sure everyone around them knows how needed they are because the two people who should care the most are never there for them.

Maybe I'm just being bitter, but that's what happens when you're used by someone and cheated out of friendship because you're not cool enough. Or maybe I wasn't athletic enough. Maybe I wasn't straight enough. Whatever the reason, people like me don't become friends with people like Mackenzie West. Instead, we get used for her benefit, because don't forget what I said about number one.

Speaking of number one, I'll end with two final truths. The first: Mackenzie West is the best volleyball player at our school and will get into whatever college she wants.

The second: No one outside high school gives a shit.

One day, everyone will graduate and move on to the real world, and volleyball is something only a select few care about. And when the world widens, so does the competition.

In the real world, no one cares about Mackenzie West.

So, congratulations, Mackenzie West. You successfully changed my life forever. Thanks to you, I live in the real world now. And in the real world, you don't exist.

I was a ball of tears by the end, feeling both better and not. I looked at the framed sign on my wall, the one with the "Question everything, assume nothing, learn the truth" quote. I was questioning everything, but I was also assuming everything. I didn't actually *know* the truth, no matter what Brie had said. And maybe I'd never learn it, but I was better than this. Also, Mx. Shannon would be so disappointed in me if that vile article ever saw the light of day. I could kiss an editor position goodbye—maybe *any* role—and I'd never let that happen. I'd worked too hard, come too far, and I wouldn't let this ruin me. And if it was all true, I wouldn't let Mackenzie West ruin me.

At least I could protect my future without lying to myself and other people. At least I could be my true self every day without shame or concern. At least I had friends who encouraged me to be myself instead of making me feel like I needed to hide. I had so much to be grateful for, and I wouldn't take it for granted.

I saved the document for my own future therapeutic needs and closed my laptop. "Come along, Pond," I said quietly to my dog, who'd been waiting patiently for me. We climbed into bed and I held her close, crying away the emotions of the past couple of months. Even if it was all a lie, it still felt like I was saying goodbye to something special.

CHAPTER NINETEEN

THE SEVERAL MISSED calls and texts the next morning reminded me that I hadn't told anyone I was leaving the party. Audrey and Isaac had tried calling, and I felt terrible for not explaining. They didn't deserve me bailing on them, especially Audrey, who'd expected a sleepover after the party. My stomach turned as I caught up.

Audrey: UM HI WTF

Isaac: What happened? You were all giddy like 10 minutes ago and now you're gone?!

Audrey: Are you sleeping over? Should I come home?

Audrey: Emma is even worried about u!

Audrey: Did Mackenzie do something?! Because I'll end her if she did!

Isaac: That's it, we're calling your dad

Audrey: This is serious Jo!

Isaac: The only reason we aren't coming over is because your dad said you're in bed so we know you got home safe

Audrey: Please explain tomorrow. We're really worried!

Isaac: Text us when you get up

Audrey: ILY

I groaned, feeling both guilty and so, *so* loved. I responded with a quick apology and said I needed a *me* day and we'd talk more on Monday. Then I looked over at Pond, who was dutifully waiting for me, no doubt needing to pee. "Okay, I'm sorry. Let's go outside."

Pond instantly sprang into action, jumping off the bed and dancing in circles while I threw a sweatshirt on over my pajama top and stepped into a pair of Tardis slippers. Knowing the parents were awake somewhere in the apartment, I tiptoed to the door and attached Pond's leash before stepping out.

The cold morning air welcomed me. Most people complained about winter in Minnesota, especially the great white north where you're basically in Canada, but I loved it. The crispness was both refreshing and threatening. It could only be enjoyed in small doses or your body would make you regret it. The frosted trees were as stunning as the coloring of leaves that had greeted me only a month ago. Winter was a reminder that all things die, but it also came with the promise of new life. There was a special kind of beauty in that.

I took out my phone after Pond had peed and we made our way to her usual poop spot. Audrey and Isaac were the most important messages to address, but I'd missed calls and messages from other people. Olivia had checked in, and Dad had texted that he was there if I wanted to talk.

But seeing Mack's name on my screen brought back everything from the party. How she looked in her Halloween costume. Her needing to excuse herself but wanting to talk to me later. Her teammates talking shit about me in her room. Hearing that I was being used. The sound of blood pumping in my ears as I ran from the party. The article I'd written because of it all.

The article I'd written.

I didn't regret keeping those words to myself. It was the right thing to do—not only for my career, but on a moral level.

My phone dinged, snapping me out of my thoughts as I opened the text thread with Mack to catch up.

Mack: Where did you go? I thought we were meeting in my room?

Mack: Hello??

Mack: Isaac said he saw you leave. Is everything okay?

Mack: Tried to call

Mack: I guess you went home?

Mack: Talk to me.

Mack: At least tell me you're okay.

I groaned again. This would've been so much easier if she magically knew what I'd heard and either had an honest explanation or left me alone. And even if everything Brie said was a lie, I couldn't keep doing this to myself. I'd do my job, attend games, write the remaining articles, but I needed a little space, otherwise, to clear my head. After that, I'd move on to another beat and not have to worry about the team again.

If everything was as I'd heard it last night, I could go back to pretending Mackenzie West didn't exist.

Mom was waiting for me when we got home, and she had pancakes and bacon on the table. This wouldn't be a terrifying image if Mom was the one who usually made our meals. "Where's Dad?" I asked after letting Pond off her leash.

"He's cleaning the shop after the party last night," Mom said, looking out of place in Dad's apron, with pancake mix in her hair. "I thought we could spend some time together."

I sighed at what should be a harmless statement. "Okay, now you're *really* freaking me out. What's going on?" My eyes widened. "Oh my god, are you and Dad getting a divorce?"

"What?" Mom's eyebrows shot up. "Why would you think that? Do you even know the man I married? I'd never give him up. He's a national treasure."

I relaxed at her words, chuckling at the last part. I knew exactly what she meant. Dad may not make a lot of money or aspire to greatness or whatever, but he was selfless and a damn good listener. "I'm sorry, I just . . . I'm not used to having you make me breakfast and wanting to hang out spontaneously." I paused. "Did you lose your job?"

"Stop assuming something is wrong," Mom said. "No one

is getting divorced. No one lost their job. And no, no one is pregnant."

"How well you know me," I muttered, because of course that was my next question. "But *can* you be pregnant? That would be kind of awesome."

Mom laughed and shook her head. "That shop is closed, but thank you for thinking that I still could be."

I eyed her as I considered other possibilities. It was nice of her to make my favorite meal and want to spend time with me, but I knew my mother better than she realized. "I still think there's a catch."

She was quiet for a moment, confirming I was right. "Well, maybe your dad told me that you came home early last night from a party instead of staying at Audrey's house, and maybe he wasn't the only one who was concerned. He needed to get back to the shop this morning, so I told him this conversation was on me. And really, I *am* concerned. You hate missing Audrey sleepovers, and you enjoyed the last party you went to."

"I did," I said, shrugging as I sat at the table. "But this one was different. And after I realized how not-fun it was, I decided to go home instead of making Audrey bail early. She had a date, and I wasn't going to take that from her."

"That was considerate of you," Mom said, smiling warmly. "You're just like your father, always thinking of other people. But who's thinking of you?"

"I am," I said, instantly feeling guilty for making it sound like I'd done something selfless. "Trust me, I still am. And my friends think of me. And you and Dad and Casey. Maybe in different ways, but I know you all do."

"I'm glad to hear you say that, because sometimes I wonder," Mom said. She didn't mean it in a self-pity kind of way that I'd need to talk her out of like she sometimes did. "Your father is clearly the more natural parent, and you two have more in common, but I still love you and your brother just as much."

"We know," I said, thinking about Mack's situation with her parents and knowing I needed to be honest. I didn't want my relationship with my mom to be like hers. "It's just . . . sometimes I feel like you don't really hear me, you know?"

"What do you mean?" she asked as she sat across from me and started serving breakfast.

Already uncomfortable, I clasped my hands together under the table. "You're really good at fighting your own battles, but you don't always let me fight mine. Like with Mx. Shannon. I told you not to do anything about that, and you still did."

"That wasn't a big deal. Mx. Shannon can handle me."

"Of course they can continue—they're amazing. But that was my business to handle. And I *can* handle it."

"I know," Mom said, pausing. "I get in the way sometimes because it's what I'm good at. Casey and I have always been more on the same level, but you and your dad . . . I can't compete with him. And I don't want to, but I do try to help. Sometimes I forget that my way isn't always the right way. I'm sorry."

I frowned. "You're not in the way, Mom. I know you care and want what's best for me, but sometimes it would be nice to trust that *I* know what's best for me. I'm not a little kid anymore. Everything changed for me when I came out. It was the hardest thing I'd ever done, and you and Dad and Casey were so supportive. You asked thoughtful questions and told me you loved me and were proud of me, and there wasn't a single negative or judgmental word. And that meant so much to me. I'll never forget it."

"You mean so much to *us*," Mom said. "You're so loved, and we needed you to know that. I might do or say things to make you wonder if I'm really on your side, but I've never wanted you to change a single thing about who are you."

"Not even my weight?" I asked hesitantly.

"Is that not a part of who you are?" Mom asked, raising a brow.

"It is."

"Well then, there's your answer."

I wanted to leave it there, but it wasn't that simple for me. "It just doesn't always come off that way. How you feel about your body is your business, but some of the things you say about yourself . . . I think you forget that I'm listening. I watch you only have a couple of bites of Dad's dessert instead of ordering your own, or focusing on salad instead of other parts of a meal. And of course there's nothing wrong with exercise, but sometimes you seem to use it as a punishment, not something you do because you want to or because it makes you feel good." I huffed out a sigh, feeling tears form. "And I know none of this means I need to act or feel a certain way, but it still hurts watching someone I love go through life like they need to fit into some unrealistic societal ideal. You don't need diets or flawless makeup or tailored clothes to be amazing. You already are just by being a good person—by being my mom."

Mom's eyes were watery, too, but there was something else. She was embarrassed, which I didn't want. "Oh, sweetie, I know that," she said, resting her hand over mine. "Your dad tells me the same thing all the time. And I'm truly sorry that my actions have made you wonder if I wanted the same for you, but I promise that couldn't be further from the truth. It's okay if you don't like salads or makeup or dressing a certain way, but I do. And some exercise is really hard—of course it feels like a punishment at my age." She laughed quietly, wiping under her eyes. "But I promise that's all for me and no one else, okay?"

I hadn't given her enough credit. I saw a woman who wasn't like me and never once considered that the differences made her feel good the way pancakes and writing and Tardis slippers made me feel good. "Okay," I said, smiling back at her. "Sorry for assuming."

"Don't be sorry," she said, wiping tears from under my eyes now. "Thank you for bringing this up. I'll try to be more mindful of how I speak about things, and please correct me if I say something that bothers you. That's the last thing I want."

"Okay." I couldn't take it anymore. I left my chair and stepped over to her, pulling her into a hug and closing my eyes. "I love you."

"I love you, too, sweet girl," Mom said, hugging me tighter. We stayed like that for several seconds before she pulled back. "Let's dig in before the pancakes get cold."

"Agreed," I said, returning to my seat. We each took a bite, and she closed her eyes as if savoring the flavor. I laughed quietly and fed Pond a chunk of my pancake before starting to eat. For the first time in a long time, I sat with my mom at the table without wishing my dad was there, too.

CHAPTER TWENTY

HAVE YOU EVER watched a movie where the main character enters a room and it's obvious everyone else knows something they don't?

That happened to me Monday morning. Isaac had gotten a ride to school from Olivia, so I pulled into my usual spot near the back of the lot alone. I had roughly five minutes to get to homeroom, which I was dreading because that meant facing Brie. But I didn't even make it to the building before realizing I had bigger problems. Several classmates circled me, trying to get my attention with various statements.

"Do you really think her parents don't love her?"

"Damn, girl, she must've really hurt you."

"I am *obsessed* with you! Will you sign my arm?"

"You have some fucking nerve!"

"I am *so* proud of you!"

I was relieved to hear the last voice as Audrey cleared a path and hugged me. "What's going on?" I asked, trying not to panic. But I was definitely panicking. "Why are people perceiving me?"

"Because you did it, girl! You finally did it. You knocked Mackenzie West on her ass and exposed her for who she really is."

"What are you talking about?" I asked.

Then it hit me.

I broke free from the group that lingered as I turned on my phone. "Please, please, please, tell me I didn't do what I think I did," I mumbled to myself as I pulled up Google Drive. I had a personal account on my phone and laptop as well as the newspaper's account, and clicking on the newspaper's account confirmed my worst nightmare.

I'd written my personal rant while still logged in on the newspaper's account. When I hit "save," I had accidentally submitted it to the newspaper.

And someone had approved and posted it.

"You're my hero!" Audrey said as she once again appeared at my side, wrapping her arm across my shoulders. "Seriously, you deserve a monument. Or at least a meal at The Diner—my treat."

I barely registered her words as I found the paper's website. My venting article was on the front page with a picture of Mack that Isaac had uploaded a couple of weeks ago during a match. I remembered it because I'd thought she looked beautiful. "I'm going to be sick," I said.

"What?" Audrey asked, looking over my shoulder at the article. "Did you have another picture in mind?"

"I had *no* picture in mind," I said, pocketing my phone and stepping away from her. "I didn't mean to save this to the school Drive. It was for *me*—I never intended this to actually publish."

"What—*Oh*. Oh my god, Jo!"

"I know!" I looked around in an attempt to figure out what to do next. And then I saw her.

Mack stood across the lawn from me, her short Sabrina hair on display and an expression I never wanted to see in my life—pure devastation. No matter what she'd done years ago and potentially done recently, I didn't want this.

"Mack," I said as she turned to walk toward the parking lot. The bell rang, and I looked back to see the other students reluctantly heading inside. Audrey offered a small smile and gestured to text her before doing the same. I shouldn't care about what had happened and should've let Mack get in her car and drive off, but I'd never been capable of fully letting her go.

So I followed her, hustling to catch up. "It was an accident," I said when I got close enough.

"Oh, so you didn't mean to write a hateful article about me and publish it for the entire school to read?"

"I wrote it because you'd *once again* broken my heart and I needed to get it out. But I never meant for it to get published. I saved it to the wrong Drive."

"Bullshit," Mack scoffed. "You've hated me for years. I should've known you'd mess with me for revenge."

"Are you fucking kidding me? You've been messing with *me* this entire year so I'd write a perfect article about your perfect life so people would read it and know how fucking perfect you are."

"You couldn't be more wrong," she said. "Yeah, sure, I'd love a nice article about me—who wouldn't? But I haven't been using you to get it. Do you honestly think I'd fake everything we've talked about and done for a story in the high school newspaper?"

Okay, her words were logical, but it still didn't add up. "At your party, Brie said—"

"Brie hates me!" Mack yelled, her eyes wild as she whipped around to look at me. "How is that not obvious to you? She's bitter because I got the captain position, which I'd never asked for and didn't even want. But that's on Coach, not me, and my parents would've lost their shit if they'd known I'd turned it down."

I opened my mouth to respond, but she kept going.

"I get not trusting me immediately, but how could you still feel that way after everything? How could you think Minneapolis meant nothing to me? That *you* meant nothing to me? Have you just been waiting for a reason to go back to hating me?"

"I . . . I don't know," I said, realizing I didn't. Like she'd said, hating her had been easier in a lot of ways. Hating her meant not being open to getting hurt again. Hating her meant not somehow hurting her in return. But there I was, dealing with both.

Mack rolled her eyes. "That's great. Well, you got what you wanted. You've confirmed you were being messed with—it just wasn't by me."

I stopped in front of her car as she fished for her keys. There had to be something I could say to fix what had happened—not just the article, but all of it. "I'm sorry," I said, needing to keep her there while I formed the right words.

"I'm sure you are," Mack said, turning to look at me. "Even if you *did* post the article by mistake, I doubt you'd write all that if you didn't think it was true. Question everything, assume nothing, learn the truth, right?"

That was the second time she'd said those words, and they'd been haunting me all semester. "How do you know about that?" I asked. We had bigger things to talk about, but I needed to know.

"I was at your apartment in April," Mack said, looking as wrecked as I felt. "Casey had a party while your parents were somewhere and you were at Audrey's. The guys were being obnoxious and I was bored, so I snuck into your room with Pond for a break. I saw the sign, and it was just so . . . *you*. It made me realize how much I missed you. Fuck, I'd missed you so much. I took a picture of it and stared at it until the words were etched in my mind."

My heart broke all over again. It was impossible not to believe her with that look on her face. How could I have been so stupid? "I'm going to find a way to make this right," I said, determined. "I promise."

"Don't bother," Mack said, opening her car door before looking back at me. "I don't exist, remember?"

My article's final line slapped me in the face as her words

echoed in my ears. She was gone before I could think of anything to say.

After standing in the parking lot for an unknown amount of time, I checked the newspaper's site again to see if my article was posted word for word, but it was gone. Mx. Shannon must've seen it, which meant I was in even deeper shit with them than I was with Mack. But I had to talk to Brie first.

I made it to homeroom but waited in the hall, not wanting to get into it during morning announcements. When the bell rang, Brie walked out after a handful of other students. "I'm surprised you showed up today," she said as she stopped in front of me. "You don't look so good."

I ignored the weak insult. "What's wrong with you? Are you so pathetic that you had to use me to mess with Mackenzie?"

Brie blinked as if confused. "I don't know what you're talking about. *I* didn't write a scathing article about her. But hey, thanks for implying that I worked hard for a shot at captain. That was really nice of you."

I rolled my eyes, tired of her bullshit. "Maybe you didn't write it, but don't pretend you weren't thrilled to see me standing on the other side of Mack's door."

"Oh, that?" Her smile quickly returned. "Yeah, I really was. But you can't blame that on me. I didn't know you'd be eavesdropping, or that you'd go as far as you did with what you'd heard. I mean, I even told you to let it go. I was trying to help you. So at some point, you'll have to take responsibility for your actions." She looked away before back to me. "This was fun, but

I have to get to class. See you around." Her shoulder hit mine as she walked off.

People passed me in slow motion as I stood in the hall. Some of them gave me a pat on the back while others nudged me Brie-style. I didn't register anything they said as I tried to think about what this meant. Brie had totally benefitted from the anger that she helped stoke in me. Maybe she didn't know I'd be standing outside the door, but she still loved seeing Mack be steamrolled in the paper.

But what really clicked was the now-obvious fact that everything that had happened with Mack was real. Maybe she wasn't out, and maybe she didn't want to talk about writing with the world yet, but she had still opened up to me about both. That alone should've told me everything I needed to know, but here I was with a new enemy, a shattered friendship, and a school full of people who thought I was either a legend or a monster.

But I couldn't dwell on that now. Before I could figure out what to say to Mack, I had two teachers to see, and it was unlikely either of them wanted to see me. Actually, that's a lie. Coach probably wanted to strangle me, and Shannon probably wanted to kick me off the paper.

Shannon got to me before I had a chance to seek them out. Or rather, Shannon, Coach, and Principal Jeffries got to me first. I was called to his office five minutes into first period. Of course the entire class knew why, and I was treated to a round of childish laughter and applause on my way out.

Walking into Jeffries's office, I was shocked to see Audrey sitting in one of the chairs. "What are you doing here?" I asked.

"Sit down, Miss Elliot," Principal Jeffries said before she could get a word out.

I made the mistake of looking at all their disappointed faces before sinking into the seat next to Audrey. They all stared back at me, having their own reasons to be upset. Well, I still didn't know about Audrey, but I had a feeling that would soon be explained.

"I didn't think I'd ever need to remind you ladies that this school has a strict no-bullying policy, but here we are," Principal Jeffries said, shaking his head. "Considering I've never had either of you in this office before now, I'm hoping it doesn't continue. But first offense or not, this is a serious situation. Using the paper and taking advantage of Mx. Shannon's trust to start a smear campaign will not be taken lightly." He eyed us in turn. "What do you have to say for yourselves?"

"Jordan is my best friend," Audrey said before I could form words. "When I saw the article posted to the paper's Drive, I thought we were taking a stand against bullies like Mackenzie."

My eyes widened as reality dawned on me. My sweet, hilarious, overly protective best friend shared my words with the entire school. "I didn't mean to post it," I said, turning to face her. "I thought I'd saved it on my personal Drive."

"Well, I know that *now*," Audrey said, letting out a sigh. "And I'm sorry, Jo, I really am. But your words were inspiring. You were finally standing up for yourself and fighting back, and I was so proud of you. So I posted it before anyone else could touch it." She looked at the principal. "What about journalistic freedom?"

"Whether intended or not, Miss Lim, the article was bullying, plain and simple," Jeffries said. "It has no place on our school's website. Mx. Shannon took it down immediately."

Audrey slumped in her chair with a sigh. "Yeah, that's fair," she mumbled. "I promise it won't happen again." She eyed them hopefully. "Can we go? I have a test next period."

"You're not off the hook just yet," Mx. Shannon said, their stare locked on us. "I'm very disappointed in both of you. Audrey, you should know better than to abuse your editor position like this. And Jordan, mistake or not, it's troubling you wrote something like that in the first place. I thought everything was going well with the volleyball team."

"It was," I said, looking at Coach. "Writing about volleyball and your team has been the highlight of my year, truly. This mess doesn't take away how much I respect you and have enjoyed being part of the team in my own way."

"I'm just so surprised," Coach said. "Mackenzie is a good girl, and I know that because she comes to me with a lot more than just ideas for the team. Whatever is going on between the two of you, she didn't deserve this."

"She didn't," I agreed, my voice full of regret as the knots in my stomach doubled. "It was a misunderstanding that got out of control. She didn't do anything wrong."

Coach nodded, quiet for a beat. "Did this misunderstanding have to do with another girl on the team?"

"With respect, Coach, I don't want to answer that. I think I've caused enough damage."

"You don't have to answer for me to know," Coach said, letting out a sigh. "I've heard enough to have an idea of what happened." She looked to Jeffries. "Let me handle this?"

"Of course." Jeffries nodded. He looked back to me and Audrey, pointedly. "Now, about next steps. We feel it's best if you girls take some time away from school this week to think about your actions, be they innocent or otherwise. We'll regroup next week and decide if further action is necessary."

"You're suspending us?" Audrey asked as my stomach knots tripled.

"I am," he said. "And let me put in your heads what's at stake here. You, Miss Lim, may lose your editor position. And you may both be removed from the newspaper for the remainder of the semester, if not the rest of the year."

"Oh my god," I said quietly at the same time Audrey yelled, "You can't be serious!"

"I'm very serious," Jeffries said. "Mx. Shannon will determine any further punishment next Monday when you both return to school, and it'll be up to them and Coach Pavek if you return to the volleyball beat, Miss Elliot."

Shit.

"But the big tournament is this weekend," I said. The main season had wrapped before Halloween, and the team was moving on to the quarterfinals, then possibly semifinals and finals. This was the most important weekend for the team to date. And

Mack was still going to look like Sabrina. Doubly shit. "I understand if I've lost your trust, but please know that I'm still good for it when it comes to covering the games."

"It's true, your writing this semester has beyond impressed me," Coach said, her eyes narrowing. "But I need to think about it and talk to Mackenzie first. If she's not comfortable having you there, or if it will distract the team in any way, you're out. I'll let you know my decision later this week."

"I understand, thank you," I said, knowing I had no room to further plead my case. "For the record, I really am sorry for what happened." I looked at Shannon. "I take my position on the newspaper very seriously, and I know Audrey does, too. I promise nothing like this will ever happen again."

"What she said," Audrey chimed in, calming down enough to be civil, or maybe she just didn't want a more severe punishment. "I'm so sorry. I don't know what I was thinking."

Mx. Shannon's expression softened. "You're good kids—we all know this. Take the week to remind yourselves of that and learn from your actions."

"We will," Audrey said, forcing a small smile, and I did the same.

"Good," Principal Jeffries said. "I'll be calling your parents to let them know you'll be on your way home and to coordinate any homework or tests you had on deck this week. I urge you both to complete everything on time so you're not scrambling to catch up next week."

"Of course, sir," I said, nodding along to whatever he threw at us. The last thing I wanted was to tell my parents I'd been suspended, especially my mom, who I'd just gotten on better terms with. But this was serious, and I wouldn't do anything to risk messing it up worse than I already had.

I also wanted to talk to both Shannon and Coach more, but our time was up until next week. We all needed to think and process, and talking to them while their defenses were up was a terrible idea. Audrey seemed to understand the same, because she stood with me when we were excused and walked out.

I waited until we'd turned a corner before saying anything. "I can't believe you'd post that article without talking to me first. Wasn't it obvious I was spiraling?"

"Um, no, Jo, it wasn't," Audrey said, giving me a *seriously* look. "You bolted from the Halloween party and wouldn't talk to me or Isaac, and then you shut off your phone. What was I supposed to do except assume something extremely shitty had happened and that you'd meant every word?"

"I did mean every word, at least at the time. But I messed up. Brie made it sound like Mackenzie was using me. And because I was so insecure about freshman year, I ate it all up without even thinking through the reality. Mackenzie is . . . I was wrong." I sighed, remembering the look in her eyes this morning. The pain. "I was *so* wrong."

Audrey was quiet for a moment. "Look, I'm truly sorry I posted it, but I thought the revenge plot was back on, and I was so proud of you. I was thinking like a best friend, not like a journalist or an editor. But I don't want you hating me for doing something I thought was genuine. I really can't have you hating me, okay? You're my most favorite person in this stupid town—probably the world."

I let out another sigh in the hope that all the shitty energy in my body would leave. "I don't hate you, Audrey. I'm just . . . The whole situation is fucked up. Brie being a legit mean girl. Mackenzie somehow being the victim of bullying. *Us* being the bullies?"

"Yeah, we've totally entered some warped time paradox," Audrey said, frowning. "But I guess we should get our shit and go before the next class lets out and we get mauled by Mackenzie's friends."

"Or get a parade thrown by all the people who seem to think I'm a legend now," I added, groaning. "I hate everything."

"Me too," Audrey said, pulling me in for a hug. "But we have each other."

"And Isaac," I added, suddenly wondering what he thought about all this. I'd have to check my phone after getting home, because this had no doubt been filling his head all morning.

"Only if he hasn't ditched us for Olivia after she convinces him we're bad news."

I snorted a laugh. "She would never. She's cooler than you give her credit for."

"I know, I just can't help but look after our little weirdo best friend."

"Same." I stepped back after a moment. "Regroup later?"

"Regroup later, though I'm sure I'll be grounded."

"Oh, totally, but has that ever stopped us?"

"Never." She grinned, ruffling my hair before turning to head to her locker.

I watched her go, grappling with mixed emotions. I was grateful to have a best friend who had my back, but I also wish she would've waited until talking to me first. We couldn't do anything about it now, and I wouldn't push her away over something that I couldn't blame her for thinking. I went to gather everything I'd need for the rest of the week from my locker, hoping that when I got home, things would be a little less uncomfortable than they'd been in Principal Jeffries's office.

CHAPTER TWENTY-ONE

HOME WASN'T AS uncomfortable as school—it was worse. Not only had Dad left the shop in the hands of his new employee, but Mom had taken the rest of the morning off to be home for our "talk." They let me put my stuff in my bedroom and meet them in the living room before making their opinions known.

"We're very disappointed in you, JoJo," Dad said.

We all knew it was serious when *he* was the one talking about disappointment. "Trust me, no one is more disappointed than me," I said, looking down at my hands as I fidgeted.

"What happened, exactly?" Mom asked. "Principal Jeffries didn't get into details, just that you and Audrey had published a nasty article about another girl at school."

"This doesn't erase what happened, but the article wasn't supposed to get published," I said, facing them again. "Yes, I wrote something cruel, but it wasn't meant for the whole school. I'd written it to get some feelings out, and I accidentally saved it to the paper's Drive instead of my personal."

"Does this have anything to do with why you left that party early?" Dad asked. "I know we haven't had a chance to talk about that yet, but your friends had sounded really worried about you. We're worried, too."

"Yeah, it has something to do with that," I said, trying to think of how to explain everything without telling them about Mack specifically. "I'd overheard some girls talking about me, and they made it sound like one of my friends was using me. And because I've had trouble trusting this friend in the past, I believed every word of it. But I had it all wrong, and the friend I ended up writing about is actually innocent."

"I was hoping we were missing pieces of the story," Dad said, a soft smile forming. "You're a really good kid, always have been. And I'm sorry this girl messed with you like that. She should be the one getting punished."

"I think she will be," I said, thinking on what Coach had said about handling Brie.

"High schoolers can be vicious," Mom said, letting out a sigh. "I'm sorry you're going through this, sweetie. But this is your issue to deal with, so I'm not going to call the school or that other girl's parents like I want to."

I chuckled at her words, proud of her and also relieved that she took our conversation yesterday to heart. "Thanks. I have a lot of work to do to make it up to the friend I hurt, but I'll figure it out. And I'll let you know if I need anything."

"That's all we ask," Mom said.

"And also, we're forced to ground you," Dad added. "A nice

change, honestly. We grounded Casey constantly, but never you."

"You're right . . . this is a first," Mom said, somehow looking proud in this moment.

"I'm glad you two are enjoying this," I said, scrunching my nose. I wouldn't try fighting them on it. Not intending to share a hate article didn't change the facts, and it didn't make me hate myself any less for letting Brie get to me and believing her over Mack. "Can I at least take Pond for her walks and to the dog park like normal?"

"Yes, as long as we don't come home from work and find out you haven't touched your homework or done your chores," Dad said.

"Yeah, that's fair," I said. "Anything else?"

"Nope, that's it," Dad said. "We both need to get back to work, so promise not to slip away to Audrey's or Isaac's just because we aren't here."

"I promise I won't," I said. "Dog park only."

"And don't invite them to the dog park," Mom added, winking at me.

Damn, they were good. But again, Casey. He was genius at skirting around language.

"No other people, period. Just me and Pond. Got it."

After they left, I checked my phone to see what else I'd missed. I started with the string of texts that Isaac had sent me this morning.

Isaac: WTF happened?!

Isaac: U ok?

Isaac: I'm really worried about u

Isaac: Can I come over after school?

I texted him back, because the parents didn't say anything about no phone. I'd have to thank Casey for the inspiration.

Jordan: I'm grounded so no company allowed sorry

Jordan: I made a huge mistake. That article wasn't supposed to post. I thought I'd saved it to my personal drive.

Jordan: Audrey posted it thinking our revenge plan was back on.

Isaac: She should've confirmed it with you first.

Jordan: 1000% agreed! But we both made mistakes, so don't be mad at her. We'll be fine. I just feel terrible because Mackenzie didn't deserve that.

Isaac: Operation Fix Everything?

Jordan: Yes, but not yet. Need to give her some space first, and I'm suspended for the rest of the week anyway.

Isaac: Damn I'm sorry

Isaac: Here for u, whatever u need

Jordan: You're the best. I'll let you know when I'm free. <3

Operation Fix Everything sounded like exactly what I needed, but it would have to wait. Mack wasn't someone you could just say pretty words to ten minutes later and everything would be perfect. She'd need time to sit with what I'd done. Accident or not, I'd gone too far.

I groaned at my own failure and messaged Audrey.

Jordan: How did it go?

Audrey: BRUTAL! They're so disappointed and I'm grounded until they decide otherwise. I've never felt this shitty!

Jordan: At least they didn't take our phones?

Audrey: Wouldn't even cross their minds lol, small victory

Audrey: Sorry again btw

Audrey: Like a thousand times sorry

Jordan: I know. We're ok

Jordan: OMG I forgot to ask! What happened with zombie Emma?

Audrey: I mean, I might be in love, but it's no big

Audrey: She insisted on coming with when we went to look for you, and she took me to The Diner after for comfort food. And then we just drove around and talked for another hour. It was magical.

Audrey: I LIKE HER SO MUCH JO!

Jordan: Yaaaassss! I love this so hard and am glad we were wrong about her

Audrey: SAME! But my mom is giving me a look so I better go. Think she's catching on to the phone part. Talk later?

Jordan: Obviously <3

I opened Instagram, finding a flood of messages from people who hadn't given a shit about me before thinking I was an icon or their enemy. I ignored them and focused on my feed. Audrey shared a picture at The Diner with Emma and a caption that read: When Tina finds her zombie. Isaac and Olivia posted different pictures with them posing in their Bonnie and Clyde costumes. I passed a picture of Brie and Marissa in their costumes, which reminded me to block them because screw them. And then I stopped at a picture of Mack dressed as Sabrina. She stood on the stairs of her house, the regular lighting replaced with candles to make the space look dark and sinister. Her caption read: The witches are coming.

I laughed at the irony of the quote, which only made me feel sicker. The witches came all right. If I'd waited for Mack downstairs, would I be in this mess? Or if I'd gone upstairs a minute later as they were leaving the room, would they have wondered why I was upstairs? Would they have come back after Mack arrived, when we were in her room alone? Would they have seen something and then told people? My stomach dropped at the thought.

Somehow, me being painted as the villain was better than the alternative. Brie outing Mack would've been so much worse. Either way, embarrassing Mack wasn't going to get her kicked off the team. If anything, Coach would figure out what happened, and Brie would be the one to go.

We should be so lucky.

My phone beeped, and I tapped on my texts to see a message from my brother.

Casey: Never thought I'd get a text saying my baby sister
is stirring up drama at school. Should I be proud or
worried?

I groaned. The last thing I wanted was for Casey to find out about what had happened. My first thought was that Brie had said something, but that would be really stupid of her considering she thought they were endgame or some shit.

Jordan: What do you know?
Casey: Someone sent me the article . . . so everything?
Jordan: Def not everything. The kicker is that I never meant to
publish it. I saved it to the wrong drive.
Casey: Rookie mistake, I'm shocked!
Casey: What did Mackenzie do to deserve your wrath?

I didn't want to sound like I was tattling on Brie, but he deserved to know the truth. If he was going to be around her next year at college, he needed to know what she was really like. So, I told him everything.

Casey: Well shit
Jordan: Sorry. I know you kind of like her or whatever, but
she's horrible.

Casey: I could've told you that.

Jordan: You knew?!

Casey: Uh yeah, everyone knows JoJo.

Jordan: Then why do you hang out with her?

Casey: She's selectively shitty, and sometimes when you're
in the same friend circle it's easier to just run with it
than disrupt the peace. It wasn't my business, but
obviously it is now. I'm sorry she messed with you.
Consider her written off.

Jordan: Wow

Casey: What?

Jordan: You might actually be a good brother. Who knew!?

Casey: shut up!

I smiled at his response. I'd never really *let* him be a big
brother, and we'd always been busy with our own friends and
activities that spending time together never lined up. But I
wanted to change that.

Jordan: Can we hang out when you come home for
Thanksgiving?

Casey: I was going to bully you into it if you didn't ask. Count
me in.

Jordan: Can't wait. :)

I put my phone in my pocket and called Pond over. I had a lot
to process, and I needed to stay distracted enough so I wouldn't

try texting Mack or doing something extreme like showing up at her house. She deserved a movie-worthy apology, but first she deserved the space to hate me. After attaching Pond to her leash, we set off to the dog park so she could play with friends and I could think about how I'd disappointed mine.

The days passed with little excitement. My Instagram messages died down after people realized I wasn't going to engage. I helped Dad at the comic shop for a few hours and took Pond to the dog park twice every day. I kept up with homework and texted Audrey and Isaac, though mostly it was Isaac catching us up on what we were missing at school.

According to Isaac's gathered intel, Mack took the rest of Monday off and returned on Tuesday, acting like nothing had happened, which made everyone else do the same. Coach had laid into Brie over her behavior and threatened to kick her off the team. The only reason she didn't was because Mack asked her not to, saying it would only hurt their chances of making the finals. I would've loved seeing Brie's face when Mack came to her rescue. No doubt she'd think twice before trying to ruin her life again.

On Wednesday night, Dad told me to pause homework and come to the living room. If that didn't sound weird enough, I found Coach standing in my apartment. "This is a surprise," I said, smiling a little despite my instantly growing nerves.

"I know you aren't *technically* allowed on school grounds until Monday, and some conversations are better in person," Coach said. "What are you doing this weekend?"

"I'm grounded, so you're looking at it," I said, gesturing to the nothingness around us.

"Not anymore. You're coming to the tournament."

"What?" I laughed in disbelief. "Are you sure?"

"I'm sure. I talked to the team, and they want you there." She chuckled when I raised my eyebrows. "They know the value of you being there and not some random kid who doesn't know anything about the sport or the team."

That made more sense. It would take a while before the girls forgave me, especially Mack. "Mx. Shannon is okay with it?"

"They said they'll want to review the story first, but yes, we agreed that you were the best writer for the job."

"Okay," I said, feeling like my life had been restored, if only a little. Volleyball would never be my passion, but I'd worked hard to understand it and build a relationship with the team. I wouldn't let some personal drama destroy that, and I was relieved I wasn't the only one who felt that way. "Count me in. It'll be my honor to write about them winning in the finals."

"That's the spirit," Coach said. "I'll see you Friday, Elliot."

"Thank you, Coach," I said genuinely. "Seriously. I don't deserve it, even if it's for the team's benefit."

Coach shook her head. "I might not know the full story, but I know enough to know this wasn't all on you. So let's focus on ending the season on a high and take it from there."

"Right, one thing at a time," I said, nodding. "See you Friday."

Coach grinned. "Don't get into any trouble until then," she said before walking out.

It wasn't five seconds before Dad reappeared. "That went well."

"You were listening?" I groaned, shaking my head. "Can't even trust me to have a conversation right now?"

"Of course I trust you," Dad said. "But that woman has an intense look to her. I had to make sure you didn't need backup."

"Right, of course." I sighed. "And I guess I should've asked before agreeing to attending the tournament, huh?"

"You should've," Dad said. "But I already talked to Coach Pavek about it. And since it's for school, I think we can make an exception. Just come home right after."

I nodded. "Of course. And speaking of my epic grounding, I better get back to my homework. My history essay won't write itself."

"Admire the dedication," Dad said, smiling fondly. "Go make me proud. And if you finish on time, we can watch a movie. Mom will be home soon."

"Perfect, sounds great. Thanks, Dad." It had only been a few days since my talk with Mom, but already things at home felt generally lighter. If she had time to hang with us, I didn't want to miss it.

CHAPTER TWENTY-TWO

IT FELT WEIRD going back to school on Friday for the tournament, but at least most of the students had cleared out by the time I arrived. Isaac was waiting for me outside the gym, camera bag in hand and a warm smile on his lips.

"Can I just say one thing?" he asked. "Then we'll put away this week's drama for good."

I'd never tried to hide what had happened, but he'd done more than his share of bringing it up over the week in our private and group text conversations. He knew there was more to what happened, but he didn't know about how strong my feelings had gotten, or that Mack shared them—or at least she did before everything happened. Who knew where her head was at now. "Sure, Isaac, let's hear it," I said, bracing myself.

"I'm really proud of you."

"What?" My eyebrows shot up. I'd expected something like *You should talk to her and apologize again* (I can't yet), or *Olivia*

267

thinks you shouldn't be here, for Mackenzie's sake (I'd agree), but no. He was *proud* of me. "Why?"

Isaac shrugged. "I'm sure it's not easy being here, but you're doing the right thing—the *professional* thing—by staying committed to the team and the paper."

"That article was anything but professional," I said, my eyes moving to my feet. "It was horrible. *I* was horrible."

"Maybe it was, but you're not. You made a mistake. You believed the wrong person. And yeah, boo you, bad Jo, but so what?"

I snorted, looking back at him. "So what? Mackenzie *hates* me. I wouldn't be surprised if most of the team does, too. The only reason I'm here is because she decided to be the bigger person. That doesn't mean I'm forgiven."

"No, but Olivia talked to her, and Mack believes the article wasn't meant to be posted."

"That doesn't make the words go away."

"I'm trying to give you a bright side. Roll with me on this?"

"Fine," I sighed. "What's the bright side?"

"If she knows you weren't trying to humiliate her, there's hope you can get through this. At least that's what Olivia thinks, and she knows best."

"That's true," I said quietly. No matter how well I thought I knew Mack at times, no one compared to a best friend. "What else does she think?"

"You and Mackenzie need to talk. She offered to help me

figure out a plan to make that happen. Operation Fix Every-thing, remember?"

I shook my head, letting out a deep breath as I forced myself not to jump at the offer. "Thanks, Isaac. And thank Olivia, too. But it's only been a few days. Even if Mackenzie knows the article wasn't meant to exist, she still won't forgive me just like that. She needs time. And honestly, so do I. If I was so ready to believe everything Brie said, that means I have some work to do with trusting Mackenzie, too. And I don't want to make a big thing about trusting me again until I know I trust her."

"You still don't trust her?" Isaac asked, groaning. "Seriously? Even after this?"

"It's complicated, Isaac," I said, hating that I couldn't tell him everything. We didn't keep secrets. "I'll let you know when I'm ready to make some big friendship move, but it's not going to be today. Let's focus on the team winning this weekend. I'll fix things when the time feels right."

"I think you're scared," Isaac said, giving me a challenging look. He didn't have to.

"Of course I'm scared," I admitted. "I'm terrified. We've both messed up a lot, and I'm not going to risk that again. The next time one of us apologizes, that needs to be it. We need to be done with the back and forth, and we aren't there yet."

"Okay, okay," Isaac said, raising his hands. "Let's just get through the tournament, like you said. And I'm not going to bring it up again, but know that I'm in your corner. So is Olivia, who, for the record, is nothing like Brie or Marissa."

"Obviously," I said, laughing. "You don't have to convince me of that. You'd never date someone like them. And thanks. You're the best."

"I am, aren't I?" Isaac grinned, resting his arm across my shoulders. "Come on. We've got work to do."

Two sets into the first game, and the team was destroying our opponent. This surprised no one considering we'd only lost one game the entire season, but we weren't out of the woods. This was only the quarterfinals. If we won, we still had the semifinal match to get through before the final. The team that had beaten us was playing this weekend, too. Had I not ruined everything on Monday, I would've been around to talk to the girls about how they were feeling and give them my positive vibes alongside Coach.

"That's my girl!"

I snapped out of it in time to see Olivia get nearly attacked by the rest of the team. The board confirmed that she'd scored the winning point. I jumped up with Isaac to cheer with the rest of the people around us, annoyed with myself for missing it. But Isaac hadn't noticed, and Olivia blew kisses at him after doing a little dance. And really, that was the main thing I needed to see—two of my friends making heart eyes and supporting each other.

"I'm going to marry that girl," Isaac said after we sat. "Like, in ten years. It's on. You just wait and see."

"Okay, buddy," I said, patting his thigh. As much as I'd love to have Olivia around for the rest of my life, we were sixteen. Thinking about forever was terrifying.

When the team walked back to the sidelines for a quick break, Isaac left me to wrap Olivia in a hug. I slipped away to use the bathroom. Of course I could've waited until after the game, but at least this way I wouldn't have to pretend to be on my phone to avoid looking at Mack.

After leaving the stall, I found Brie waiting by the sinks. "Shouldn't you be with your team?" I asked, trying to hide my alarm at her obviously waiting for me.

She glared back at me. "I almost got kicked off the team. Do you know how humiliating that would've been?"

"Probably about as humiliating as having a friend write an awful article about you when you didn't do anything wrong," I said as I stepped up to the sink, turning on the water to wash my hands. "What do you want, Brie?"

Brie sighed, quiet for a moment. "Look, I'll admit that I've wanted to knock Mackenzie down a few pegs this year, but I didn't know it would get so out of control."

"Okay?" I laughed quietly, confused by whatever angle she was taking. "Well, it did, and you still talked a lot of shit about me in the process, so I don't think there's anything else to say." I turned off the water and grabbed a couple of paper towels.

"There is, though," she said.

"Go on, then," I said after considering walking out. I dried my hands while she spoke.

"I'm sorry," she said. "I doubt it means anything right now, but I am. I *really* wanted to be captain, thought I'd earned it, and it sucked being looked over for a junior. Then you came in and had this fast bond with Mackenzie and Olivia, and it felt like I couldn't do anything right. And what happened with you was shitty, but I just . . . wanted some kind of control in my life again. But it's no excuse, and I'm sorry."

I stared at her in disbelief. A part of me understood her—fighting hard for something you thought was inevitable, not getting it, and having to reassess everything. Yes, she'd reacted all wrong, and no, I didn't trust her, but I understood the disappointment, the desperation. And even though we weren't going to be friends, we could put everything aside for the sake of the team.

"Wow, that must've been hard for you to admit," I said, tossing the towels in the garbage. "Are you sick or something? Aliens invade your brain?"

Brie rolled her eyes. "No matter what's happened, you've been good for the team. Not just the articles. And I'm sorry for the part I played in messing with that. Okay?"

"Okay," I said slowly after a pause. Coach had definitely told her to apologize, but I hoped she'd come to the conclusion on her own that being a mean girl wouldn't get her anywhere in life. "My brother already knows what happened."

"Yeah, we talked," Brie said. Her brief defeated expression told me Casey had done what he said he'd do, and she'd never ask me for advice related to him again. What a gift. "Anyway, I have to get back."

"Yeah, go help get us to the finals," I said.

"You know it," she said. She lingered for a few seconds, like she wanted to say something else, but then she walked out without another word.

I exhaled a deep breath, shaking away my nerves from the confrontation. I waited another minute before leaving the bathroom, returning to my seat next to Isaac, who had now removed himself from his girlfriend to be a somewhat professional photographer.

I tried my best to focus throughout, but it was damn near impossible with Mack right there in front of me. She was in her element, flawlessly serving and scoring points as if nothing had happened earlier that week. It was torture having her this close and not being able to joke with her between sets or cheer as loudly as I wanted for her. And in true punishment form, she didn't look at me once, didn't make eye contact with a single spot away from the game.

The opposing team won the next set, but we came back in the fourth and won the match. After the players shook hands and Olivia got a couple of minutes in with Isaac, we headed to my car. Olivia had family dinner plans and needed to focus and sleep for game prep the next day, so I was on Isaac-driving duty.

"That was incredible," Isaac said after I started driving. "I'm sad the season is almost over."

"Did you manage to take any pictures, or did you just stare at your girlfriend the entire time?" I asked, glancing at him with a grin.

"Shut up," he laughed. "You know I was taking pictures. You saw me do it."

"Yeah, yeah." I ruffled his hair. "So, Brie kind of cornered me in the bathroom after the second set."

"What?!" Isaac's eyed bugged out. "Was there a brawl? You look fine. Did you take her ass down?"

"Oh my god, obviously not," I said, rolling my eyes. "She actually apologized. It was awkward, but at least I know she won't try to mess with me again this year."

"But *do* we know that?" Isaac laughed. "I mean, it's Brie."

"I think Coach laid into her enough for her to finally know better."

"Okay, fair. That woman could scare me to death."

I laughed under my breath. "She's actually pretty amazing, and the only reason I'm here tonight. I think Shannon would've blocked me from writing anything else this semester if they'd had it their way."

"That's rough," Isaac said. "You're, like, their favorite student."

"Okay, that's bullshit," I said easily, giving him a look after stopping at a light. "If that were true, I'd be an editor like you and Audrey. I'd be writing what I wanted to write, and I'd be building a solid portfolio for college applications. I haven't even had time to think of other stories to pitch them because of how focused I've been on volleyball. It's infuriating."

"You're already building a solid portfolio," Isaac said. "Maybe it's not exactly what you'd had in mind a few months ago, but you're still writing incredible stories. And if you get a chance to write a real feature on Mackenzie, that story alone will get you into whatever college you want."

My stomach dropped at the reminder. I didn't know if Shannon would let me write the feature story, even if I did have them read it first, but that was next week's problem. "Still, I'm not Shannon's favorite," I said as I started driving again.

"I disagree," Isaac said. "They let you write a story about lawn gnomes, Jo. That should tell you everything you need to know. But if it doesn't, think about everything that's happened this year. They took care in finding you a beat that could be both a challenge and an opportunity. You have all of senior year to be an editor. And they had every reason and opportunity to kick you off the paper but didn't."

"They still could," I said, knowing it was technically an option.

"But they won't," Isaac said, nudging me. "They believe in you, even if you don't see it. So just keep doing what you do best and don't get wrapped up in more drama. You'll be an editor next year if you stay focused."

I smiled at his words. "Thanks, Isaac. Let's hope you're right."

"If I'm wrong, we'll stage a coup," Isaac said, grinning. "I won't start senior year unless we're all editors. You can quote me on it."

I knew he would, too. He'd walk away from the paper and never look back. I'd never allow that, of course, but it was comforting know how dedicated he was to having my back. "Not necessary, but thanks. I'll let you know if Operation Coup needs to happen."

"Yessss," Isaac said in a whisper, forming a victorious fist.

I laughed and shook my head. We finished the drive in silence so Isaac could stare at his phone and I could sit with my thoughts. When we got back to the apartment complex, we agreed to leave early tomorrow and stop at the Quilted Bean first. If we ended up watching two games tomorrow, I'd need the fuel.

CHAPTER TWENTY-THREE

THE FUEL WAS *definitely* needed. The semifinal match went into five sets to break the two-two tie. Isaac groaned over the knowledge that the coffee we'd gotten this morning wouldn't be enough, and I agreed. We were dragging, so the team was surely dragging. But you wouldn't know it looking at them. I'd never seen them so determined to win. Having a team that was hard to beat probably helped, but still. They really had to prove themselves this time.

As the final set was about to start, my eyes followed Mack to the court. Like yesterday, she hadn't acknowledged me. If I was going to convince her to give me another chance, I'd have to think of something huge.

Marissa served first, and we got two points before the opposing team took possession of the ball. The girls played as well as they always did—better, even—but it wasn't enough to sweep the opposition. After taking turns serving every couple points, Mack was up. She smacked the ball with such determination and force that the other team had no chance at returning it. I saw the smallest of smirks form on her lips, like she knew they were in trouble.

I was in trouble, too. I had no right staring at those lips and thinking about kissing them, but I couldn't help it. She was impossible to ignore. And maybe it would never happen again, but that night in Minneapolis would live in my head rent-free forever.

Mack managed multiple serves, putting us far ahead of the other team. After they had a short run serving, Brie led us to victory with a few final serves. When the win was confirmed, the girls cheered, danced, and hugged. Time slowed as Brie and Mack faced each other. They both knew the truth of what had really happened on Halloween, and Mack had made sure Brie didn't lose her spot on the team, but I didn't know what had come after that. In the end, they shook hands, which felt like they were saying all wasn't forgiven, but the team mattered more.

I'd kill to get even that much from Mack right now.

Once the teams had all shaken hands and the girls had a moment with Coach, Isaac hopped off the stands to praise Olivia. I hung back so I could jot down some final notes as people around me left for a break. Two other teams played next, so we had a decent amount of time before needing to be back. Another coffee run was needed.

"You have a lot of nerve showing your face here."

I looked up to see Mack's mom standing not five feet from

me on the sidelines. I was surprised to see her there considering she and Mack's dad hadn't shown up to a single game throughout the season. There had always been some excuse like work or a meeting or "other plans" that were somehow more important than cheering on their daughter.

Apparently, making it to the semifinals warranted their presence. Or maybe she just wanted to yell at me in person and thought this was an appropriate setting.

"I write about the team for the newspaper," I said, focused on staying logical and giving no emotions away. "I have to be here, Mrs. West."

"Don't think I don't know about what you did to my daughter," she said, ignoring my response. "You should've been expelled."

"With respect, I wasn't responsible for the decision Principal Jeffries made," I said, trying to ignore my shaking hands as my discomfort grew. "But I'm trying to work right now, so if you have any concerns, please take them up with him or Coach."

"You think I didn't try?" she scoffed. "What kind of mother would I be if I didn't look after my daughter?"

"What kind, indeed," I muttered.

Her eyebrows shot up. "What did you just say?"

"Mom, stop," Mack said as she arrived at her side. "I told you to leave her alone."

"And I told you that what happened is unacceptable," Mrs. West said, her eyes shifting to her daughter. "I won't stop calling your principal until he decides to take this more seriously and gives this girl a proper punishment. And to think, I let her into our home."

Mack took me in, really looked at me for the first time in days, then focused on her mom again. "I think she's been punished enough."

"A week off from school is hardly punishment," Mrs. West said.

Mack groaned, clearly annoyed and embarrassed. How could her mom not see that? "If you don't stop, I'll quit the team."

Mrs. West rolled her eyes. "Oh, don't be so dramatic, Mackenzie."

"I'm serious," Mack said firmly. "If you don't let this go, I'll hand in my jersey and leave right now."

Mrs. West paused before letting out an exasperated breath. "Fine, I'll let it go. But if she pulls another trick like that again, I won't stop until she's expelled."

"Understood," Mack said.

Mrs. West took out her phone and walked off to a different part of the gym. Mack headed toward the exit without so much as another glance at me. I should've stayed in the gym and let her go, but my feet were moving before I could stop myself. "Thank you," I said after catching up. "You didn't have to do that."

"I didn't do it for you," Mack said, her voice lowering. "I broke your heart twice, and you expressed how that made you feel. Consider us even."

"That's not what the article was," I sighed, frustrated all over again.

"You're right. It was all about how you believed someone who hates me because you have such little trust in me. And sure, a few months ago that made sense, but I thought things had changed. I thought *we* had changed. I guess none of it mattered."

"Of course it mattered," I said, looking around to make sure no one was listening for her sake. "How can you say it didn't matter?"

"I don't know," Mack said, facing me. "How can you say I don't exist or that I'm impossible or any of the other shit you said?"

"I made a mistake." My voice lowered as I moved a little closer. "But I'm trying to make it right."

"Well, don't," Mack said, shaking her head and stepping back. "If we win later and go out to celebrate, you can come, but that's it. I don't want to be around you for a while. It was so hard having you so close before that article came out, and now it all feels unbearable. So please, just leave me alone, okay?"

"Okay," I said quietly after a pause, my heart racing. My stomach was all over the place, but I couldn't fix this—not right now. "I'm sorry."

"I know." Mack's eyes remained on me for a handful of seconds before she continued toward the bathroom.

Once she was gone, I turned to see Isaac and Olivia watching with concerned faces. "Still hates me," I said after meeting them halfway, shrugging at Olivia. "But great game, seriously. You were amazing."

"Thanks," she said, her smile not reaching her eyes. "I'm rooting for you, okay? She still cares about you. Give her time."

I chose not to read into her words. As far as I knew, Mack had only come out to me. Assuming Olivia knew could get me into even bigger trouble, and I wouldn't risk that. "Thanks, Olivia." I looked at Isaac. "Coffee run?"

"Yes!" he cheered. "As thrilling as it is watching my girl-friend smack a ball around, I'm dragging."

"You two have fun," Olivia said, leaning up to kiss Isaac's cheek. "I'm going to go check on my bestie. See you at the finals?"

"You know it," I said.

"See you soon, cutie," Isaac said before following me out for round two at the Quilted Bean.

After refueling, calling Audrey to update her, and teasing Isaac about wanting to be a child groom, we returned to school for the final match. It hadn't started yet, so Isaac went through his photos while I read through my notes, adding bits and pieces as I thought of more.

If we won the final, the article would be easy to write. If not, I still had ideas for how to make it feel special to the team. I'd focus on their strengths and family-like camaraderie, because that's really what mattered to Coach. She was like a fun, athletic aunt to a dozen nieces, and a story about their family would top anything I could write about them winning. But if they won, I'd obviously talk them up for that, too.

Isaac's phone buzzed, and he pulled it out to read a text. "We're invited to the after-party or pity-party tonight—whichever they end up throwing."

"I'm not going," I said. "It would be too weird. The team has been generally decent toward me since everything went down, but I don't feel right being there. I'm still grounded, too, and I don't think a volleyball party is what Dad had in mind when he said I could cover the tournament for newspaper."

"Okay, that's all fair," Isaac said. "But once you're done being grounded, we need to do something with Audrey that doesn't involve volleyball."

"Agreed," I said, smiling at the plans already forming in my head. We used to have the best movie nights with homemade snacks, potluck-style, with dance party breaks in between viewings. The year was flying by, and a lot of it was good, but I didn't want to miss out on trio hangs. Even if things had changed, I still needed that semblance of normal with my besties.

We quieted as the teams walked onto the court. Our opponent had beaten us earlier in the year, which no doubt made our team feel on edge. But if they were nervous, they didn't show it. They looked like they did before every other game that season—determined to win.

Like the semifinals, the final match went into five sets. Unlike the semifinals, we'd barely won our two sets. I was close to biting my nails as the fifth set kicked off, and it took everything I had not to look at Coach or the girls on the bench, because they no doubt felt the stress harder than me. It didn't help that Isaac muttered about plays and form like he was the coach as the ball moved around the court. But he managed to take pictures while muttering, so I couldn't tell him to be quiet. Instead, I focused on my job and took notes about stellar moves, points scored, and whatever else I could think to add.

The other team had more points as the tournament neared an end, but something changed before they could claim victory. Mack was made for this moment, serving up her best game of the season. Not only did we come back to tie, but we passed the other team. The Wildcats worked in perfect formation to keep the ball moving, and Mack set them up for success.

In the end, we won by three points. I was sure I saw a few of the girls on the other team cry. Their coach was definitely crying. But so was ours. She'd had winning teams before, but not like this. Even if things were still a little rocky between me and the girls, I was proud of them. They'd earned this moment.

"You did it!" Isaac yelled to Olivia as she ran to him, taking pictures of her until she was in his arms, nearly knocking him over. "That was incredible!"

"We won!" Olivia cheered as she wrapped all her limbs around him. "I can't believe we won!"

"I can!" Isaac said like the perfect boyfriend that he was.

I left them to their moment and walked over to Coach, who'd just finished being congratulated by the other team's coach. "Looks like you're going to get another glowing article," I said, holding out my hand. "Congratulations."

"Thank you, Elliot," Coach said, taking my hand and shaking it firmly. "I'm glad you were able to join us this weekend to see the wins firsthand."

"Me too," I said genuinely. In that moment, there was nowhere else I'd rather be. "Can I get a quote for the paper?"

"Of course," Coach said, waiting for me to turn on my recorder before continuing. "The team had an impressive season, and we saw that here this weekend. Every girl was instrumental in each win, and I'm very proud of them. I couldn't ask for a better team."

My smile grew as she spoke. I could feel her commitment and pride in every word she spoke. The girls were lucky to have her. "Perfect, thank you," I said after she finished. "Have fun celebrating."

"You're not joining us?" she asked, brows raised.

"I'm still grounded." My eyes moved to Mack before back to Coach. "And I think it's better if I don't, you know?"

She didn't have to look to get it. "In that case, see you next week."

"Can't wait," I said, borderline giddy at the idea of returning to school. Things would be different, but at least my punishment would be partially over. I glanced at Mack again before leaving the gym for home, knowing it was better to disappear than to try being a part of something I'd only meant to observe from the sidelines. No matter how harsh it had sounded, Brie was right. I wasn't one of them, and I was done pretending to be.

CHAPTER TWENTY-FOUR

Girls Varsity Shines at Volleyball Finals

BY: JORDAN ELLIOT

The girls' varsity volleyball team played in the season's final tournament last weekend. The crowd was glued to the court as the ball flew back and forth between our very own Davenport Wildcats and the Bemidji Lumberjacks during the final match. The first two matches were against the Hermantown Hawks and Duluth East Greyhounds, with final scores of 3–2 each.

With the support of the entire team, Captain Mackenzie West finished out the final game with seven impressive serves in the end of the fifth set. Coming from a concussion earlier in the year, it's clear that the junior didn't let it slow her down. "It was truly magical how she brought us from being behind to winning in the final set," senior Brie Carlson said of her captain. "She moves effortlessly, so of course some of that magic rubbed off on the rest of the team this year."

Coach Sheila Pavek looked ecstatic by the wins, which happened in part as a result of her leadership. "The team had an impressive season, and we saw that here this weekend," Pavek said. "Every girl was instrumental in each win, and I'm very proud of them. I couldn't ask for a better team."

For a few players, this tournament last weekend was their final high school game. "It's bittersweet for sure," Carlson said. "Spending a few years of your life with the same coach and some of the same girls is a special, rewarding experience. I'm going to miss them next year."

The final win placed the Wildcats in first for their division and will help set many players on a path toward successful college careers. If you missed the tournament and other games this season, come back next year when Coach Pavek, Captain West, and the rest of the Wildcats return to wow us with their fiery serves and fierce dedication.

I watched Mx. Shannon as they read the article, hoping they let me post it. There was nothing dramatic or suspicious about it, so in theory we were good to go. I'd even unblocked Brie on Sunday to get quotes. But a part of me feared Shannon would change their mind and not let me publish anything ever again. If that happened, I wouldn't blame them. Principal Jeffries getting involved had no doubt put Shannon's job and the integrity of the paper on the line. I'd step down if it meant preserving both.

"Brie Carlson is the one who inspired you to write that article about Mackenzie West, right?" Shannon said, glancing at me after reading the story.

"Yeah," I said, wanting to die. Coach and Shannon must've talked, or Shannon had spies everywhere. That was a running theory among the paper staff, so anything was possible. "I thought it would look good having a member of the team who'd been . . . unenthusiastic about the team's captain be the one to speak well of her. Plus, she kind of owed me."

Shannon snorted, shaking their head. "That's one way of looking at it," they said, studying me for a moment. "This is a solid article, though I'm not surprised given your work the last couple of years. We can publish this after the editors do their thing."

I stared back at them, surprised by how easily things were shaping up. On Sunday, my parents told me I was no longer grounded as long as I promised not to write any more scathing articles—accidentally or otherwise. But I hadn't expected Shannon to let me back in so soon. Maybe I really was their favorite student. "Are you sure?" I asked before I could help it. "I mean, I *really* messed up."

"You did," they agreed easily. "But Pavek told me about how professionally you'd handled everything since our meeting, and I heard you completed all your assignments early or on time last week. You're clearly taking this seriously, so I see no reason to further punish you. I still want to read and approve anything else you write for the rest of junior year. After that, we'll consider your punishment over."

A weight lifted as they spoke. I'd prepared for the worst, expected it even, and here was Shannon being better than I deserved. "Thank you," I said sincerely, pausing as I thought about my best friend. "What about Audrey?"

"Audrey will still be writing and editing, but she lost her privileges to hit 'publish' on articles for the rest of the semester," Shannon said. "Your article may have been an accident, but her choosing to publish it wasn't. I had to take that seriously."

"I understand," I said, knowing Audrey did, too.

"Good," Shannon said, smiling a little. "Anything else, or are we good?"

I had another question that needed to be asked, but that didn't mean I wanted to ask it. "Um, am I still allowed to write a feature story on Mackenzie? Obviously you'd read it first, and Audrey won't be involved."

Shannon considered my question. "I guess that depends on what you want to write," they said. "Do you have an angle that doesn't involve bringing up absent parents or wanting attention?"

Okay, I'd deserved that. Removing the article quickly from the paper's site hadn't erased it from people's minds. Screenshotting was a talent among my generation, and content lived forever. "I don't have an angle yet, but I promise it won't be anything like the last article."

"It better not be," Shannon said. "But yes, if you can find a positive angle worthy of our paper, I will happily let you publish it."

I nodded, figuring that answer was as good as a yes. "Perfect, thank you. She deserves a real feature story, especially after everything that happened this year." Not only did I destroy her trust in me and make her look horrible in front of the entire school, but she'd also gotten a concussion and had generally shitty parents and a couple of fake friends. Mackenzie West deserved a win that had nothing to do with serving a ball, and I wanted to give it to her—even if it didn't change anything between us.

"I agree," Shannon said. "Focus your class time on that story, and help out some of the freshmen when the editors are swamped."

I smiled at them giving me a fraction of responsibility. It wasn't an editor title, but it was a step in the right direction. "Got it, will do." I gathered my things. "Thanks again, Shannon."

"Of course," Shannon said. "And Jordan? You know you can talk to me if you need help with anything, right? That article was alarming coming from you."

I'd hoped to avoid that part of the conversation, but they knew me too well to let what I'd done go unnoticed on an emotional level. "I know. I think I've got it figured out now, but thanks."

Shannon nodded, and I took their silence as an okay to leave. I wasn't two steps out the door before Audrey and Isaac flanked me.

"How did it go?" Isaac asked.

"Yeah, are you okay?" Audrey added. "Do we need to talk to

Shannon on your behalf or start planning Operation Newspaper Revolt?"

"It's Operation Coup," Isaac said.

"Oh my god," I said, laughing quietly. "Everything is fine, you goofs. There will be no more schemes, at least not ones that hurt people. Okay?" I gave Audrey a pointed look.

"Yeah, okay," she said, linking her arm with mine, and Isaac did the same on my other side. "But say the word and we're there."

"I know," I said, trying not to let any feelings show. I'd been through enough of them lately. "Thanks, besties."

Isaac nodded. "Yeah, yeah. But more importantly, Audrey and I were talking, and we think a hang this Saturday is needed. You in?"

"Oh, I'm totally in," I said, grinning at the invite. "As long as no one has plans with their girlfriend . . . Wait, is Emma a girlfriend?"

"Honestly, I don't even know," Audrey said, laughing a little. "We talked almost all weekend while you two nerds were obsessing over volleyball, and I still don't know what we are. But I don't care. I just know I'm having fun with her but also want to have fun with my best friends, so she'll have to live without me on Saturday."

"Same with Olivia," Isaac said. "She's all for us having a trio hang. She has plans anyway. Top secret, apparently."

I wanted to ask if her plans were with Mack, but it wasn't my business. Even if time passed and she forgave me, we couldn't get to that point if I pried and moped. I needed to let time heal the initial wounds before I could sweep in and . . . well, I still didn't know what to do, but I'd figure it out. One way or another, I'd get Mack to be my friend again.

"What about now?" Audrey asked when I didn't say anything. "Anyone free for The Diner or QB?"

"Can't. I have a group project for English," Isaac said, scrunching his nose.

"And I have to get home and help Dad with dinner and do my homework like a good daughter who has never done anything wrong," I said.

"I thought you weren't grounded anymore," Audrey said.

"I'm not, but I don't want to give him any reason to think I'm out doing something sketchy on a school night. But Saturday?"

"Saturday," Audrey said, grinning as we turned the corner. "There's your volleyball champion."

I looked, but of course it was Olivia waiting for Isaac. "See you tomorrow, Isaac," I said, hoping they hadn't seen me looking for—no one. I was looking for no one.

"Bye, fools," Isaac said, jogging to meet Olivia. She waved at us before letting Isaac scoop her up and kiss her.

"They're so disgusting sometimes," I said fondly as I waved back.

"The worst," Audrey said, giggling. "But fair warning, you might have to deal with the same thing when Emma is around—if anything comes from all this hanging out, I mean."

"The girl dressed as a zombie for you, took you to The Diner, and spent all of last weekend talking to you," I said pointedly. "Even if you aren't labeling it, she's obviously into you."

"Yeah, she is, isn't she?" Audrey grinned, pulling me in for a hug. "Love you. Go home and be a good daughter."

"Love you," I said. We exchanged cheek hearts as she stepped back and walked off, taking a different door so she didn't have to pass by the other two who were still making out. I laughed and followed her, feeling happy for both my best friends despite having no one to make out with, which was fine. Well, it wasn't fine, but I wasn't someone who needed a relationship. Having Mack not hate me would be good enough, but that was a problem for future Jordan.

My final volleyball article published on the paper's site the following Wednesday, and it was received like most sports articles. Other than newspaper staff and the volleyball team, few people mentioned my words about the tournament. My new fans had slithered back under the surface when it became more and more clear that I hadn't tried to sabotage Mack, and the people who'd hated me were working toward forgiveness. I didn't get a single dirty look from any of the volleyball girls, but I also didn't get an invite to hang after school or eat lunch with them.

Mack and I made brief eye contact in the hall before she looked away again, lost in a conversation with Olivia, Emily, and Kalie. Olivia waved and gave me an encouraging smile that said *don't give up*, and I waved back before carrying on.

Not being able to talk to a girl I'd made out with and shared a bed with not even two months ago was on a scale of torture that I'd never experienced before now. Having Olivia in my corner made me feel confident that Mack would let me back in eventually, but that in-between time was enough to confirm I'd learned my lesson.

A different torture welcomed me the next day when Brie sat next to me in homeroom. "Hey, girl," she said, smiling a little. "No tricks today, promise. I just wanted to thank you for letting me have a few words in your article. I'm still kind of on the shit list with the team, but it's getting better. They even added me back to the group chat."

Of course the team had a group chat. I could only imagine what they'd said about me recently. "I didn't do it for you," I said. "I just hope you learned something from all of this."

"So much," she said, her tone sounding genuine. Shocker. "Mainly, don't be an asshole. And don't try to sabotage your team."

Groundbreaking. "Yes, those are very good, very low-bar learnings," I said. "This isn't *Gossip Girl*. Too Midwest and middle-class."

Brie snorted. "Agreed."

I waited for her to turn away, but when she didn't, I realized she was looking at me expectantly. Of course there was more. "My brother isn't going to date you after what you did, but I'm sure he'd be your friend again if you prove you're changing. He's too chill to hold a grudge forever."

Brie let out a sigh of relief. "Oh good, I didn't want to go to college with no friends," she said. "Could you ask him to stop ignoring my texts?"

It meant a lot to me knowing Casey hadn't backed down from his cutting-Brie-out stance. But if I'd learned anything from the past few years, it was that no one was beyond forgiveness if they were willing to admit they messed up and promise to try harder. "He'll be home for Thanksgiving. I'll tell him then," I said, laughing when she gave me a look. "Oh my god, okay, I'll tell him now."

"You're the best," Brie said, taking my hand and squeezing it. "I mean it. Thank you."

"Yeah, you're welcome," I said, moving my hand away to text Casey that Brie was off the villain list and that he should reach out if he wanted. I added "Thanks for being a good brother <3" before putting my phone away as the homeroom teacher started announcements.

Having Brie off my back for good made me feel a lot better about the article I had yet to write about Mack. If there were any obstacles, at least Brie wouldn't be one of them.

The next week moved at a glacial pace. It didn't help that I no longer had volleyball games to attend or stories to write about it. My only remaining article before winter break was Mack's feature, and I still didn't have an angle. I had a couple dozen Post-it notes taking up space on the inside of my closet door that I pondered over when I had time, but none of them felt good enough. I had less than a month to get my shit together. I hoped for under-the-wire inspiration, but for now I had Thanksgiving break to focus on.

Casey was home by the time I got back from school the day before the holiday. With school life behind me for a while, I was glad to have time to focus on family and friends. Thursday and Friday were for family, Saturday was for friends, and Sunday was for me. It wasn't nearly enough time, but it was better than nothing.

"Fancy seeing you here," I told Casey as I took off my backpack and coat.

"Fancy that," Casey said, laughing as he walked over and pulled me in for a hug. "How are you?"

"I'm good," I said, embracing the hug for the first time in forever.

"Something tells me that's not entirely true." Casey gave me a squeeze before letting go. "What's up?"

I groaned. "Can we not get into my recent drama the second we see each other? Let's talk about you, or at least let me get something to drink first."

"I wasn't trying to get into anything, JoJo," Casey said, shaking his head. "But yes, go get a drink, and I can tell you all about my life, if that's what you want."

"It is," I said, frowning at the reminder that I didn't need to go at him all the time. "And sorry. It's just been a long few weeks."

"I know," he said, smiling a little. "It's okay."

It wasn't, but I understood what he meant. After heating

up a mug of apple cider, I joined Casey on the coach. "Okay, brother of mine, tell me things."

Casey snorted. "Okay, sister of mine. School is going well, top grades and all that. Work is work—nothing too exciting there. No girlfriend, but I've been on a couple of dates since I saw you last."

"So really everything is as expected in life for Casey Elliot," I teased, pausing to sip my drink. "What about Brie? Did you talk?"

"We did." Casey nodded. "We're chill again, and she's going to visit in the spring to tour campus, assuming she gets accepted and all that."

Despite her personality flaws, Brie was as smart as Casey, so I had no doubt she'd get accepted to the U of M. "That's cool," I said. "She's a . . . very interesting person."

"That's one way of looking at it. She causing more problems, or is it all good?"

"I mean, we were never 'all good,' but she's left me alone on the drama scale since we talked last. We're on an acquaintance level now, which is good enough for me. She's not really my type as far as friends go."

"Yeah, I get that," Casey said. I'd generally liked his friends, but Mack had been the only one I'd been friends with, and technically she'd been my friend first. And Casey liked my friends, but he never hung out with us. "What about our mutual friend? Or do I need to think about more stuff to talk about on my end first?"

"To be fair, you hardly talked about yourself, but I guess we can talk about Mackenzie," I said, drinking more and low-key wishing the cider was spiked. "She still hates me."

"I find that hard to believe," Casey said. "You mean a lot to her."

I laughed at his words. "How would you know?" I asked. "Also, you're almost creepishly invested in my nonfriendship with her. Why do you care so much? What's the deal?"

"There's no deal," Casey said, rubbing the back of his neck. "Okay, maybe there is a deal."

I set down my mug and turned to give him my full attention, beyond curious. "Explain."

"Okay, so, summer after your freshman year, I asked her out at a party."

"What?" I asked loudly. "Casey! Why didn't I know about this?"

"I'm getting there—give me a minute," Casey said, laughing quietly. "I'd gotten to know her that year because she hung out with Brie and other mutual friends, and she was just so, I don't know . . ."

"Special?" I guessed, smiling weakly.

"Yes, special." He nodded. "Anyway, she turned me down and said she just wanted to be friends. And honestly, I probably would've told you about it so we could have a laugh or something, but she asked me not to. She said it would really upset you, and she didn't want to hurt you more."

"Why would I get hurt over her turning down my almost-perfect brother?" I joked in an attempt to calm my racing heart.

"That was my question, too," Casey said, grinning gently. "It didn't make any sense. Like, I knew you'd had some kind of falling-out, but I didn't know it would be shitty of me to ask her out. But then earlier this year I had a party, and it all started making sense when I found her in your room."

"She mentioned the party," I said, thinking back on her saying she took a picture of the sign Dad had gotten for me. "And hanging out with Pond."

"Yeah, well, did she mention that I found her curled up on your bed crying?"

I blinked, my mouth feeling dry as I replied. "No, she conveniently left that part out."

"I'm not surprised," Casey said, smiling a little. "Look, JoJo, I know none of this is my business, and I didn't make it my business for a long time. But it was obvious back then that she missed you, and it's obvious now that you miss her. So I'm going to tell you what I told her when I found her crying. If she matters that much to you, you need to put aside whatever shit is going on and fight for her."

I held back a laugh at his words. It was easy enough to say it when he thought "fighting for her" meant being friends again. Our situation went way beyond that. If Casey knew everything, he might have different advice. "But she didn't fight for our friendship," I said after a moment. "That party was in April, and we didn't talk again until we had to for the paper."

"But you did become friends again, right?" Casey asked, raising his eyebrows. "Who cares how long it took. The point is that you both figured out how to be friends again. You both messed up, but it doesn't matter whose fault it is or how much time has passed. Focus on moving forward. You'll never heal and be friends again if you can't let all that past shit go. You're not fourteen, JoJo."

I sighed, knowing he was right. The foundation of our problems started when we were different people, and we've been letting that be the reason for our current problems. But her ghosting years ago really didn't matter anymore. I knew I trusted her again when I showed up at her house after her concussion. When we kissed in Minneapolis. When I went to her Halloween party. Her being scared didn't make me not trust her, and neither did Brie. My own fear did that.

"I'm working on it," I said. "But what I did to her, intentional or not, is still a new wound. She knows it wasn't on purpose and that I'm sorry, but I need to give her time. And I *am* working on a plan to fix things, so don't worry about that."

Casey smiled a little. "Well, whatever your plan is, make it a good one. She's kind of awesome, and I'd feel better about being her friend if you were, too."

I nodded, hoping I could give him that one day. "Me too," I said, matching his smile. "Thanks for telling me everything. I missed her back then, too, even if it was easier hating her."

"Hating someone is always easier," Casey said. "But if she's important, fight for her." His phone buzzed, and he took it out to read over a text. "I have some plans tonight, but maybe we can do something tomorrow before the big meal?"

I knew better than to tell him we should stick around to help Dad with prep because Dad had been shooing us out of the kitchen for years. He loved getting bragging rights over being the one to make the entire meal—minus the pies, of course. Those were all me. "Yeah, that sounds good," I said. "Have fun."

"Oh, I will," Casey said, grinning. "See you later."

After he left, I took Pond to the dog park. She immediately ran off to play with Brego and Cedar, two adorable shibas we'd met a few weeks ago, leaving me to overthink my conversation with my brother. He deserved a medal for making me realize more and more each day how lucky I was to have him.

CHAPTER TWENTY-FIVE

WHEN IT COMES to Thanksgiving, I'm like the superior stepsister in *Ever After*—I'm only here for the food. I make that clear to family every year before agreeing to bake the pies. Pie duties were passed down to me when I was twelve, after Grandma Elliot died. I was properly educated on the real history of Thanksgiving two years later, and ever since, I'd been reluctant to participate. But I couldn't *not* eat the meal.

After putting the pies in the oven, I left Dad to do his thing and checked in on social media. A little scrolling led me to a picture of Mack and Olivia hugging each other. Mack was the type of person who posted what she was thankful for every year, which usually included the volleyball team, her friends, or Sabrina.

I scrolled to read the caption: A lot has changed since last Thanksgiving, and through it all I've had my friends by my side. Special thanks to you both for being there for me when I didn't know how to be there for myself. You're incredible humans, and I don't know what I'd do without you. I also don't know how to write a "coming out" post, but this is mine. I'm a lesbian, and I'm done hiding it. I hope everyone has a good holiday weekend. Be kind to each other.

A second glance at the picture showed me that their cheeks had rainbows painted on them. It was clearly staged for this post, but the fact remained: Mackenzie West was officially out.

Several thoughts swam in my head. I was surprised. I was proud. And most importantly, I was hopeful she'd be able to breathe better after carrying such a heavy load for so long. Regardless of my feelings, the ache I felt at not getting to celebrate with her, I knew what a big deal this was. She'd found the courage I knew she had in her all along, and she did the damn thing. Whatever came next, I was beyond happy for her.

After reading the post a couple more times, I noticed there was more than one picture and a mention of "both" in the caption, so I swiped over. The second picture was the same, but instead of Olivia, Casey was next to Mack. And yes, he had a rainbow painted on his cheek, too. The third picture was of the three of them, and they held a sign with hearts and rainbows on it that said *Happy Thanksgiving!*

I remembered Casey saying he had plans yesterday. I didn't know if I wanted to kill him or kiss him, but in the very least, my brother deserved props for keeping Mack's secret—even from his sister, who already knew about it.

Hundreds of likes and dozens of comments followed the post—all of them positive. People from school and people I didn't know were praising Mack for her bravery and sending encouraging words. The comments wouldn't make all her fears disappear, but at least she'd know people supported her.

And I needed her to know I was one of them. Instead of adding to the growing list of social media comments, I texted her.

Jordan: I'm still leaving you alone, but I saw your post and I'm really proud of you.

She didn't respond right away like she normally would, and I wasn't surprised. Whatever she was going through, it had nothing to do with me. She'd come out for *her*, not me or anyone else, and that was truly magical.

I went to Casey's room and knocked loudly on the door. He needed to get moving so we could hang out, but also I had words to say to him.

"Morning," he said through a big yawn after opening the door, his hair askew from sleep. "What's up?"

I choked out a laugh at his casual greeting and held my phone up so he could see the post with the picture of him on it.

He looked at my phone, a grin forming on his face. "Well, there you go," he said after a moment. "The big secret is out."

Shock was no doubt written all over my face. "How long have you known?" I asked as I put my phone in my back pocket. I never realized they'd been close enough for Mack to share something so serious with Casey, but maybe he'd hidden that fact for my sake.

"When I saw her crying on your bed over you, it was kind of obvious that there was something else going on," Casey said, shrugging. "So she told me everything. I mean, it was a rambling, blubbering of words, and she'd had a little to drink, but after saying she missed you, she explained the real reason why." He grinned again. "I guess the Elliot siblings are easy to open up to. Or maybe it was because she had a major crush on my sister and thought telling me would help her be brave. But I guess she needed you for that."

I shook my head, knowing that wasn't true. "I had nothing to do with it."

"You had everything to do with it, from what I understand," Casey said.

"What are you talking about?"

"I obviously don't know every detail because I wasn't there, but I guess when you were at the dog park for an interview, you told her you were really proud of her, and that whenever she decided to come out, you'd be there for her no matter what happened."

My heart sank at his words. I remembered the conversation clearly. She'd pretty much shut down after I'd said it and, after that, I hadn't expected her to take my words to heart. And then she did. "And then that article came out and I ruined everything," I said, shaking my head. "Have you ever fucked up this bad?"

"Nope," Casey said, laughing despite how not funny the situation was. "But so what? Between what you've already said to her and the conversations she's had with me and Olivia, I think you two are going to be fine. You just have to find a way to prove that it's worth putting her heart on the line again."

I narrowed my eyes at him. "How are you so wise? Better yet, how are you single? You're a walking romance novel."

"Call it a choice, baby sister," Casey said, poking my shoulder. "But stay focused. You have work to do."

"I know, I know," I sighed.

"Then go do it!"

"I can't yet! It needs planning."

Casey groaned. "Oy with the planning already. Romantic gestures don't need planning—they need action."

I rolled my eyes. "This one needs planning."

He let out a dramatic sigh before smiling again. "Fine, fine. Let me know if I can do anything to help."

"Thanks, but I think you've done more than enough by being a good friend to Mack," I said, still grateful for that. "She deserves people like you who support her no matter what."

"Yeah, well, I have some experience in that department, so it wasn't too hard being a decent human," Casey said.

He meant me, and I pulled him in for a hug. "You're going to get a really good Christmas present this year," I said, unable to find the right sentimental response.

"Remind me to be decent more often," he teased before hugging me back. "And if you're not going to go sweep Mackenzie West off her feet, let me take a shower before we find something fun to do."

"Okay," I said, glad he was still free to stick with our plans.

I went back to my room to wait and saw group texts from Audrey and Isaac.

> **Audrey:** Tell me y'all saw Mackenzie's Instagram!!!
> **Isaac:** whaaaaat?! This is huge!
> **Isaac:** And your brother knew????
> **Audrey:** ICONIC!
> **Jordan:** I guess he did! So weird
> **Jordan:** How do you two feel about turning Saturday into a new Operation?
> **Audrey:** Seriously? We get to scheme again!?
> **Jordan:** Scheming for a good cause, but yes
> **Audrey:** I AM SO IN!!!
> **Isaac:** Same! What are we calling this one?

I stared at the question, thinking on it for a moment before texting back.

> **Jordan:** Operation Heart Eyes

Instead of going somewhere, Casey and I decided to stay in for an extended *Lord of the Rings* marathon. To our surprise, Mom joined us for all of it. Dad watched when he wasn't working on meal prep, and we paused only to eat. But I had trouble focusing on anything as Saturday's plans stuck in my mind. All I wanted to do was devise the best apology ever, but instead I spent two days with my family, which, admittedly, was more fun than I'd had with them in a long time.

When Saturday afternoon rolled around, Isaac and I drove to Audrey's house with snacks and drinks from the Quilted Bean. I made him promise not to mention Mack until we were with Audrey, so instead we talked about Thanksgiving and Isaac's next date with Olivia. They were going ice skating at a local rink, which I'd pay good money to see. I got a hard nudge when I told Isaac that.

"Did you know Mack was a lesbian before she posted about it?" I asked after passing her house on the way to Audrey's. It may have been a block out of the way.

"I thought we weren't talking about her," Isaac said.

"It's just one simple question," I said, rolling my eyes. "How long did you know? Because apparently my brother knew since April, so I'm just curious."

"I didn't know," Isaac said. "But it makes more sense now. Olivia hasn't stopped talking about needing y'all to fix your shit, so she must've known."

"Yeah, probably." I didn't know why it even mattered. Olivia likely didn't tell Isaac for the same reason I didn't, and the same reason Casey didn't say anything to me. It wasn't our thing to tell. At least Mack had people in her life who respected her privacy.

"Uh, are we going to get out?"

I blinked and looked at Isaac before turning forward again.

Apparently I'd autopilot driven the rest of the way and parked in front of Audrey's house without realizing it. Cool. "Yeah," I said, laughing a little. "Let's go."

Isaac grabbed the snacks while I took responsibility for the drink carrier. Within ten minutes, we were eating and drinking on a pillow-and-blanket pile in Audrey's basement as *Dash & Lily* played on Netflix. It came with a lot of memories and feels, and I needed to remember the good times with Mack if I was ever going to fix things.

"Okay, before we get to work, I need to confess something," I said as I took out a notebook we'd used for all our previous operations. Some of the content in the notebook would no doubt result in another grounding. At least this time the scheming was all positive.

"You're in love with Mackenzie West," Audrey said. "And we're planning on helping you win her heart. Anything else?"

I blinked at them. "How did you know?"

"Uh, Operation Heart Eyes," Audrey said, laughing. "It was kind of obvious."

"Yes, but I'm *in love* with her," I said, as if she didn't hear herself. "That's not just a crush or wanting a girlfriend. It's so much bigger."

"Hi, yes, I'm almost seventeen. I think I know what love is," Audrey said, making a face. "In theory."

"I know what love is," Isaac said proudly. "And that's definitely where you're at, my friend. You've got it bad."

"Oh, so does that mean you know about us making out

during the Minneapolis tournament, too?" I asked in an attempt to prove a point, and of course their eyes bugged out.

"Excuse me?" Audrey laughed. "You made out with Mackenzie West and didn't tell us?"

"I'd never *out* someone, Audrey."

"Okay, obviously, but . . . okay, yeah, that makes sense. I take it back."

Isaac chuckled before giving me a light shove. "You're in love! This is worth celebrating. Maybe we should throw a party."

"I'd totally throw a party for that," Audrey said. "Would it be like a coming out party? How does someone throw that kind of party?"

"No one is throwing a party," I said, groaning.

"Okay, fine, but at least tell us more," Audrey said, bouncing a little on her pillow. "How was it? I mean, obviously amazing because here we are, but I need details."

"You're *not* getting details," I said. "I'm only sharing what's necessary for us to figure out where I go from here."

"No fun," Audrey said, pouting.

Isaac narrowed his eyes at her before grabbing my notebook. "Tell us the necessary information then. I'll take notes."

I watched him write *JORDAN LOVES MACKENZIE* under where I'd already written *Operation Heart Eyes*. My stomach did a thing. "Okay, well, I had a crush on her that summer but obviously didn't do anything about it because I didn't know she was a lesbian. And I found out recently that she'd liked me back then, too."

"And she obviously still likes you," Audrey added, grinning like a fool.

"We don't *know* that."

Audrey and Isaac made eye contact before focusing on me. "We know that," they said in unison.

"Fine, okay, let's say she still likes me, then," I said, smiling at how in sync we could be sometimes. "I'm done being mad about freshman year, so the thing we're really up against is the article situation and how she probably doesn't trust me anymore, which is obviously a big thing. And I already apologized for that, so just saying sorry isn't going to work. It needs to be bigger than that."

"Confess your feelings in the paper," Audrey said. "Shannon is secretly a romantic. They'd totally go for it."

"Amazing idea, but I can't do that," I said. "I already robbed her of one feature story, so I'm not going to turn the other one into a confession of my feelings. But I do think I should post her feature story first to kind of tee up whatever big thing I do. That way she knows I took the article seriously and can forgive the last one. Maybe. Hopefully."

"Perfect," Audrey said, nodding. "So now we just need something big enough to explain your feelings and how you'll never do something shitty again."

"I would've said that another way," Isaac said as he continued taking notes. "But yes, I think that's what we're getting at."

"For sure." I glanced at the TV to see Dash reading the lyrics to Joni Mitchell's song "River" at the Strand, and a memory slapped me in the face. "Oh my god!"

They followed my eyes to the TV, and Audrey laughed. "Right? I love this scene."

"Yes, it's great. But I know what I need to do."

"We're listening," Isaac said, and Audrey nodded eagerly.

"The summer before freshman year, Mackenzie said this was one of her favorite Netflix shows, so we watched it even though it was eighty degrees outside and nowhere near Christmas," I explained, my heart racing at the idea forming in my head. "I told her I'd be terrified to have to do something like that, but she thought it was super romantic. And then she said she loved those scenes where people propose in a big crowd because they're risking a lot and showing everyone else how much they love that person. Of course I made fun of her for it at the time, but it's perfect, right? I need to do something like this."

"No, you need to do *exactly* this," Audrey said, beaming now. "Not at the Strand, obviously, but you should totally read the same lyrics so she knows what you're doing and that you remember her favorite show."

"Yes, I love this," Isaac agreed as he continued taking notes. "You have to do it, especially because the idea scares you."

"Okay." I nodded along, glad they were on board. "But there isn't a place where something like that would make sense. I'd say the school, but as much as she's worth a second suspension, I'd prefer to avoid that."

"You could do it at her next party," Isaac said, his face scrunching up. "But it's not until we kick off winter break."

Audrey groaned. "That's too long! We can't make true love wait, like, three weeks."

"No, it's perfect," Isaac said, looking at me. "You should keep giving her space and let it sink in a little longer that you're sorry. And publishing her feature story first will help her see that you're trying without being in her face about it."

"That's . . . okay, yeah, that's good," Audrey said.

"But what about Chrismukkah?" I asked. "Your parents won't let you skip the festivities. Shit, *I* wouldn't let you either."

"First of all, they absolutely would if your heart is on the line. Second, Hanukkah doesn't start until Christmas Day this year, so it's fine. Third, please just admit this idea is genius instead of trying to get out of it already."

The idea *was* genius, but something about it didn't feel right. It wasn't enough for Mack to know I was willing to act like a fool for her. Joni Mitchell was an icon, but I needed to do something that was personal to us. I looked at my friends, then to the TV, then back to my friends. "I'm going bigger," I said. "I know what I need to do."

"Yes, girl, tell us!" Audrey said.

"No, I don't want to chicken out," I said, blushing a little as the idea sunk in more. "But you'll see at the party, and I promise it'll be good."

"Then that's enough for us," Isaac said, holding up his sugary coffee drink. "Cheers to Operation Heart Eyes."

"Cheers!" Audrey and I echoed, tapping our lattes to Isaac's before drinking.

We went back to watching the show, but I couldn't focus. I was overcome with nerves at the thought of a romantic gesture, and because I'd said out loud that I was in love with Mack. Finally, it was no longer a jumble of messy feelings in my head.

I hadn't actually said those words out loud before, not with either of my exes. I'd liked both of them, but not *that* much. But what did I even know about love? I knew that seeing Mackenzie West for the first time in the dog park had turned my world upside down. I knew that kissing her felt like I was floating on a cloud. I knew that her laugh sent chills up my spine. I knew that losing her the first time had been a nightmare, and the thought of losing her again was unimaginable.

I knew that whatever love was, this was it, and I was going to prove it.

My bedroom turned into a tornado of paper the next day. Every Post-it I'd ever written, every word in my notebook, every thought I'd had about Mackenzie West that year was laid out on my floor. After eating breakfast with the family and saying goodbye to Casey with a long hug, I left Pond with the parents and got to work.

I'd told Casey about the plan minus my secret twist, and he thought it was genius. He even knew the *Dash & Lily* scene I was talking about, so he got a few extra cool-brother points. He promised not to say a word about the plan to anyone else, as did Isaac and Audrey. This was a high-security, covert mission, and we couldn't risk anyone else finding out.

Hours passed as I pored over the notes and recordings. Fortunately, I'd already drafted snippets over the past couple of months, but that didn't mean I had an article. Knowing Mack was out changed nothing about me being unwilling to write about it, mainly because I wasn't going to ask her if she wanted to talk about it. It was a part of who she was, and I was proud of her, but the story needed to primarily focus on volleyball.

I'd been trying so hard to find an angle that I'd overlooked that the purpose of the article *was* the angle. Because she wasn't just like every other volleyball player. She *was* special. Her parents knew it. Coach knew it. The team knew it. Hell, even *Brie* knew it. I knew it, too, and my biggest mistake in all of this was acting like it wasn't enough.

After combining everything I wanted to say in a document, including quotes from Mack, Coach, and Olivia, who'd emailed me some interview responses recently, I got to work on writing a feature story on Mackenzie West. And this time, it was worthy of her.

CHAPTER TWENTY-SIX

Student Feature: Mackenzie West, Girls Varsity Volleyball Captain

BY: JORDAN ELLIOT

Have you ever met someone and immediately known they'd change your life forever? That's how people feel when they meet Mackenzie West. I had the privilege of spending the semester with the girls' varsity volleyball team, and it was clear on the first day how deeply valued West is by all of them.

"I knew she was special from day one," Coach Sheila Pavek said. "You get that feeling about kids like her. They just have the kind of raw talent and confidence that falls off of them and latches onto you. I didn't know anything about her going into the tryout, but by the end of it, I knew we needed her."

The positivity doesn't stop there. "She's an inspiration," junior Olivia Davidson said. "While she was out for two weeks with a concussion, she made sure to text us words of encouragement. Not only is she the best player I've ever met, but she's also the kindest."

When it comes to volleyball, West is completely focused on her team. "It doesn't matter if you're popular or how much money you have or how smart you are," West said. "I don't carry the team. We all do, and I love that. You can't win without everyone giving it their all."

But West's dedication doesn't stop when she leaves the court. After learning a couple of girls couldn't afford the costs associated with joining the team last year, she started a fundraiser initiative to help. "We've done a lot of work to make sure anyone who has the talent but lacks the funding is able to play," Pavek said. "Money shouldn't be a barrier when you have talent like these girls."

West's love of volleyball started from a young age, inspired by her parents, who were in a league during her childhood. "I'd go to their practices and matches when I was little," West said. "There are pictures of me holding a volleyball during their events. Volleyball came naturally because of [them], but I also loved it on my own. I love the feeling of smacking the ball over the net, the uncertainty of where it'll land but knowing it'll land *somewhere*. I love having something I can depend on and improve on. I love feeling in control of myself, feeling grounded."

"I'm really proud of her," Pavek said. "She has impressed me since day one, but she has still come a long way. And wherever she ends up after high school, she'll succeed."

Regarding her plans after high school, West hopes to attend university on the East Coast and continue playing volleyball. But no matter what she does next, it's clear from speaking to those who know her that she'll go far. And we wish her all the best.

I hand-delivered my article to Mx. Shannon that Monday after school for approval. Their eyebrows raised after reading the first couple of sentences. "This sounds a lot like the last article, Jordan."

"I know," I said, giving away no emotion. "Keep reading."

They continued. The seconds turned into minutes, feeling like an eternity. I wasn't worried about Shannon rejecting the article because I knew it was solid, but I worried about what Mack would think. I worried it wouldn't be enough—that *I* wouldn't be enough.

"You got some really solid quotes," Shannon said after finishing. They set the article on their desk. "I like that you let them carry the article."

"I thought it was better to keep my personal thoughts out of it this time," I said, letting the smallest of smiles form.

Shannon laughed. "A wise decision," they said, tapping the paper. "Send it to the editors. This is approved on my end. Fantastic work, Jordan."

"Thank you," I said, finding relief in their words. Of course I wasn't off the hook yet, and maybe I'd never be an editor, but at least I still had my spot on the paper. I wasn't completely screwed. "And thanks for giving me another chance."

"You got it," Shannon said. "I know it may not feel like it, but you're one of the best reporters I've ever had. And as long as we don't have any more shenanigans like your accidental article, I think you'll be very happy with how things turn out next year."

They meant senior year and not a few weeks from now, but I could wait. Whatever they had planned, I'd be ready for it. "Thanks, Shannon. I'm looking forward to it."

"Me too," they said, smiling back at me and looking like they wanted to say something else. And then they did. "So, about Mackenzie West."

I groaned, but not because I wasn't comfortable confiding in them. In a way, they were like an older sibling, and this wouldn't be the first time we'd had a discussion that had nothing to do with the paper. "What about her?" I asked.

"I heard about her personal life update," Shannon said. "Is that somehow related to everything that happened this semester and you two being so-called enemies?"

Okay, Shannon *definitely* had little spies everywhere. But at least their sources were correct. "Yes and no. We met the summer before freshman year and became really good friends, but then high school started and she ghosted, acting like we didn't know each other."

"That's rough."

"It was *humiliating*," I said. "We managed to get back on good terms this semester, and then everything got complicated."

"Complicated how?"

I gave them a look. "That's where her life update comes into play. We recently admitted to liking each other as more than friends that summer, even though I didn't know she was a lesbian until the Minneapolis tournament, and then we admitted to still liking each other. But because she wasn't out yet, we obviously didn't do anything about it. And it sucked, but that wasn't why I wrote that article. Like, it was a factor, I guess, since I wanted to date her, but coming out is a huge deal, so I'd never pressure her to do that. But between her wanting to keep us a secret and her ghosting me two years ago, I let someone else's gossip convince me Mackenzie still hated me and was just using me for . . . I don't even know what. A good article? Just because? It's ridiculous hearing myself talk about it now."

I blinked, realizing how much I'd just shared. But Shannon didn't look alarmed or upset. "So you wrote to get out your feelings," they said.

"Exactly. And of course I wasn't paying attention because I was upset and just threw it into a Docs folder without confirming *which* folder."

"And here we are."

I sighed, leaning against the chair. "And here we are."

Mx. Shannon nodded, quiet for a moment. "Well, considering

everything, I think you've handled yourself pretty well. And you owned up to your mistake and braved the wrath of the volleyball team in order to stay committed. There's a lot to be proud of there." They smiled a little. "I assume you still like her, then?"

"Yeah," I said, matching their smile. "I kind of love her. It's infuriating."

They laughed, shaking their head. "Yeah, that sounds about right. But you'll figure it out. You always do. And according to your article, that girl always succeeds at what she does. So, even if the odds feel stacked against you, I think you'll both be fine."

My smile grew at their words, feeling confident in my chances for the first time. "Thanks, Shannon," I said, standing. "You always know exactly what to say."

"It's a gift," Shannon said, grinning now. "See you tomorrow, Jordan."

I nodded, grabbing my bag and coat. "See you."

After leaving the newspaper room, I checked my phone to catch up on texts and social media from the day, but the results came up short. Mack still hadn't replied to my message about being proud of her—not that I'd expected her to. But she deserved a heads-up that her feature article was still coming out, so I sent her a new text as I walked to my car.

Jordan: Your feature article was approved and will publish sometime before break.

Once I was in my car and had blasted the heat, I emailed the article to Casey to get his opinion just in case he found something I should tweak before sending to the editors. Because apparently he knew Mack so well or whatever. That part was still a lot to take in. After adding a disclaimer not to share it with anyone, I sent the message and left the parking lot for home.

Operation Heart Eyes was officially in motion, and I prayed to whatever gods existed that it worked. I didn't know what I'd do if it didn't.

Over half the newspaper staff had submitted stories the same week as me, and the editor in chief didn't want too much hitting the site at once. My feature story wasn't deemed important enough and was pushed off, not posting until the Monday before winter break. Rude. But considering neither Casey nor the editors had any suggestions or edits, I felt like I'd written the best article I possibly could have, given the circumstances.

That left four days for the story to sink in before facing Mack at her party, and those days felt both too soon and like a lifetime. Mx. Shannon's words stuck in my head in the hopes that I could manifest a positive outcome, but the more days that passed, the less I believed it.

By Wednesday, I'd received compliments from most of the volleyball team about the article. The few who'd been giving me the stink eye for weeks were now smiling at me in the hall again. But Mack did nothing to acknowledge the article. No texts. No calls. No in-school conversations. Not even a smile the handful of times I'd seen her in the hallway. It was like I didn't exist, which only added to my concern about the party.

"It'll be okay," Olivia said after school on Thursday outside the newspaper room, where she was meeting Isaac. We let her in on the plan to help make sure Mack was in the right place at the right time. "This is going to be super romantic."

"I hope you're right," I said, smiling as I looked down at my vibrating phone. "Oh, I guess Coach wants to see me in her office."

"Yeah? Great!" Olivia said easily, grinning now. She knew something.

"Oh god," I groaned. "Should I be worried?"

"I wouldn't be smiling if it was bad," Olivia said, tugging Isaac's hand. "See you later!" she added in a singsong voice as they turned to leave.

I looked at Isaac for some kind of sign, but he was just as confused as I was. Reluctantly, I walked to the other side of the school until I reached Pavek's room, and I knocked before walking in. "Hey, Coach," I said, smiling tentatively and looking around as if she was somehow scheming with Mack to get back at me, but of course it was just the two of us.

"Come in, Elliot," Coach said, nodding to an open chair on the other side of the desk from her. "I wanted to talk to you about a couple of things."

"Okay," I said, trying to sound more relaxed than I felt as I sat down. "What's up?"

"First of all, congratulations on the feature story. I was really impressed with how you handled it, even if you failed in making me not sound sappy."

I hadn't forgotten her request. "Hard to fight the truth, Coach," I said, shrugging.

She barked a laugh. "Of course, of course," she said. "Anyway, the second thing and real reason you're here is a request. Open that box."

I looked to the plain white box she nodded toward on her desk, not noticing it until now. "Okay," I said slowly, confused. I slid the box over and lifted off the top, my mouth dropping. A matching set of Wildcats volleyball sweatpants and hoodie were inside. "Oh my god, I thought that was a joke."

Coach grinned. "Well, I hope you seriously like them, because I can't return it."

I took both items from the box, seeing my last name written on the back, accompanied by the number eleven. "Is the number significant?" I asked..

"Apparently," Coach said, shrugging. "Someone told me you'd know what it meant. Something about a doctor."

"Matt Smith?" I asked almost immediately. *"Doctor Who?"*

"Yeah, that's it," Coach nodded. "You like it, then?"

"Are you kidding me?" I laughed quietly. "I *love* it. I mean, I'm not exactly sure I'm *worthy* of it, considering I caused a lot of problems this year, and you're probably thrilled to be done with me at this point, and—"

"Elliot."

I looked up at her firm voice. "Yes, Coach?"

"Just say thank you."

"Thank you," I said, my voice shaking. "But I really did mess up. I'm not part of the team, not really. I'm not one of them."

"You *are*," Coach said. "Your role doesn't matter. Being perfect or imperfect doesn't matter. You gave it your all, and you didn't give up when it got hard. That's what counts. And no matter what happened with that article, I know you care about those girls as much as they care about you. All of them."

Tears fell from my eyes as she spoke, her final words breaking me as I thought about Mack. I looked away, wiping at my cheeks, trying to calm down. "Thank you," I said between breaths. "That . . . means a lot to me."

"Yeah, I can tell," Coach teased. "Here. We don't want you crying on your new gear."

I choked out a laugh, taking a tissue from the box she'd held out to me. "Thanks." I dabbed under my eyes, releasing a few slower breaths. "Seriously, this is the best gift."

"Is it good enough to convince you to cover volleyball next year?"

I stared at her, considering the question. Editors were still allowed to cover beats, of course, but I'd planned on trying for more serious topics or world events. But after the semester we'd had, I couldn't imagine not writing about it. I'd have spring semesters to cover other stories, and I could still make room for another article or two next fall. It could work. I'd make it work. "It's more than enough," I said, smiling more. "If the team will have me."

"Oh, they insisted," Coach said. "So if you're in, we're in."

I nodded, practically hugging the clothes to my chest. "I'm in," I said, already excited for next fall. "I'm *so* in."

CHAPTER TWENTY-SEVEN

MACK'S WINTER BREAK party was ugly-sweater themed, because of course it was. This worked in favor of my plan to dress as a tree like how Lily had done in *Dash & Lily*—green sweater with tinsel and lights wrapped around it, and black leggings. Mack and I had agreed it was a solid look a couple of years ago, so it was worth a try.

To get in the spirit, I started the show after eating dinner while I got ready for the party. By the third episode, I was ready to leave. By the fourth, it was time to leave. By the fifth, I was going to be late. By the sixth, I was a thousand percent panicking. I texted Casey.

Jordan: I can't do this.

My phone rang almost immediately, and I reluctantly answered. "What do you mean?" Casey asked over the sound of music. He'd gotten home from college a few days ago, which of course meant he was at Mack's house. As if I wasn't nervous enough, I'd be performing a romantic gesture in front of my brother.

Kill me.

"I mean this week didn't go as planned," I said, standing up to pace with Pond at my heels. "I thought she'd eventually text me back or say something to make me think I had a chance. But nothing."

The music quieted, and a door shut before Casey responded. "Listen, JoJo. I've never seen you this fired up about someone. Yeah, you've had girlfriends, but you weren't nearly as into them as you're into Mack. She's going to see that and remember why she liked you in the first place."

"But what if she doesn't?" I asked, staring off at the TV as *Dash & Lily* saw each other at the Christmas Eve party. "What if I'm trying to make this into some kind of fairy tale that isn't going to have a happy ending?"

"First, you're not even seventeen yet, so let's not talk about happy endings," Casey said. "And second, you won't know until you try."

I sighed, hating when he used pillow-stitch phrases against me. "I'm scared," I said, frowning as the truth of it came out.

"I know," Casey said. "But your friends and I will be right here. And if for some reason she doesn't react how we all think she will, we'll help you get through it. But no matter what happens, it'll be okay. *You'll* be okay."

I nodded to myself and stopped in front of my full-length mirror, looking at the effort I'd put into making tonight happen.

I thought about everything I'd done to get here. It was all for a girl who frustrated me at times, but a girl I loved all the same.

Casey was right. I wouldn't know until I tried. And one way or another, I'd be okay.

"Hello? JoJo?"

"Sorry," I said, coming back down to earth. "What did you say?"

"If you aren't at this party in twenty minutes, I'll drag you here myself."

"Calm down. I'll be there soon, promise."

"Good, because I'm already two beers in, so I shouldn't drive anyway."

"Wait to start a third. Would hate for you to embarrass me in front of a room of people."

"I would never," Casey said. "Twenty minutes!"

"Okay, bye!"

I hung up and grabbed my purse before running out of the apartment, yelling to the parents along the way that I was leaving. They said something about being safe and having fun before I shut the door.

And just like that, I was going to get my girl.

Or humiliate myself trying.

Sixteen minutes later, I stood in front of Mackenzie West's house—maybe for the last time. I'd texted Casey that I was there so he didn't call with another fake threat, and I'd texted Isaac and Audrey so they could coordinate with Olivia to turn down the music in the right moment and make sure Mack was in the living room.

My mind wandered in a fast-motion montage sort of way to everything that had happened this year. Mack giving me shit in the bathroom the first week of school. Not making editor. The news of me having the volleyball beat. The reality of what that meant with Mack. Hiking at Jay Cooke. Reading *Persuasion* to Mack as her concussed brain healed. The night in the hotel room. Brie acting like a friend before showing her true colors. The aftermath of my mistake. Reconnecting with my mom and brother. Watching Isaac fall in love and Audrey head in that direction. Stolen glances. Feet touching in the dog park. Broken hearts.

A laugh from inside slapped me back into reality, and my heart was ready to burst. "You won't know until you try," I said quietly, letting out a deep breath before opening the door.

The decorations and music were holiday themed, and a massive Christmas tree was aggressively decorated in various lights and bulbs by the fireplace. As planned, a chair was set out for me between the two, and I hoped it was sturdy enough. The last thing I needed was me breaking a chair in the process of breaking my dignity.

I checked my phone to see replies that everything was ready, and I sent a thumbs-up emoji before putting it away and approaching my pseudostage. On cue, the music stopped right after I stood on the chair and faced the crowd. I waited until the voices quieted before speaking.

"Hello." I looked out across the room at several people I knew and some I didn't. A few of them looked amused, but most of them were curious. "Sorry to interrupt your holiday cheer, but I've been inspired to share a reading."

My eyes wandered until they locked on Mack. She stood at the bottom of the stairs next to Olivia, Isaac, Audrey, Emma, and Casey.

It sunk in again that I'd be doing this in front of my brother. His encouraging smile was the only thing keeping me on the chair, and I smiled back.

"So read already!" someone from the crowd yelled.

"Right," I said, reaching into my purse to pull out the paper, staring down at it for a moment. I'd taken the lyrics to Joni Mitchell's "River" and changed them to work for me and Mack. It might not be good enough for her, but I wouldn't know if she agreed until I tried.

I looked up again, not actually needing the words. "It's coming on Christmas. They're going to parties. They're drinking some cheap beer and singing songs of joy and dreams. Oh, I wish I had a time machine I could whoosh away on." My eyes returned to Mack as I read my lyrics out loud just as Dash had done at the Strand, my heart racing faster with each word. I couldn't read her expression, but if I looked anywhere else at this point, it would be over.

I fought back tears as I wrapped up. "I'm so hard to handle. I'm messy and I'm sad. Now I've gone and lost the best girl that I never had. Oh, I wish I had a time machine I could whoosh away on . . . It's coming on Christmas." I stopped at the same line that Dash had been cut off, in hopes that it was even more obvious what I was doing.

If she knew, she didn't let it show. She just . . . looked at me, and my heart sank. Everyone had been wrong. Determination wasn't enough. Love wasn't enough. And I'd just embarrassed her in front of the entire school.

Again.

"Sorry," I said quietly before getting off the chair and walking to the door, certain I'd spontaneously combust before I could get home. The music resumed as I closed the door behind me, and I paced the length of the porch, needing a minute to shake these emotions before being able to drive. And of course I'd forgotten my coat at home, and of course it was fucking freezing outside.

It didn't register that the door had opened until it clicked shut, and I turned to see Mack standing there. I'd memorized all her expressions, understood them, but her current one was a mystery.

"Why did you do that?" she asked after what felt like an eternity.

"I was doing a thing," I said, but I stopped explaining when she took a step closer.

"I know exactly what you were doing," she said. "I have memories, too, you know. I'm asking *why* you did it."

I took a step closer to fill in some of the space between us. "Have you ever met someone and immediately known they'd change your life forever?" I asked, repeating the first line I'd written in my accidental blast article and the real feature story.

"That doesn't answer my question," Mack said.

"Then how about this," I said, taking another small step forward. "It killed me when that article got posted, and I've hated myself every day since. All I could think about after that was finding some way of making it up to you because . . . because I love you, Mackenzie West. I love you so much I can't stand it. These last couple of months have been absolute torture not being able to be with you and show you exactly how sorry I am and how much I want to kiss you again and lie with you and read to you." I laughed quietly. "I just did something absolutely terrifying and risked breaking a chair in the process because I know how you feel about romantic gestures. Because I know you and I'm so sorry and I love you and—"

She closed the rest of the space between us and kissed me before I could finish, and I was taken back to the first time. But now we weren't shy or tentative. Mack's hands found my waist among the tree tinsel and tugged me against her, and my hands slipped from her cheeks into her hair as the kiss deepened. We carried on like that until we were nearly out of breath and the cold had become too much.

"Just to be clear, I came out for me," Mack said after we finally pulled apart.

"I know," I said, letting out another deep breath. "And I'm so proud of you for that."

"Yeah, I saw your text." A small grin formed on her lips.

"But now that I'm out, I want you to know that I love you, too, and I want you, and I don't give a shit who knows about it."

I opened my mouth to respond, but the door swung open before I could get a word out.

"Thank god, I thought it would never happen!" Audrey said from inside.

"Audrey," I said as my cheeks flooded red from more than the cold. "You just interrupted the most romantic moment of my life."

"You'll get over it," Olivia chimed in as she walked out behind Audrey. "Did it work? Is everyone happy and in love now?"

"You knew about this?" Mack asked, looking as shocked as me by our friends spilling out of the house.

"Of course we knew," Casey said, looking at me. "But let it be known that I wasn't watching from the window like the rest of these creeps. You're my sister, and I love you, but I don't need to see you kissing people."

"Oh my god, I'm going to just sit down and die right now," I said, not thinking it was possible to be so quickly mortified after the cutest moment of my life.

"That would kind of defeat the purpose of a romantic gesture," Mack said, taking my hand before looking back at our friends. "Let's bail and go to The Diner. I want real food, and a moment alone with this one on the way."

"Won't people get mad?" Emma asked.

Mack glanced at the window, shrugging. "I've always hated

these parties," she said. "The only people I want to hang out with are right here."

"Awe, romantic gestures make you cheesy," I teased.

Mack looked nothing short of proud. "I said what I said. Are we in or not?"

"Oh, we're in," Isaac said, grinning. "You two go ahead. We'll get everyone else out of the house and be right behind you."

"I'm riding with you, my guy," Casey said, clapping Isaac on the shoulder. "We'll call you Designated Isaac."

Isaac groaned. "Don't ever call me that again."

I laughed at the visual of Isaac hanging out with my brother for even five minutes. Couldn't wait for that story. "Thanks, Isaac," I said, looking at the group and smiling more. "And everyone."

"We got you," Olivia said, winking at me before taking Isaac's hand and leading everyone back into the house.

I offered to drive since Mack's car was in her garage, which was blocked by all the partygoers' cars, and we were quickly on the road after that, our hands clasped together between us. "I know we're riding a high right now, but I want to apologize again about everything," I said after a minute of comfortable silence.

"I know." Mack squeezed my hand. "I've had a lot of time to think, and honestly, I was pretty close to caving and telling you to stop giving me space."

"Guess I should've waited," I teased. "I mean, you were supposed to be the one to work for it after coming out and all that."

"Shut up," she laughed, making me feel even warmer. "So, we're all good, then? No more blaming each other for past mistakes or believing bitter volleyball girls or ghosting or anything like that?"

"We're all good," I agreed. "From now on, it's all honesty, all the time."

"Absolutely. Question everything. Assume nothing. Learn the truth."

"You're obsessed with that quote," I said, grinning.

"Hell yes I am. I'm going to get it tattooed somewhere one day."

"I'm sure you are," I said, completely incapable of keeping my mouth from exploding in the biggest smile. "I love you."

"I love you, too," Mack said, bringing my hand to her lips, kissing my palm.

I turned my hand to rest against her cheek, brushing her skin with my thumb as I did my best to focus on the road.

Audrey, Isaac, and I had planned several operations over the course of our friendship. We'd had victories and many, *many* failures. But if I knew anything for sure, it was that Operation Heart Eyes would go down as our greatest success.

ACKNOWLEDGMENTS

IF YOU'RE READING this, that means I survived the second book slump. After over a year of writing, editing, editing, editing, and more editing, the final pages were turned in, the team let out breaths they knew they were holding, and a book was printed. This book, to be exact. I still can't wrap my head around the fact that this has happened twice, and I'm all kinds of grateful. Please bear with me in these final pages as I thank so many wonderful humans.

Thank you to my agent, Mike Whatnall, for being on this journey with me for the last few years. I flew into your inbox the day you opened to queries, and it remains one of the best decisions of my life. Thank you for your collaboration, for helping me strengthen my writing, and for answering the same questions multiple times because my memory is terrible and my folder structure is even worse. I don't know what I'd do without you!

Thank you to the rest of the Dystel, Goderich & Bourret team, including Michael Bourret, Andrew Dugan, and Nataly Gruender, for being the agency of my dreams. I'm beyond lucky to be represented by you and have the support of so many talented, kind people.

Thank you to my incredible editor, Alyssa Miele, for seeing something in me and my stories, and for giving me a home at Quill Tree. From helping me elevate my books and think about writing differently, to supporting me through publishing uncertainties, I'm so grateful to you. You're truly one of the best in the business (I'm only a little biased). We'll always have Cool Dad and Eataly!

Thank you to the managing editorial, marketing, and publicity teams at Quill Tree Books/HarperCollins who helped make *We Got the Beat* what it is today. Special thanks to executive managing editor Gwen Morton, senior production editor Jai Berg, copyeditor Sarah Mondello, proofreader Jacqueline Hornberger, senior marketing director Audrey Diestelkamp, and publicist Samantha Brown.

Thank you to Carina Guevara for bringing my children to life and for creating such a stunning cover. And thank you to Laura Mock for adding your design skills and touches to the book. You're both so incredibly talented, and I couldn't have been in better hands.

Thank you to my best friends (in order of the day we met so no one gets offended this time) Brian Koenig, Amanda Piller, and Janice Davis. (You're welcome for also including last names.) Y'all have been putting up with me for a LONG time, and I honestly don't know why. I'm happy about it, just confused. Anyway, thanks for being by my side since elementary and high school. It's been a ride, and there's no one else I'd rather be on it with. (OK, maybe Cate Blanchett, but I digress.) What I'm trying to say is that my best friends get a longer shout-out this time because they think they deserve it. (And they do.) I love and admire the hell out you and wouldn't be doing the damn thing without you. And if you're crying . . . #crushedit.

Thank you to my family for showing up every step of the way to support me, from my agent announcement, to the book deal, to *Out of Character*'s publishing day, to today. I think about how lucky I am to have family who love me for who I am and who'll never let me forget how awkward I am. Special thank you to my little sister, Hannah, for sharing her volleyball wisdom with me so I could make it sound like I know what I'm talking about. I love you all.

This is where we take a break so I can acknowledge the dog. Izzy, you're a little monster whose bark pierces our home and whose Stage 5 Clinger behavior makes me cringe. But you also love so hard and have the cutest little face, and there's nothing better than coming home to a dog who throws her tiny body into your arms with joy. Thank you for reminding me to take breaks so I can play with you and give you scratches. You're a mess, and I couldn't ask for a better fur baby.

OK, back to regular programming . . .

Thank you to my most enthusiastic critique partners and friends, Janice Davis, Emily Miner, and Kalie Holford. You've all been by my side since day one of this journey, and your support is next level. Your wisdom, compassion, and friendship mean everything to me. I can't wait for shelves to be full of your books!

Thank you to my OG writing group, Team Trash. I can't believe we've been flailing through this writing life together for four years. Y'all were there for the entire WGTB journey, and I couldn't be luckier to have you little gremlins by my side. To my fellow raccoons in a trench coat (Crystal, Elle, Jenna, Mallory, Melody, Michelle, Monica, Shoshana, and SJ), thank you.

Thank you to my other author pals who've helped me get through these past few years of being a baby author: Christen Randall, Shelly Page, Jenna Voris, Jen St. Jude, Camille Kellogg, M. K. Lobb, Trang Thanh Tran, Jenny Perinovic, Page Powars, Cat Bakewell, Meredith Tate, Elle Gonzalez Rose, Edward Underhill, Courtney Kae, Carlyn Greenwald, and Alison Cochran. Y'all are so incredibly talented, and I'm honored to be sharing stories among such icons.

Thank you to the WFHS *Packer* newspaper staff (2003–2006) for the shenanigans, late-night layout sessions, NIPA conferences, and, of course, the stories. If anyone has a copy of my lawn gnome story, please send it my way. The world deserves to read my masterpiece.

This book wouldn't exist without the many, *many* teachers who kicked me into shape over the years and believed in me when I didn't believe in myself. Nelson, Metcalf, Neugebauer, Gredesky, Preston, and Grooters (RIP), thank you for making my high school years bearable and memorable. I wouldn't have gotten through it without you.

We currently live in a world that threatens marginalized people and their stories every single day. My sincerest thank-you goes to the educators, librarians, and individuals who fight to keep these important voices on shelves. Your dedication, support, and kind hearts don't go unnoticed. You're the real heroes, and I'm so immensely grateful to all of you.

Last but never least, thank you to the many readers I've met online and in person who've made this author journey truly special. It's an honor to write fat, queer stories, and it means the world to me to have you read along. No matter where you are on your personal journey, you're valid just as you are. Thank you, thank you, thank you.